3 01320

D0626383

RARY

ed

Murder Out of Tune

Murder Out of Tune

Lesley Cookman

Published by Accent Press Ltd 2014

ISBN 9781909624962

Copyright © **Lesley Cookman** 2014

The right of **Lesley Cookman** to be identified as the author of
this work has been asserted by the author in accordance with the
Copyright, Designs and Patents Act 1988.

The story contained within this book is a work of fiction. Names
and characters are the product of the author's imagination and
any resemblance to actual persons, living or dead, is entirely
coincidental.

All rights reserved. No part of this book may be reproduced,
stored in a retrieval system, or transmitted in any form or by any
means, electronic, electrostatic, magnetic tape, mechanical,
photocopying, recording or otherwise, without the written
permission of the publishers: Accent Press Ltd, Ty Cynon
House, Navigation Park, Abercynon, CF45 4SN

To the memory of Caryl Ann Knight
November 1947 - July 2014

Acknowledgements

My thanks once again to my son Miles who provided the suggestion of a ukulele group as a viable setting for murder. None of the ukulele players I am acquainted with are murderers or victims, as far as I know, although I have heard threats …

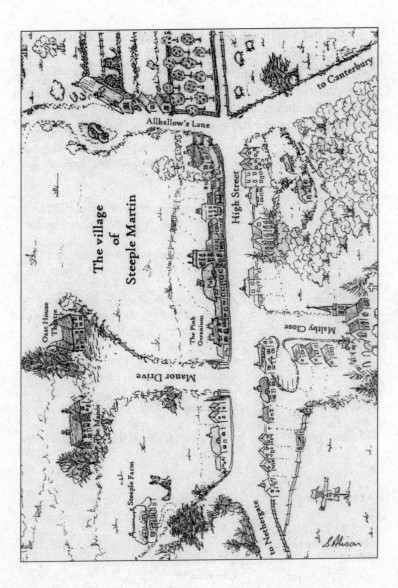

The village
of
Steeple Martin

Allhallow's Lane

to Canterbury

High Street

Oast House Theatre

The Pink Geranium

Manor Drive

Maltby Close

The Manor

Steeple Farm

to Nethergate

S Alison

WHO'S WHO IN THE LIBBY SARJEANT SERIES

Libby Sarjeant — Former actor, sometime artist, resident of 17, Allhallow's Lane, Steeple Martin. Owner of Sidney the cat.

Fran Wolfe — Formerly Fran Castle. Also former actor, occasional psychic, resident of Coastguard Cottage, Nethergate. Owner of Balzac the cat.

Ben Wilde — Libby's significant other. Owner of The Manor Farm and the Oast House Theatre.

Guy Wolfe — Fran's husband, artist and owner of a shop and gallery in Harbour Street, Nethergate.

Peter Parker — Ben's cousin. Freelance journalist, part owner of The Pink Geranium restaurant and life partner of Harry Price.

Harry Price — Chef and co-owner of The Pink Geranium and Peter Parker's life partner.

Hetty Wilde — Ben's mother. Lives at The Manor.

DCI Ian Connell — Local policeman and friend. Former suitor of Fran's.

Adam Sarjeant — Libby's youngest son. Works with garden designer Mog, mainly at Creekmarsh.

Lewis Osbourne-Walker — TV gardener and handy-man who owns Creekmarsh

Sophie Wilde — Guy's daughter.

Flo Carpenter — Hetty's oldest friend.

Lenny Fisher	Hetty's brother. Lives with Flo Carpenter.
Ali and Ahmed	Owners of the Eight-til-late in the village.
Jane Baker	Chief Reporter for the *Nethergate Mercury*. Mother of Imogen.
Terry Baker	Jane's husband and father of Imogen.
Joe, Nella and Owen	of Cattlegreen Nurseries
Reverend Patti Pearson	Vicar of St Aldeberge's Church
Anne Douglas	Librarian, friend of Reverend Patti

Chapter One

A breeze rustled through the heavy branches of the old yew tree and moved moon shadows over the body that lay quietly stiffening between the gravestones. Voices drifted back to disturb the silence, gradually petering out to be replaced by the sounds of car engines being started up, until, at last, peace returned to the graveyard and its most recent occupant.

'I don't care,' said Libby Sarjeant mutinously. 'I can't play the bloody things. They hurt my fingers.'

Her friend Peter Parker regarded her with amusement. 'And you don't want to cut your nails.'

'Well, no.' Libby regarded her newly varnished nails with satisfaction.

Harry Price, Peter's life partner and owner-chef of The Pink Geranium restaurant in Steeple Martin's high street, peered at her hands.

'So what were you talking about anyway?' he asked, sitting down at the pub table.

'The ukulele group,' said Ben Wilde, Libby's significant other, returning from the bar with drinks. 'You know.'

'I don't actually,' said Harry, accepting a pint of lager. 'Oh, I know there is one – isn't Lewis part of it? – but I'm not sure what it's all about.'

'It's a craze,' said Libby. 'These groups have sprung up all over the country and because ukuleles are cheap to buy and fairly easy to play, they've become really popular, especially with the – er – older market.'

'Pensioners,' explained Ben. 'People looking for something to do with their time and who like playing the old songs.'

'Like that cleaning windows bloke?' said Harry.

'Similar,' said Libby. 'Anyway, this chap from Canterbury had a group going and decided to start another one here.'

'Why here?'

'Because it's a fairly large village with a decent church hall,' said Libby.

'Initially, he tried to use the theatre for his rehearsals, until we explained that it was so often in use he couldn't and the hire rate would be the same as for the theatre. That peeved him a bit.' Ben smiled at the memory. 'So he uses the church hall.'

'So why were you going to join?' Harry turned back to Libby.

'I wasn't. Somehow, as you said, he's persuaded Lewis to join to raise the profile, and Edie's joined too. She used to play the banjo in her salad days, apparently, and she's really enjoying it, so she wanted me to join too, to keep her company.'

'And you don't want to.'

'No! I wasn't at all sure about the people – I went once with Edie – and the strings hurt my fingers.'

'And now they're going to be part of the big Christmas Concert at the theatre,' said Peter.

'Andrew's charity concert?' said Harry. 'But haven't you got some famous people in that? Won't they show themselves up?'

'We've got some pro singers and musicians and your Andrew is going to read some Dickens,' said Ben. 'You knew that.'

'Pro musos won't take kindly to a bunch of geriatric strummers,' said Harry.

'Don't be so rude, Harry Price!' Libby bent a baleful eye on her friend. 'It's for a very good cause, and Andrew will keep everyone in line.'

Sir Andrew McColl was a friend met fairly recently, after the death of someone close to both he and Harry. A theatrical knight, married to a theatrical dame, he had professed himself delighted with the Oast Theatre, of which Ben was the owner. Peter and Libby were both directors of the company. It was he who had suggested the concert, in aid of a homeless charity.

'How was panto rehearsal tonight?' Harry changed the

subject. 'Still having trouble with the chorus?'

'Not my problem any more,' said Libby. 'Susannah's taken them over lock, stock, and barrel. She's making them sound quite good now. And we've got proper dancers again, so they're doing their stuff in Lorraine's studio until we stick them all together.'

'I don't know Lorraine, do I?'

'She's a dancer with her own studio in Canterbury. She takes private pupils, and still appears in TV ads, but says she's too old now for the West End. She's bloody good, and hilarious,' said Peter. 'I'm sure I pointed her out to you the other day. That furniture polish ad.'

'Oh, her,' said Harry. 'You are getting posh. And is Susannah's old man quite happy to be doing all the baby-sitting while she's out gallivanting?'

'He is,' said Libby. 'After all, we're paying her.'

Susannah's brother Terry Baker had introduced her to Libby and the Oast Theatre some years before when they were planning a special birthday party for Ben's mother Hetty. Susannah was a professional singer and pianist, who, since she'd become a mother, was less keen to do the touring that went with the job. She'd happily settled in to the Oast company as almost permanent musical director.

The barman leant across the bar.

'You talking about the ukulele lot? That's some of 'em come in just now.' He jerked his head in the direction of the other half of the bar, where some of the pantomime cast were also drinking.

Peter and Libby craned their necks to try and see round the corner.

'Don't recognise any of them,' said Peter, 'but I can't see properly.'

'Lewis isn't there, then?' said Libby.

'He'd have come looking for us,' said Ben.

Lewis Osbourne-Walker had come to prominence as a handy-man on a television make-over show and now presented a whole variety, from country documentaries to lifestyle

3

programmes. His own series had featured the make-over of his garden by Libby's son Adam and Adam's boss, Mog. He divided his time between London and Creekmarsh, an old house a few miles from Steeple Martin, where his mother Edie had the former housekeeper's flat.

'Well, I'm ready to go home now,' said Libby. 'I've got an appointment with our wardrobe mistress in the morning which I'm not looking forward to.'

'Why?' asked Ben.

'She always wants to make the costumes *she* wants, rather than the ones *I* want,' said Libby. 'I wrote the bloody thing, I know what I want the cast to look like.' She stood up and wandered into the other bar to say goodbye to the rest of the cast.

'And why did you do that?' asked Peter, when she came back to collect her coat. 'Just to have a look at the ukulele people?'

'Of course she did,' said Ben with a grin. 'I wonder she doesn't join them just out of nosiness.'

Libby sniffed. 'I told you, the strings hurt my fingers. Anyway, I've got far too much on with the panto.'

Lewis Osbourne-Walker appeared in the doorway of the pub. He waved distractedly to Libby and her friends but called loudly to the ukulele group in the other bar.

'Old Vernon in here? His car's still in the car park.'

A stillness fell over the bar.

'No,' said one male voice hesitantly. 'He never comes to this pub.'

'That's what I thought,' said Lewis. He turned to Libby.

'Any of you lot seen him? Oldish bloke, reddish hair, thinning on top, glasses.'

'That could be anybody,' said Peter.

'Nobody's been in this bar but us,' said Ben.

'Where is he, then?' said Lewis. 'His missus just rang me to say his mobile keeps going to voicemail. What's happened to him?'

Chapter Two

They found out what had happened to Vernon Bowling the next morning. Harry rang as Libby was having her third cup of tea and Ben was about to leave for the estate office at the Manor.

'You know that bloke Lewis was looking for last night? Well, they found him.'

'Yes? Oh, good.'

'Not so good. Dead as a dodo in the churchyard.' Harry sounded cheerful.

Libby gasped. 'Poor man. What was it? A heart attack?'

'No, ducky. Murder.'

Libby sank down into her chair and made a face at Ben. 'I simply don't believe it.'

'True. Blue-and-white tape across Maltby Lane and the doctor's car park half full of police cars.'

'That doesn't necessarily mean murder,' said Libby. Ben had come back to the table and sat down again.

'Flo's already been across to tell me. All the old dears in Maltby Close have had an officer at the door, and our Ian's been seen.' Detective Chief Inspector Ian Connell was an old friend.

'Oh, dear.' Libby shook her head. 'Tragic. At least we've got nothing to do with it this time. But why bring it right home to our village? That's not fair.'

'I don't suppose he meant to get killed in your village, lovey,' said Harry. 'Anyway, I've got prepping up to do. I'm looking forward to being full at lunchtime when the gawpers arrive.'

'That's shocking, you ghoul!'

'No, just sensible. Pop in for a chat if you're passing.' Harry ended the call, and Libby looked across at Ben.

'Did you get all that?'

'Lewis's missing man? I gathered. Where?'

'In the churchyard. Ian's there, apparently. Flo told Harry.'

'Don't get involved,' warned Ben, standing up again. 'Nothing to do with you.'

'No, of course not,' said Libby. 'I've got enough to worry about.'

'Have you?' Ben raised one eyebrow. 'What, exactly?'

'The panto, of course,' said Libby in exasperation. 'I've got the wardrobe meeting in half an hour, and you know I'm not looking forward to it.'

After a gruelling hour with the formidable wardrobe mistress, whom Libby did not dare push too far in case she took up her scissors and left in a huff, Libby put her folder of sketches into her brand new bag, the latest successor to her old favourite, the basket, locked the theatre and made her way down the Manor drive towards The Pink Geranium.

'Had a call from Andrew this morning,' said Harry, coming forward with two steaming mugs of coffee.

'Did you? Why?' Libby frowned.

Harry shook his head at her. 'What do you mean, why? Why do you think? About the concert.'

'Oh!' Libby was enlightened. 'I thought you meant the other Andrew.'

'Why on earth would Andrew Wylie call me? And we haven't seen him for ages, anyway.'

'He came to last year's panto, and he helped out over that business at Dark House,' said Libby.

'Well, we'll have to find a way to tell them apart,' said Harry.

'Easy, I suppose. Sir Andrew and Professor Andrew.'

'But not to their faces.'

'No. But I would love to see them together. They're both small and neat, aren't they?'

Harry laughed. 'I suppose so. And much the same age, too.'

'Oh, no,' said Libby indignantly. 'Andrew Wylie's at least ten years younger.'

'All right, all right. I didn't tell you about Andrew's call to get into a discussion about his age.'

'What, then?'

Harry topped up their mugs. 'He'd already heard about our murder.'

'What?' Libby was bewildered. 'But we've only just heard …'

'On the news, apparently.'

'I didn't hear it,' said Libby.

'On the *proper* news, dear heart,' grinned Harry, 'not the three-second headlines you listen to.'

'Oh.' Libby digested this. 'I expect it will be on the local news this evening.'

'I'm sure it will.' Harry nodded towards the window. 'Isn't that your mate's outfit?'

Libby looked round to see the large blue-and-white Kent and Coast Television van drawing up beyond the police tape.

'If you mean Campbell McLean, he's not my mate,' she said.

'I thought you and Fran got to know him quite well?'

Libby shrugged. 'A bit.'

'Well.' Harry grinned again. 'You're going to get the chance to know him a bit better. He's headed over here.'

Sure enough, the bell over the door tinkled and Campbell McLean, still looking like an old-fashioned geography teacher, appeared.

'Hello, Libby – I thought I recognised your back.' Campbell nodded to Harry, who held up an enquiring coffee pot. Campbell's face broke into a grin. 'Oh, I'd die for a decent coffee.' He turned back to Libby and pulled out a chair. 'So what do you know about all this?'

'All …?'

Campbell waved a hand at the window. 'This. The murder.'

'Nothing,' said Libby. 'Harry's only just told me – well, a bit earlier.'

'Really?' Campbell looked from Libby to Harry and back again. 'Oh, come on, don't give me that.'

Libby scowled. 'Why does every bloody murder in the district have something to do with me? Well, it doesn't. I don't

7

know anything about this, or even who the victim is.' She glared at Campbell. 'Do you?'

He was taken aback. Harry put a mug down in front of him and patted him on the shoulder. 'Never mind, mate, her bite's much worse than her bark.' He winked at Libby.

'Actually, I do know,' said Campbell slowly, 'but I thought you must know because of this group he's in.'

'Do you mean the ukulele group? They're nothing to do with me.'

Campbell raised his eyebrows. 'No? Then why did the wire say "rehearsing for a concert in Steeple Martin's well-known Oast Theatre"?'

Libby sighed. 'It's a charity concert. It's been hired by an outside hirer.'

'Yes – Sir Andrew McColl. How did he hear of you?'

Libby saw Harry's face darken. 'Old friends,' she said hurriedly. 'And how come you've got so much information already?'

'I told you – it was on the wire. Apparently your friend Lewis Osbourne-Walker's involved, too.'

Libby nodded gloomily.

'So you could hardly blame me …'

Libby sighed. 'No all right but, truly, I know nothing about it. All I know is Lewis came into the pub last night to ask the ukulele group if any of them had seen someone, then Harry called me this morning to tell me a friend of ours had been questioned in a house to house.'

Campbell brightened. 'Questioned?'

'Because she lives over there. They talked to everyone,' said Harry.

'Really?' Campbell swivelled in his chair and tried to peer past his own van into Maltby Close.

'It's a sort of private retirement complex,' explained Libby. 'There were barns there, and someone turned them into self-contained units for the better-off over-fifty-fives. There's a community hall and, of course, the doctor's surgery at this end.'

'Oh, so not likely to be involved?'

'They're all over sixty-five, let alone fifty-five,' said Harry.

'So that community hall, is that where this rehearsal was?'

'No, in the church hall, at the back of the church. I know that, because we turned them down and they asked us to suggest somewhere else. The Carpenter Room is only used by the residents of Maltby Close.' Libby drained her coffee mug. 'Sorry Campbell, but this time, you've got the edge on us. So who was the victim?'

'Vernon Bowling.' Campbell looked from Libby to Harry. 'Ring any bells?'

They both shook their heads.

'Top government scientist. No?'

'No,' said Libby. 'Why would we know that?'

'Unless he's been involved in scandal of some sort,' said Harry.

'Well, it looks as though he might have been now, doesn't it?' said Campbell eagerly. 'I'd better get over there and see what's going on.'

'Off you go then,' said Libby. 'Good hunting.'

They watched him trot across the road and disappear behind the big van.

'Scientist,' said Libby. 'Playing the ukulele?'

'There's a gay television builder, too,' said Harry. 'Takes all sorts.'

'Do you think this is going to bring the media down on us?' Libby rested her chin in her hands and peered through the window.

'That was what I was going to tell you. Andrew heard it – or saw it – on the news this morning and wanted to know if we knew any more about it. He was pretty sure the media will pay us some attention –'

'Oh, no,' groaned Libby.

'And that it will do us good,' finished Harry triumphantly.

'I thought the tickets were already selling quite well?'

'The punters will be falling over themselves now,' said Harry. 'Andrew reckons we might have to put it on for another night.'

Libby frowned. 'Does he mean the Sunday as well as the Saturday? I can't see that being popular with the artistes – it's the Sunday before Christmas. A lot of them will have stuff planned.'

'He meant the Friday,' said Harry, looking a little nervous.

'My last rehearsal?' exploded Libby. 'You must be joking!'

'I told him that, but he still wanted me to ask.'

'He's a pro – he knows we open on the 29th. I've had to let everybody have Christmas week off, or I wouldn't have a cast, so I can't afford to lose any more rehearsal time. As it is the cast are coming in on the 28th to do a final run.'

'I know,' sighed Harry. 'I told him.'

'Anyway,' said Libby piously, 'it's awful to have to profit from a murder.'

'I can think of quite a bit of profit made out of murder round here,' said Harry, collecting mugs.

'What?' Libby glared at him.

'You and Ben, Fran and Guy. Even Flo and Lenny in a way. And young Jane and her Terry.'

'That's not profit. Not money profit.'

'You've also made friends with the dishiest cop in Kent,' said Harry, nodding once more towards the window. 'And guess where he's coming?'

Chapter Three

Detective Chief Inspector Ian Connell pushed open the door of The Pink Geranium.

'Coffee?' said Harry.

'No, we don't know anything about it,' said Libby.

DCI Connell looked amused. 'Yes, to the coffee, Harry, and no, I didn't think you did, Libby.'

'Oh.' Libby deflated.

Harry brought a mug for Ian and sat down at the table. 'What, then?'

'I simply wanted to know how much you know about this ukulele group. They were in touch with you, weren't they?'

'Only to ask if they could rehearse in the theatre,' said Libby. 'Ben put them on to the church hall. Andrew's had the most contact with them.'

'Professor Wylie?' Ian frowned.

'There, see,' said Libby, turning to Harry. 'He did it, too.'

'Not him, no,' said Harry. 'My Sir Andrew.'

'Ah.' Ian was enlightened. 'McColl. I forgot he was a Sir.'

'Well, he's the one organising this concert, you see.'

'So he asked a local amateur ukulele group to appear at his Christmas Concert?' Ian's eyebrows disappeared into his hairline. 'I don't believe it.'

'I think they asked him,' said Harry. 'Putting the emphasis on Lewis.'

'Ah, I heard he was involved.' Ian sipped coffee and seemed to relax. 'So that's all you know?'

Libby shrugged. 'Afraid so. Can you tell us what happened?'

'Only what you can read in the papers later, or hear on the news. Vernon Bowling was found in the churchyard this morning by the sexton. His wife had actually reported him

11

missing last night when he didn't come home from a rehearsal.'

'Yes, Lewis came into the pub asking for him,' said Harry. 'We didn't know who it was, though.'

'And I still don't,' said Libby.

'You don't?' Ian seemed surprised.

'Campbell McLean thought we ought to know, too,' said Libby. 'He was over here just before you.'

'I saw,' said Ian. 'That's why I came. Anyway, Vernon Bowling was the man who was involved in the scandal at Dellington, remember that?'

'Er ...' Libby's eyes swivelled towards Harry.

'Dellington!' Harry's chair rocked backwards. 'Yes. That experiment place.'

'That's it.' Ian looked at Libby. 'Bowling was one of the scientists at Dellington, which was a top secret government testing base.'

'Oh – like that Porton Down?'

'That's it. And they were found to be testing lethal substances, which only came to light after a couple of the volunteers died.'

'Horrible.' Libby shuddered. 'So is that why you think he was murdered? In revenge?'

'It looks unlikely,' said Ian. 'It was a long time ago, and Bowling's been out of the public eye for years. But,' he sighed, 'we'll have to go through the other members of the group with a toothcomb.'

'You shouldn't be telling us,' grinned Libby.

Ian smiled ruefully. 'I know. It's come to be a habit. Anyway, you don't know any of them, so it really doesn't matter.'

'We do,' said Harry. 'We know Lewis and his mum.'

'Oh, no. Is she a member, too?'

'Yes. I went with her once to keep her company.' Libby bit her lip. That wasn't meant to come out.

Ian frowned. 'I thought you said you didn't know any of them?'

'I don't. I went once with Edie because Lewis couldn't go

12

that week, and she so enjoyed going, but she didn't know any of the other members, so I didn't actually meet them, either.'

'Well,' said Ian, getting to his feet, 'I might show you a list of the other members when I've got it, just to see if you do know any of them. Or anything about them.'

'And we won't tell the Chief Constable,' said Harry, also getting to his feet and holding the door open. 'It's Wednesday tonight, and we'll be in the pub.'

'If I'm not still sleuthing, I'll see you there.' Ian gave a wave and set off back to the crime scene.

'Well, that's a first,' said Libby. 'Ian asking for our help.'

'No, it isn't,' said Harry. 'He's done it before.'

'But not when we had no possible connection.'

'But you *have* got a connection. The theatre and the concert.'

'That's very tenuous,' said Libby, getting up and collecting her basket. 'I'll see you tonight. And you can tell *Sir* Andrew he can't have the Friday.'

On Wednesday evenings, the Reverend Patti Pearson came to Steeple Martin to have dinner with her friend Anne Douglas at The Pink Geranium, after which they had formed the habit of joining Libby, Ben and Peter at the pub. Ian often joined them, especially if Libby was involved in something unsavoury. This evening, he arrived at the same time as Harry, who had left the closing of the restaurant to Libby's son Adam, who occasionally worked for him.

'What have you been up to now, Libby?' said Patti, as Harry went to buy himself and Ian beer and coffee respectively.

'Nothing,' said Libby with a sigh. 'Why does everyone automatically assume I'm involved in something?'

'Because there was a murder here last night it follows as the night the day,' said Anne, moving her wheelchair to allow Ian to pull up a chair.

'In this case,' said Ian, 'Libby actually isn't involved. And as we're all here, I might as well let you all see this list of names.'

'What names?' Ben peered across the table as Ian brought out a piece of paper.

'The people in the ukulele group. If any of you know

anything about any of them, perhaps you'll tell me? Uniform have spoken to most of them by now, but they're all saying they didn't know the victim very well.'

'Well, they would,' said Libby. 'What does his wife say?'

'Not a lot yet. She's not even sure how he got involved with the group, just that he'd become obsessed with the instrument.'

'Who was the victim?' asked Anne.

'Vernon Bowling,' said Ian

'Vernon Bowling? Wasn't he that scientist back in the seventies who killed people with drugs?' said Patti.

'At Dellington, yes.'

'How do you all remember him? It was years and years ago,' said Libby.

'There was a scandal at the time, and then it was referred to Operation Antler.'

'Eh?' said Harry.

'It was the police operation looking into chemical weapons test participants who weren't properly informed about the possible dangers.'

'Like those poor atom bomb people?' said Libby.

'Who were they?' asked Patti.

'Military people who were at the nuclear testing sites in the fifties. They had no protective clothing and were just told to turn their backs. They suffered awful effects from radiation exposure, and they've never been given any compensation.' Libby's voice had become indignant.

'Well, not quite like them, but similar. In fact some of the Dellinger and Porton Down victims did get compensation – or rather, their relatives did. The victims themselves were simply sent to the families in sealed steel coffins.'

'Bloody awful,' muttered Peter. 'Caring society we live in, don't we?'

'If Bowling was involved in that I'm not sure he didn't deserve to die,' said Ben.

'Ben!' Patti turned a shocked face to him. 'You can't say that! I expect he was under orders, anyway.'

'It does suggest a motive, though,' said Libby.

14

'Well, it isn't going to be an outraged parent at this distance,' said Ben.

'It could be,' said Ian, 'the parents would be in their eighties. But it could also be a sister? Brother? Even a niece or nephew.'

'Bit far-fetched,' said Anne. 'Let's have a look at that list.'

They all peered at Ian's list.

'Ron Stewart – is that Screwball Stewart?' said Patti.

'No idea,' said Ian. 'Who's he?'

'An old ex-rock star. He lives in Shott. Well, Bishop's Bottom, actually.'

'Does he now? Yes, that sounds like him.'

'How do you know an old ex-rock star, Patti?' said Libby.

'Shott comes within my parish boundary. His name crops up now and then.' Patti laughed. 'You all looked so shocked!'

'So you don't actually know him, then?' said Ian.

'Oh, I've met him a couple of times, but we're not exactly on visiting terms. So I can't go and do undercover snooping for you!' Patti grinned mischievously.

'Screwball Stewart,' said Peter. 'I remember him, don't you, Ben?'

'He was the drummer with Jonah Fludde. Drugs victim, wasn't he?'

'Jonah Fludde – I've heard of them,' said Harry. 'Seventies, weren't they?'

'Weren't they all drugs victims then?' said Ian. 'Sorry – that's generalising. Anyway, we'll talk to him. Seems odd for a seventies rock star to be in a ukulele group, though, doesn't it?'

'Perhaps he was asked to be a draw, like Lewis?' suggested Libby.

'I don't recognise any of the other names,' said Ben. 'Anyone else?'

They all shook their heads.

'Are any of them from here? From Steeple Martin, I mean?' said Libby. 'I mean, it seems odd if they're rehearsing here that none of the members are local. Who's the organiser?'

'I can't remember,' said Ben, pulling the paper back towards him. 'Who is it, Ian?'

'This one –' Ian pointed. 'Dr Eric Robinson.'

'Is he a real doctor?' asked Harry.

'What do you mean?' Ian grinned at him.

'I mean, a medical doctor? Or a doctor of something else?'

'No idea – again,' said Ian. 'I'll try and find out for you. Now, how's the panto coming along?'

Everyone accepted the change of conversation, but Libby was obviously still thinking about the murder as she and Ben walked home to Allhallow's Lane.

'I don't buy that old seventies story as a motive, you know,' she said. 'It's too old.'

'I'm sure Ian will dig something else up,' said Ben. 'And anyway, didn't someone once say the motive was the least of the problems? It's the "how" that's the most important.'

'Well, that's easy,' said Libby. 'He was hit on the head.'

'But how was it done? Who has an alibi? Was anyone seen? That's what they'll be looking for.'

'I still think the "why" is important. Anybody could have walloped him after their rehearsal and just slipped away with everyone else. They could even have been in the pub when Lewis came in to ask. I think looking into all the members to see who had a link to the victim is the only way forward. That's why Ian came to us – to see if we knew anyone on the list.'

Ben looked dubious. 'If it was, then he'll be doing it – looking into the suspects. Not you.'

'Oh, of course not,' said Libby, suspiciously innocent.

The next morning, as soon as Ben had gone off to his office in the Manor, Libby was on the phone to her friend Fran Wolfe.

'Ian did come to the pub last night!'

'Eh?'

'I told you he said he might. He told us a bit more about the murder.'

'He did? Why?'

'I told you yesterday,' said Libby with a sigh. 'Everybody seemed to assume I knew something about the victim and I didn't, but Ian brought a list of the members of the ukulele group to the pub to see if anyone knew anything about some of them.

And guess who did?'

'Patti,' said Fran promptly.

'How did you know that?' Libby was indignant.

'Because of the way you said it. It had to be the least likely person.'

'But you'll never guess who it was she knew! Screwball Stewart!'

'Screwball – who?'

'Ron Stewart – known as Screwball. He was the drummer in Jonah Fludde.'

'Jonah – oh yes, I remember. They were prog rock, weren't they?'

'Wow, Fran! I'm surprised you know that!'

Fran laughed. 'I wasn't always middle-aged any more than you were!'

'No. Funny though, I can't think of Jonah Fludde being middle-aged.'

'I rather liked them. They used fiddles – and didn't they have an oboe? I rather think they're still going in a revised form.'

'Really? How do you know that?'

'I've seen their name on a couple of festival posters.'

'How,' said Libby, 'do you get to see festival posters?'

'Oh, I don't know,' said Fran vaguely. 'Lucy goes to them.'

'With the children?'

'Oh, yes. I gather there are lots of families. Anyway, how does Patti know this person?'

'He lives in a village that is one of hers. A place called Shott. Do you know it?'

'I've seen it on signposts. So don't tell me this Stewart's a parishioner?'

'No,' said Libby, 'she said he just crops up. She's met him. I expect the village trot him out as a tame celebrity now and again.'

'And you say he's in the ukulele group? How odd!'

'Well, yes. But what I was thinking was – how do you fancy a little drive out to Shott?'

Chapter Four

'Libby!'

'What? All I asked was –'

'I heard what you asked,' said an exasperated Fran. 'You want to drive out to Shott and snoop around. Why, for goodness' sake? You won't find anything out just by being in the village – such as it is – and it's absolutely none of your business anyway.'

'I just thought –'

'I know what you just thought,' said Fran. 'You are incurably nosy. And when you called me yesterday to tell me about it you said it wasn't fair bringing a murder right to your own doorstep. Which, incidentally, isn't the first time.'

'No, I know.' Libby sighed. 'It's become automatic, I suppose.'

'Being nosy?'

'Well, yes.' She was silent for a moment, then brightened. 'But there's nothing to stop me going for a little drive in the country, is there?'

Fran sighed. 'If you're determined, then I'll have to come with you.'

'Why "have to"?'

'Because if I'm not with you you'll do something stupid.'

'I'm not going to resent that remark,' said Libby loftily, 'because I should prefer to have your company rather than going alone.'

Fran sighed deeply again. 'I'll pick you up,' she said.

The road to the village of Shott led off the Canterbury road in the other direction to Steeple Cross and Keeper's Cob.

'This is a bit like Dark Lane,' muttered Libby, as Fran manoeuvred round a narrow bend bordered on both sides by tall,

19

bare trees and tangled undergrowth.

'Not as intimidating, somehow,' said Fran. 'Look, here's Itching.'

'Bloody strange names they've got round here,' said Libby. 'Do we go straight through Itching?'

'Signpost,' said Fran. 'There.'

Libby peered out at the small black-and-white metal signpost that indicated a right turn to Shott and Bishop's Bottom.

'Down there,' she said. 'Shott Lane.'

Shott Lane led downhill between more heavy vegetation. As the first thatched cottage appeared before them on their right, to the left Libby saw an old chapel with a drunken "For Sale" sign outside.

'I bet that would be lovely if you converted it,' she said. 'Look – a pub.'

The lane widened out to divide round a small green. Between two cottages opposite they could see an obviously Norman church, and nearer, on the corner of another road, a long, low pub, its swinging sign announcing it to be "The Poacher".

'I'll park on the forecourt,' said Fran. 'It's after opening time, so we could get a coffee.'

'The idealised view of English rural life,' said Libby, getting out of the car. 'No shop, no post office, no transport ...'

'You're wrong there,' said Fran. 'Look.' She pointed across the green to a small building looking like a Portakabin, "Shop" proudly displayed across its front.

'A community one, do you think?' asked Libby. 'Like the one in Patti's village?'

'Looks like it. Come on, let's go inside. We don't want them to think we're taking advantage parking here.'

The pub, like so many of its ilk, had turned itself into a restaurant for the most part. Libby and Fran approached the bar through a forest of empty tables and chairs. A rather surprised-looking landlord greeted them.

'Morning, ladies. What can I get you?'

'Could we have coffee, do you think?' asked Libby.

'Sure. How do you want it?'

When they had negotiated the niceties of the coffee menu, the landlord put their mugs in front of them and cocked an enquiring eyebrow.

'So, don't get visitors here at this time of the year,' he said. 'What brings you here?'

'We found you by accident,' said Fran hastily, before Libby could put her foot in it. 'Fascinated by the names of the villages.'

'Yeah – a lot of people are,' said the landlord. 'Mind you, good for us in the tourist season. And we get a lot of Americans and such like looking for their ancestors.'

'Are there a lot of local names still here?' asked Libby. 'We've got some in my village – a lot of Hoads for instance.'

The landlord nodded. 'We've got some Hoads, here, too. And a lot of Hoddens. Vicar reckons they was all one family one time.' He grinned. 'And a right bunch they are, too! Mostly farmers and labourers and the like. And half of 'em live down Rogues Lane an' all!' He laughed uproariously.

'Really?' Libby smiled, a little disbelieving.

'No, true.' He nodded. 'Rogues Lane's over the green. Goes up to Bishop's Bottom. Got Hoads and Hoddens living down there. Used to be Hodden Farm.'

'Isn't the farm there any more?' asked Fran.

'Nah. They built some great new house there instead.'

'Who? The Hoddens?' said Libby.

'No. Last owners sold the land. Some of the Hoads was sitting tenants in the cottages, but the Hoddens had all bought theirs. So they stayed. New owner got the big house.'

'New owners built it?' said Fran.

'Some builder built it.'

'Not Ron Stewart?' asked Libby.

The landlord looked surprised. 'You know Ron?'

'Well, no, only who he was. We did know he lived here.'

The landlord's eyes narrowed. 'So that's why you came here? Now, old Ron keeps himself to hisself these days. Don't want no fuss.'

'No, of course not.' Fran was soothing. 'It's my fault. I've driven along the Canterbury road from Nethergate and passed the sign for "Itching, Shott, and Bishop's Bottom" so often, I just had to come and see what they were like.'

'Oh, ah.' The landlord took down a glass and began to polish it unnecessarily. 'Well, Ron don't live in the big house, anyway.'

'Is the shop a community one?' asked Libby, desperately trying to save the situation. 'A friend of ours helps run one over at St Aldeberge. It's very successful.'

'Yeah.' The answer was somewhat grudging. 'Opens every day except Sunday. All volunteers, o'course.'

'Yes, Patti's is, too,' said Fran.

'St Aldeberge?' The landlord now looked up. 'That's our Rev Patti, isn't it?'

'Yes!' said Fran surprised.

'Oh, I remember, now,' said Libby. 'Shott's one of hers, isn't it? She said something about parish boundary.'

The landlord had now become friendly again. 'That's it,' he said. 'Poor lass has more than enough to cope with. This is the parish of St Aldeberge, Shott, and Bishop's Bottom. Then she's got those villages the other side.'

'The mining villages,' nodded Libby. 'She does get a bit overworked. But she comes to see us nearly every week on her day off.'

'So you're friends of our Rev Patti. Oh, well, that's nice.' He leant his elbows on the counter. 'Nasty do over at St Aldeberge's the other year, though, wasn't it?'

'Very nasty.' Libby shivered, remembering.

'You wasn't involved in that, was you?' said the landlord, his eyes growing round.

'A bit,' said Fran uncomfortably. 'She's a friend. We did what we could.'

'Oh, ah.' The landlord suddenly leant across the bar and peered into their faces. 'Got it!' He snapped his fingers. 'That play! In that church place – there was a murder there, too, wasn't there?'

'Er – yes.' Libby was now even more uncomfortable than

22

Fran. 'Well, it was nice to meet you, Mr – er –'

'Sid Best.' He held out a hand.

'My –' began Libby, before Fran broke in.

'Fran Wolfe,' she said shaking Sid's hand, 'and this is Libby Sarjeant. Now we must get on. If we go through Bishop's Bottom we can get through to St Aldeberge, can't we?'

'Yes, straight up Rogues Lane. You'll see the big house on the left.' He grinned. 'Give my best to Rev Patti.'

'Not the best idea to tell him you have a cat called Sidney,' Fran reproved as they went back to the car.

'I didn't!'

'You were just about to,' said Fran. 'So what did you learn?'

'That Ron Stewart is protected by the village and Sid Best saw the play last year at St Eldreda's. He recognised us.' Libby glanced at her friend. 'Quick thinking of mine to introduce Patti.'

'You didn't, really. He was the one who took it up. And yes, it was lucky.' Fran started the engine. 'We'll drive round the green slowly and have a good peer at the houses.'

The few houses round the small green were all beautifully kept and rather smug.

'Second homes, do you reckon?' said Libby. 'It's almost too perfect to be true.'

'Commuter homes, wouldn't you think?' said Fran. 'Nice church, what we can see of it.'

'Oh, this is more like it,' said Libby, as they turned left into Rogues Lane, where a row of flint cottages flanked the right side of the road, looking as though they'd grown out of the ground.

'The Hoddens' cottages, I suppose,' said Fran, 'and look. That must be the big house.'

Just beyond the cottages, on their left, a large, neo-Georgian house in red brick with white pillasters stood on a slight rise, screaming its newness to the world.

'Wonder who lives there?' said Libby, as they drove slowly past. 'Not Ron, obviously.'

'And our Sid didn't tell us, either,' said Fran. 'Are we really going on to see Patti?'

'No, of course not. She's probably up to her ears in parish work and wouldn't thank us for dropping in.'

'We could ring,' said Fran.

'We could offer to take her to lunch,' agreed Libby, pulling out her phone.

'But not here,' said Patti, after Libby had issued the invitation. 'How about The Red Lion in Heronsbourne?'

'Shall we pick you up?' asked Libby.

'No, I'll drive over, then you don't have to make a detour to take me back. See you in – what? Half an hour?'

'It'll be nice seeing George again,' said Libby, putting her phone back in her pocket. 'That's another of Patti's churches, isn't it? St Martha's?'

'George told you it was,' said Fran. 'Now, how do we get to Heronsbourne from here?'

'After we go through Bishop's Bottom, shouldn't we hit that narrow lane that leads off the Canterbury road to St Aldeberge? Then we can turn right on to that.'

'Oh, yes, and it comes out almost opposite the road to Heronsbourne, doesn't it?'

Bishop's Bottom, which proved to be as small as, or smaller than, Itching and Shott, was nothing more than a crossroads with a couple of large houses on the outskirts, one of which was the twin of the big house in Shott.

'Same builder,' said Fran. 'Here's where we turn right.'

Libby and Fran had first been to The Red Lion in Heronsbourne some years ago when looking into another murder. George, the landlord, had subsequently provided them with odd snippets of information in the course of their other adventures. He beamed a welcome as they entered the bar.

'And what is it now?' he asked as he handed over two large coffees. 'Had a new murder, I hear.'

'No,' said Fran. 'We're taking Patti to lunch.'

'And we went to another one of her villages earlier,' added Libby. 'Shott – do you know it?'

'Course I know it. Sid Best has The Poacher over there.'

'Yes, we had coffee there, too,' said Fran.

George narrowed his eyes. 'Ah. You *are* looking into it, then.'

'What do you mean?' said Libby.

'Ron Stewart lives there.'

'Yes?' prompted Fran.

'He belonged to that group. Where the bloke was found dead. In your village,' George said to Libby, who sighed.

'No fooling you, George, is there? But we're not actually looking into it. I was just being nosy. We didn't know it was one of Patti's churches until she told us when she said she knew Ron Stewart. Well, not knew exactly, but she'd met him.'

'He gets wheeled out for the odd event,' said George. 'We have a joint Villages Show in autumn, Shott, us, and St Aldeberge, and old Screwball presents the odd prize. He's donated a cup for something or other. Can't remember what.'

'What's he like?' asked Fran.

'Quiet bloke,' said George, turning to serve another customer. 'Looks the part, though.'

'How do you mean?' asked Libby.

'Oh, you know, leather jacket, T-shirt, jeans, big boots. Longish hair, although he's going a bit bald now. Leastways, he was when I saw him back in October.'

'At the village show?'

'No, he came in here. Gawd knows why. He uses The Poacher mostly.'

'Was he on his own? Perhaps he had a friend who lives here,' suggested Fran.

'He was with someone else, but I didn't know him,' said George. 'Look out – here comes the vicar!'

Patti hurried up to the counter.

'I've just found something out,' she said, in a breathless voice. 'Vernon Bowling lives in Shott too.'

Chapter Five

When Patti had been provided with coffee and they had all ordered, they settled at a table in the window.

'I suppose it's not so surprising, is it?' said Libby. 'Some of the members of the group are bound to live in the same villages.'

'Who set it up in the first place?' asked Fran.

'I couldn't remember who it was who got in touch with us in the first place, but Ian told us last night it was Doctor Robinson, and I can't actually remember if they approached Sir Andrew before they asked us or the other way round.'

'*Sir* Andrew?' said Fran.

'So we don't confuse him with the other Andrew. Prof Andrew.'

'D'you know, I hadn't thought of that,' said Patti. 'And I've met them both.'

'Well, while Sir Andrew is messing about down here, I suggest we don't bring Prof. Andrew over, or we'll get terribly confused,' said Libby. 'And it's quite easy to confuse me at any time.'

'So, if Vernon Bowling and Ron Stewart both lived in Shott and were both members of the ukulele group, we can assume they're friends,' said Fran, returning to the original conversation.

'There may be others who live there, too,' said Libby. 'How did you find out, Patti?'

'One of the churchwardens rang to tell me. We'll have to include him in the intercessions. I'm not due there next Sunday, but I'll have to go over and talk to Mary.'

'Mary?'

'The churchwarden. She says that Mrs Bowling is a churchgoer, although not particularly regular. I suppose I ought to call.' Patti's usually smooth forehead was wrinkled with

27

worry under her heavy fringe.

'I wonder who else comes from your villages,' mused Libby. 'I mean, George here knew about it. Perhaps there's someone here?'

'He'd have told us,' said Fran. 'No, the only ones from this side of the Canterbury road are Lewis and Edie.'

'And I wonder why it was Lewis who Mrs Bowling rang on Tuesday night? Was he a friend?'

'We don't know it was Lewis,' said Fran. 'It was Lewis who went into the pub, you told me, but he could have been told about the phone call by someone else.'

'Oh, so he could,' said Libby. 'You're so logical, Fran.'

Libby's phone warbled from her pocket.

'Hello, Hal. Fran and I are having lunch with Patti. What can I do for you?'

'Andrew's coming down this evening and he's called a meeting of the ukulele group and you.'

'Eh? Me?'

'You, Pete and Ben. I think he wants to talk over the advisability of allowing the uke group to continue in the concert. Oh – and your cousin's just arrived.'

'My c … Oh, God!'

'You'd forgotten, hadn't you?' Harry sighed gustily. 'Luckily we haven't started on the building work upstairs. She can stay in the flat.'

'Is she OK? Oh, how could I have forgotten? What an idiot.'

'Yes, you are. So you'd better come home pdq. I'll feed you all here tonight as you won't have got anything in. Andrew will be here, too.'

'OK, but can I finish my lunch?'

'Yes, but hurry up about it.'

Libby switched off her phone just as their sandwiches arrived accompanied by a garnish of crisps.

'Andrew's holding a meeting with the ukulele group and me, Ben, and Pete tonight, and my cousin Cassandra's arrived.' Libby poked gloomily at her tuna sandwich.

'Your cousin –?' Fran and Patti looked surprised.

'Yes.' Libby sighed. 'We arranged it ages ago. We haven't seen one another for a year or so, so it seemed sensible to arrange a long weekend before the panto and Christmas got in the way. I don't know how I forgot.'

'I didn't know you had a cousin,' said Fran.

'Of course I do. Most people have, haven't they?'

Fran's brow wrinkled. 'I don't think I have.'

'I have,' said Patti. 'They are not the nicest of people. My extended family do *not* believe in women priests, let alone anything else.'

'Well, Cass is one of the nicest people I know. Her husband died years ago, far too young, and her children all live miles away, so I ought to have kept in touch better.'

'Where does she live?' asked Patti.

'London, and one of her children is in Liverpool and the other in Scotland, so she doesn't see much of them.'

'Does she work?' asked Fran.

'No, she retired at sixty. She must be nearer to seventy now, but she does a lot of voluntary work.'

'Well, you'd better hurry up and finish your sandwich,' said Fran, 'and I'll get you back home.'

'Harry's put her up in the flat,' said Libby, 'which is jolly nice of him, as I haven't got the spare room ready. He's going to feed us tonight, too.'

'You do fall on your feet, Mrs S,' said Patti. 'If it had been me, I'd have found the poor woman trailing round the village in the snow.'

'Oh, Cass knows all about Harry and Pete and the caff. She's been here before, but not for years. Must have been not long after her husband died.'

'Before I knew you?' asked Fran.

'Oh, yes, and before Ben and I were together. She's met Ben, because we've been up to see her a few times, when we've been to London to see Bel and Dom.'

'Bel and Dom?' repeated Patti.

'My other two kids,' explained Libby. 'Belinda and Dominic. Didn't you meet them last Christmas?'

Patti shook her head and finished her sandwich. 'Come on, eat up. You're in a hurry.'

Fran went to the counter to pay for their lunch and Libby shrugged herself into her coat.

'Sorry that was a bit cut short, Patti. I'd invite you over to meet Cass, but you're bound to have a wedding or something on Saturday and services on Sunday.'

'You're welcome to bring her over if you're short of things to do,' said Patti, and turned to Fran. 'Thank you for the lunch, Fran.'

Twenty minutes later, Fran was pulling up outside The Pink Geranium. Harry came to the door with a key and let them into the street door of the upstairs flat.

'She's fine. I sent her up lunch and wine, and Ben called her from the timber yard.'

'Oh, dear,' said Libby. 'I do feel guilty. Thank you so much, Hal.'

She started up the stairs, followed by Fran, who had also been given shelter in this flat some years ago before she moved to Coastguard Cottage.

'Cass – it's me! I'm so sorry!'

A tall woman with grey hair wound untidily round her head appeared at the top of the staircase. She grinned broadly.

'I'm not in the least surprised, you daft bat! Come here and give me a hug.'

Disentangling herself, Libby turned to Fran.

'This is Fran Wolfe, Cass. You've heard me talk about her.'

Cassandra held out her hand to Fran. 'Indeed I have. And have you been out investigating? Harry tells me there's a current murder.'

Libby sighed, and perched on the arm of the sofa. 'No, not really. Just being nosy. I'll tell you all about it if you like. But what about coming home with me now for a cup of tea?'

'I'd like that, Lib, but I'm going to stay here over the weekend. Harry offered, and it will keep me out your way.' She turned to Fran. 'Are you coming for tea, too, Fran?'

'I'll give you both a lift,' said Fran.

With Libby still profusely apologising, Fran drove them the short distance to Allhallow's Lane, where Sidney ignored both Libby and Fran and made a terrific fuss of Cassandra.

'So you'll go to this meeting after we've eaten with Harry?' asked Cassandra, when Libby had finished explaining about the evening's plans.

'You can come with us, if you like,' said Libby. 'You haven't seen the theatre since it was finished, have you?'

'Wouldn't your Sir Andrew mind?'

'Of course he wouldn't, would he, Fran?'

Fran shook her head. 'Really nice man. Not a bit starry.'

'Well, I'd like to, if you're sure,' said Cassandra. 'Wonderful actor, isn't he?'

'He is,' agreed Libby.

'How do you come to know him?'

'He and Harry had a mutual friend who died recently,' said Fran easily, while Libby floundered.

'Matthew was a mutual friend of ours, too,' said Libby.

'Well, yes.'

Cassandra squinted at her cousin. 'I sense there's something you're not telling me, but I won't pry. Now, what are you working on at the moment?'

'Working?'

'Painting? You're still painting, aren't you?'

'Er – well,' said Libby guiltily.

'She's supposed to provide originals for sale in my husband's little gallery in Nethergate, but she always seems to be behind,' said Fran.

'There's always so much else to do,' said Libby. 'And they're only potboilers, anyway.'

'They sell,' said Fran. 'OK – not for millions, but they do sell.'

'And people do like having an original on their walls,' said Cassandra. 'You'll have to come up and paint my garden.'

'Next summer?' said Libby. 'When it's at its best?'

'I was thinking of after Christmas and your panto,' said Cassandra. 'It looks lovely in winter.'

'Oh, OK,' said Libby doubtfully. 'Won't it be cold?'

Cassandra and Fran laughed.

'You can see how devoted she is to her art,' said Fran.

'Theatre comes first, Lib, doesn't it?' said Cassandra. 'And then murder investigations.'

'Well, now ...' said Libby uncomfortably.

'She can't help herself,' said Fran. 'Even with this one, she had to go nosing round this morning, and it's nothing to do with us at all.'

'Do tell,' said Cassandra, tucking her feet up under her. 'Sounds intriguing.'

Fran related the events of the morning.

'Shott?' said Cassandra thoughtfully. 'That's an unusual name. Is there a nursery there?'

'I don't know,' said Libby, surprised. 'A playgroup, you mean?'

'No, a plant nursery. I get things from there, and the owner is incredibly helpful.'

'You've been down here without coming to see me?'

'No, I get them by mail order. Of course I'd much prefer to buy them in person, but he's one of the only suppliers of certain types of plant, and it's too far just to pop down for an afternoon.'

'You need to move down here,' said Libby. 'What's keeping you in London? The kids aren't there any more.'

'But when they come to visit they can use me as a base and see other old friends,' said Cassandra. 'If I moved somewhere else they'd have to make a special Mum-only visit.'

'How often do they come and see you?' asked Fran. 'One of mine lives in London, and I swear the only reason she comes to see me is to bring the children to the seaside.'

'I go to them more often these days. I spend Christmas with one or other of them and their families. They come down once – maybe twice – a year.'

'Well, there you are,' said Libby. 'And you could get a lot for your money if you sold the Palmers Green house. You'd get at least ... well, you'd get a lot, wouldn't you?'

'I don't know,' said Cassandra. 'I would miss the theatre and the ballet, and my gardening group.'

'Well, think about it,' said Libby. 'I promise not to involve you in anything you don't want if you do come.' She grinned at Fran. 'Would I?'

Fran laughed and stood up. 'I'd watch it, if I were you, Cassandra. Look, I must be going. Let me know what's happening, won't you?'

'I will, but I don't suppose much will happen tonight. Just a decision to cancel – or not. I'll ring you tomorrow.' Libby turned to Cassandra. 'Shall Fran drop you off at the caff? And we'll see you later.'

Chapter Six

Sir Andrew had opted to hold the meeting in the auditorium of the theatre and asked Peter, Ben and Libby to sit in the front row. He greeted Cassandra charmingly, then went to stand at the foyer doors to greet the rest of the visitors. A large man in tweeds was seated in the front row next to Peter, and introduced as Doctor Eric Robinson, the leader of the group. Libby, craning round to see who else had arrived, waved to Lewis and Edie who waved back and sat at the back of the auditorium.

Eventually, Sir Andrew mounted the stage and his audience went silent.

'Ladies and gentlemen,' he began, 'I'm sorry to have dragged you out again after last night, but in view of the circumstances, we have to discuss the advisability of continuing with your appearance in the Christmas Concert.

'The dreadful murder of Vernon Bowling has already brought the media down on our heads, and I'd like to ask if any of you have been contacted today?'

'I have.' Lewis put his hand up. 'Didn't say anything.'

'Thank you, Lewis, that would be inevitable as you were part of our promotional literature.' A small guilty chuckle rippled through the audience. 'Is Mr Stewart here? I would imagine they will have tried to get in touch with him also.'

But it appeared that Screwball Stewart had not put in an appearance. Instead, Dr Robinson put up his hand.

'Local paper and TV people got in touch with me. I didn't say anything, either. Didn't really know the man.'

'Anyone else?' asked Sir Andrew. 'No? Well, in that case, I would ask you all not to say anything if you're approached. But now we come to a rather indelicate subject. It could be said that the – ah – murder could bring a degree of notoriety and perhaps more interest in the concert.'

'You mean – sell more tickets?' asked someone.

'I mean just that. However, this is a one night only event, and although I did ask if the theatre was available –' he glanced down at Libby with a smile, '– it isn't. However, most of the other guest artistes who have agreed to perform couldn't have given us another night anyway, so the question is moot. What you, as a group, have to decide is whether or not you feel you ought to continue.'

There was a flurry of responses and, in the end, Dr Robinson climbed up on the stage beside Sir Andrew and held up his hand.

'One at a time please,' he said. 'Now, Lewis?'

'I think we should carry on,' said Lewis. 'If it's appropriate, we could dedicate the performance to Vernon. Can't see what we would gain by cancelling.'

There was a murmur of approval, a woman held up a hand.

'Wouldn't it be disrespectful?' she asked. 'I mean – what would his wife think?'

'Can't see that,' said another voice. 'If he'd just – er – died, we wouldn't cancel, would we? Isn't as if we can't do without him.'

Shocked mutterings greeted this, but Dr Robinson spoke again.

'That's right. There are plenty of us, and it isn't as if he was actor in a play who couldn't be replaced, is it?' He turned to Sir Andrew, who smiled ruefully.

'Any actor can be replaced,' he said, 'but in this case I agree with you. And I don't think it would be disrespectful at all. I'm sure, as they say, "That's what he would have wanted".'

'So how about a show of hands?' said Dr Robinson. 'Those for continuing?'

Most hands in the auditorium went up.

'And against?'

Three hands went up.

'Thank you. If those of you who feel it would be disrespectful wish to withdraw from the concert, that's fine, otherwise, motion carried. We go on.'

To a smatter of polite applause, the doctor resumed his seat beside Peter.

'Very well,' said Sir Andrew, 'and now we come to the management of the theatre.' He looked down at Libby, Peter, and Ben. 'How do you feel about it?'

Ben looked first at Libby, then at Peter, and stood up.

'We feel it would be a pity for the group not to perform. Locally, they've been a draw for their friends and family, and I think we might have to refund quite a lot of tickets if they withdrew.'

Relieved laughter rang out and Sir Andrew smiled.

'Thank you, Ben, that wasn't an aspect I'd considered. So there you are, ladies and gentlemen. We carry on as before. Sorry to have dragged you out for what, happily, proved to be a short meeting, but I couldn't take the risk of making decisions without all your support.'

More polite applause, and Sir Andrew came off the stage to join Ben, Peter and Libby, who bounced up to take his place.

'Ladies and gentlemen,' she called, 'we are opening the bar in the foyer if you'd care to have a drink before you go home.'

There was an enthusiastic response to this, and Peter pushed his way through to get to the bar before the thirsty ukulele players.

'Well done, Andrew,' said Ben, 'although I can't see why you had to have a meeting.'

'I do,' said Libby. 'If he hadn't, there would have been phone calls between the members of the group, and not everyone would have agreed, or known what the others were saying, and in the end a decision would have been taken without a consensus and there would have been all sorts of grumbling and argument. And then they might have gone to pieces.'

'Really?' Ben raised his eyebrows in disbelief.

'Libby's right,' said Sir Andrew, 'so I wanted to get them together and see what the mood was. I must admit the return of the tickets hadn't occurred to me, Ben, and that would have been a blow.'

'Look,' said Libby, 'I must go and help Pete in the bar. Ben, will you look after Cassandra for me?'

But Cassandra was peering over heads towards the people pushing through to the foyer. 'Don't worry about me,' she said. 'I think I've seen someone I recognise.'

Everyone turned to her in surprise.

'You remember I told you about the nursery in Shott?' she said to Libby. 'Well there's a picture of the owner on the website and in the catalogue.' She pointed. 'And I think that's him, over there.'

Libby saw a tall, rangy man with untidy grey hair just about to go through the auditorium doors.

'Well, go after him, then,' she said. 'In case he runs away.'

Cassandra grinned, and began to push through the remaining members of the ukulele group, with Libby behind her. When they arrived in the foyer, Libby went behind the bar to help Peter, and Cassandra buttonholed the tall grey-haired man. As Libby watched, he at first looked puzzled, then surprised, and finally delighted. Libby smiled and turned her attention to the next customer awaiting service.

When the queue died down, Libby went to join Ben, who was chatting to Sir Andrew and D r Robinson.

'... just an off-shoot of my Canterbury group in the beginning,' Dr Robinson was saying, 'then it took off in its own right.' He shook his head. 'I don't know any of the members, really. I'd met Ron Stewart, and I suppose you could say I talked him into it. He brought along Vernon Bowling, I think. And Lewis Osbourne-Walker only came with his mother in the first place.' He turned and frowned at Libby. 'Didn't you come with her once?'

'Yes, because she didn't want to come on her own and she didn't know anyone else.' Libby squinted up at him. 'She didn't feel it was a very friendly atmosphere.'

'Oh, dear, really?' Dr Robinson looked round the bar and spotted Lewis and Edie talking to Peter at the bar. 'Perhaps I'd better go ...'

'Don't worry about it now,' said Libby. 'Now you've got the concert to look forward to it seems people have banded together more. No pun intended.'

Dr Robinson looked down at her, puzzled. 'Oh, I see ... Well, I suppose ...'

Ben grinned and Libby sighed.

'Would you excuse us?' said Ben. 'We must just –' He hustled Libby away. 'No sense of humour, that man.'

'We've left poor Sir Andrew with him,' said Libby. 'Oh, well, I suppose he can cope. But actually I wanted to pump him about the other members.'

'Stop it, Lib. Not your business.'

'No ... oh, Edie!' Libby gave the older woman a hug. 'Lovely to see you. Have you got a minute to pop over and see Hetty?'

'Just going,' said Edie. 'Lewis'll come and get me when he's ready.' She smiled all round and bustled off towards the door.

'Grand old girl, ain't she?' said Lewis, fondly. 'Now, Lib, what did you want to ask me?'

'Eh?'

'Go on, you can't fool me. There's this here murder – you're bound to be investigatin'. Or pokin' your nose in, anyway.'

'No, I'm not!' said Libby indignantly.

'Yes, she is,' said Ben. 'I've told her not to.'

Lewis patted Libby's arm affectionately. 'Lost hope, she is. She'll carry on anyway, you know that.'

'Oh, well,' said Libby, shooting Ben a guilty look. 'I just wanted to know why Mrs Bowling rang you the other night and not Dr Robinson – or – or someone else.'

'Oh, because I came into the pub? No, she didn't ring me, she rang Screwball. He didn't want to go into the pub, so I went instead.'

'Oh, yes. Dr Robinson said it was Stewart who brought Vernon Bowling to the group. Mates, were they?'

Lewis shrugged. 'Suppose so. They always sat together and I think they used to sometimes share lifts.'

'But not that night?'

'Statin' the bleedin' obvious, no.'

'Do you know any of the other members?' asked Peter,

suddenly appearing from behind the bar.

'Not really, nor does Mum. There was a bit of interest when I first turned up, but after that they seemed to take a delight in almost ignoring me. Snobs, every last one of 'em.'

'Don't want to be seen as fawning fans,' said Libby. 'But I bet they watch your programmes, even if they pretend not to.'

'Libby.' Cassandra's voice called over the chatter of the now dispersing crowd. Libby turned and saw Cassandra coming towards her, the grey-haired man in tow.

'Libby, Ben, this is Mike Farthing from Farthing's Plants. He knew Vernon Bowling.'

Chapter Seven

Mike Farthing shook hands all round. Tall, with a slight stoop, his blue shirt looked a little rumpled, the beige trousers more suited to summer than mid-winter.

'Cass said she'd been using your mail order service for some time,' said Libby. 'She seems most impressed.'

Mike Farthing smiled down – not an easy feat – at Cassandra. 'One of my best customers,' he said. 'I'm very pleased to meet her in person.'

'And you knew Vernon Bowling?'

'He was a customer, too. He was planting up his garden and I was helping him.'

'Was it a new garden?' asked Ben. 'Are you designing it?'

Mike smiled deprecatingly. 'We-ell, just suggesting you know ...'

'Was it a new house?' asked Libby. 'We saw a couple of new houses between Shott and Bishop's Bottom.'

'Yes,' said Mike, looking surprised. 'Neo-Georgian, just along Rogues Lane.'

'We saw it,' nodded Libby. 'Looked a bit bare, up on that rise all on its own.'

'Yes, he wanted quick-growing trees and hedging. I was trying to steer him away from Leylandii.'

'What was he like?' asked Peter. 'He was a scientist, wasn't he?'

'He had been. I don't think he liked to talk about his past.' Mike shook his head.

'Dellington, of course,' said Libby nodding sagely despite the fact that twenty-four hours ago she had no idea what Dellington was.

'Have the police spoken to you?' asked Ben. 'They asked us

41

if we knew any of the members of the group.'

'Oh, yes. A very polite constable came round this morning. Apart from Ron Stewart I suppose I knew him as well as anyone did. In fact it was Vernon who introduced me to the group.' Mike laughed. 'Said I needed to get out more.'

'Was he right?' said Cassandra.

'I suppose so.' Mike shrugged. 'I spend most of my life with plants. The only thing I do apart from that is occasionally attend the bigger shows. Which I hate. I pop down to the local now and then, and then of course, there's our Joint Villages show.'

'Oh, we heard about that this morning from George at The Red Lion in Heronsbourne,' said Libby.

'You know George? He and Sid at The Poacher are mates.'

'We've met Sid, too,' said Libby.

Everyone turned and looked at her.

'You've been investigating.' Ben frowned.

'You knew Fran and I went out this morning,' said Libby. 'Harry phoned while we were having lunch with Patti at The Red Lion.'

'I didn't know quite what you were doing,' said Ben. 'You didn't tell me.'

'Or me,' said Peter.

'Well, she told me,' said Cassandra. 'Which is why I brought Mike over.'

Lewis, who had drifted away, now drifted back.

'I'm going to fetch Mum now. She doesn't like to stay out too late these days.' He made a vague salute towards Mike. 'See you next rehearsal, mate.'

Most of the other members of the group had also now gone, and Sir Andrew came towards them while Peter went to close up the bar.

'So we go on,' he said, and turned to Mike. 'Sorry –?'

'This is Mike Farthing, Andrew,' said Libby. 'Mike, Sir Andrew McColl.'

'Pleased to meet you,' said Mike as they shook hands. 'Very decent of you to let us be part of your concert.'

Sir Andrew smiled. 'Well, we really did need some kind of

local connection, rather than just trotting out my professional mates, and I have to say that having Lewis Osbourne-Walker and Ron Stewart was a draw. I just hope it hasn't all backfired.'

'Look it's early, yet,' said Ben. 'Why don't we adjourn to the pub. Mike – will you join us?'

Mike Farthing's face brightened. 'I'd love to, thank you.' He smiled at Cassandra, and Libby was secretly pleased to see faint colour come into her cousin's cheeks. Oho, she thought. Perhaps I won't have to do much more persuading to get her to move down here.

Sir Andrew was staying at the pub, as he usually did, despite Libby and Ben's attempts to get him to stay at the Manor, and Peter and Harry's standing invitation to stay with them. He always maintained he didn't want to be a nuisance. Now, he walked up to the bar and insisted he buy the first round.

'My concert,' he told them. 'My fault, in a way, that this has happened.'

'Oh, hardly,' said Ben. 'The group were already in existence. It could have happened any time.'

'I just wish it hadn't happened at a rehearsal,' said Mike. 'And away from our usual haunt. That really narrows it down to members of our group.' He sighed.

'On the other hand,' said Libby, 'it could be the other way round. That someone here recognised him.'

'But he hadn't been seen in the village,' said Mike. 'We parked at the church, went into the hall and that was it. None of us have gone into the village at all.'

'Now,' said Sir Andrew, as he returned to the table accompanied by the barman with a tray, 'let's not talk any more about the murder. It's depressing enough as it is, and good though you are at solving mysteries, Libby dear, let's forget it for the moment.'

'Are you?' said Mike, looking interested. 'Good at mysteries?'

'Oh, she's well known locally,' said Cassandra, with a grin. 'The local Miss Marple.'

Libby shifted uncomfortably. 'I'm not.'

'She's nosy,' said Peter. 'Our favourite nosy old trout. She and her friend Fran have a habit of getting involved in anything vaguely unsavoury around here.'

Cassandra darted a look at her cousin. 'I'll bring Fran and Libby over to see you tomorrow,' she said. 'I'm dying to see the nursery for myself.'

Mike smiled at her. 'I'd like that. I'm always there, so0 anytime.'

Shortly after that, the party broke up. Mike refused another drink, saying that the road to Shott was bad enough sober, and Cassandra saying she was tired. As they stood to leave, she said in Libby's ear, 'I thought you probably wanted to ask him more questions. Did I do right?'

Libby beamed and kissed her cheek. 'My favourite cousin!' she said.

Asked the following morning if she wanted to join Libby and Cassandra on a trip to Farthing's Plants, Fran declined, saying she did have a life, you know, and had Libby realised it wasn't long until Christmas.

'It's not like her,' said Libby, as she manoeuvred Ben's four-by-four out of Allhallow's Lane. 'I mean, she's always trying to stop me getting involved with things, but she usually gives in and gets as interested as I do.'

'She's right, though, Lib,' said Cassandra. 'After all, this isn't a job, is it? And Fran does help Guy with the gallery and shop, so she has other things to do.'

Libby sighed. 'I know she's right. And I know that I'm simply incurably nosy.' She brightened. 'But sometimes I'm asked for help – even by the police. Well, by Ian, anyway.'

'Is he your tame policeman?'

'I wouldn't say tame, exactly, but we became friends after Fran helped him with a murder investigation some years ago. He was very interested in Fran for a while, but she came down on Guy's side in the end.' Libby glanced across at Cassandra. 'Pity you're not a bit younger. You would have done very well for Ian.'

'Well, thanks! I'm sorry I'm not younger, too! But I wouldn't

44

worry about me. I'm used to living on my own, and I don't think I could stand a man around the place after all this time.'

'That's how I felt when I got together with Ben,' said Libby. 'But – I don't know – we sort of slid into living together. He'd stay overnight, and then it would be two nights, and some of his stuff would appear in the cottage and there we were. He did try and persuade me to move into Steeple Farm a while ago, but it didn't feel right.'

'Steeple Farm?'

'Where Ben's Aunt Millie – Peter's mother, you know – lived. It technically belongs to Peter and his brother James, but Ben renovated it, you knew he was an architect, didn't you? And now it's let. It used to be short-term lets only, holidays and stuff, but that was too much like hard work, so now it's let to a permanent tenant.'

'Why didn't you want to go? What's wrong with it?'

'Oh, nothing. It's lovely and much bigger than my cottage, but I hated its eyebrows. You know, those little slitty windows in the thatch. I always felt it was sinister.'

'So who has it now? Are they there for a long time?'

'Why?' Libby shot another look at her cousin. 'Not thinking of taking it on yourself are you?'

'No, of course not,' said Cassandra, looking guilty. 'Just wondered.'

'Well, the truth is, I don't know. Now I don't have to do any of the cleaning between lets I don't get involved with it. Ben deals with it all at the Manor, in between looking after the tenant farmers and the woodyard. Not that he has much to do. I think he escapes up there to get out of my way. And his mum loves to have him there.'

'That's Hetty, right?'

'Yes, she's lovely. I expect you'll meet her sooner or later. Look here's the turning for Shott. Where did you say Mike's nursery is?'

Mike's instructions led them round the village green and back up Rogues Lane past the big new house Libby now knew belonged to Vernon Bowling. A turning on the left had a small metal sign pointing to Farthing's Plants at its side, and Libby turned the 4x4 cautiously into the lane.

'Don't know how he gets delivery trucks in here,' she muttered as they bounced over the rutted surface. 'It's more like a farm track.'

'Farm tracks have delivery lorries,' said Cassandra. 'Think of the animal transporters. Look, here we are.'

The track finished in a wide sweep of gravel before what had once been a farm building. To their right, huge glasshouses stretched away.

Cassandra climbed out of the car and strode towards the farm building without waiting for Libby. Her grey hair was, as usual, escaping its moorings, and with her sensible combat trousers she wore equally sensible walking boots. Her duffle coat had definitely seen better days, and Libby smiled fondly. If Cassandra was interested in Mike Farthing as more than a plantsman, as Libby suspected, she certainly wasn't using any feminine wiles to attract him. She locked the car and followed.

Before she could catch up, Cassandra was out of the building and pointing to the glasshouses.

'Somewhere in there, apparently,' she said. 'But they didn't know which one.'

'They?'

'Two lads. They were making up parcels. Come on.'

The first glasshouse was considerably warmer than the outside, and Libby undid her cape, while Cassandra sloughed off the duffle coat. They wandered between rows and rows of plants in various stages of development, until they came across a small, elderly lady who pointed them in the direction of the next glasshouse, where Cassandra's superior height gave her the ability to spot Mike at the far end. At the same time he saw them, and waved. They met somewhere in the middle, and Libby was pleased to see the obvious delight he and Cassandra had in meeting for a second time.

'Let's go into the shed and have some coffee,' he said. 'No one will disturb us there. It's a bit like an allotment shed.'

He led the way out of the glasshouse across a muddy yard

and into a shed of considerable antiquity. Inside, it was, as he'd said, very like an allotment shed. A deckchair and two stools, a kettle, mugs, and various books made it the ultimate retreat, Libby thought, remembering her grandfather's allotment, where she had been taken as a special treat every now and then.

'Now,' he said, as he spooned instant coffee into mugs. 'What did you want to ask me, Libby?'

48

Chapter Eight

Libby squirmed. 'Um – well – we – er – Cass wanted to see …'

'Yes, I know that.' Mike grinned at Cassandra and handed her a mug. 'But we're actually talking about Vernon Bowling's murder, aren't we?'

Libby sighed. 'All right, I admit it. But Ian's policemen only skim the surface and all they would have asked was if you knew him well, did he have any enemies – that sort of thing.'

'Who's Ian?' asked Mike.

Libby explained. 'So it's good to get a more – er – *in-depth* idea from someone who actually knew him. And if you know anyone else in the group.'

Mike frowned, his weather-beaten face crinkling like an old apple. 'Well, I suppose I know Ron. He lives in the other house.'

'The other house?' said Cassandra.

'At Bishop's Bottom – same builder did his and Vernon's.'

'Oh, Fran and I saw it on the way to Heronsbourne,' said Libby. 'I wonder why Sid didn't tell us that? Or that Vernon Bowling lived in what he called "the big house".'

'Protecting them, I expect. After all, you turn up a couple of days after Vernon's murder …'

'He didn't say anything about Vernon,' said Libby, 'he was protecting Ron Stewart. I suppose he gets a lot of people asking about him.'

'Some,' agreed Mike, 'but not many people except the locals know he lives here. The occasional manic Jonah Fludde fan, of course.'

'So did he and Vernon know each other well? They shared the same builder, after all,' said Libby.

'I thought it was just coincidence,' said Mike, 'but yes, they knew each other. Used to share lifts to the uke group, but I don't know anything else. I did some of Ron's garden, too.'

'What's he like?' asked Cassandra.

'Ron? All right, I suppose. Quiet, likes to look the part.'

'That's what Patti said. Ripped jeans, leather jacket, big boots.'

Mike grinned. 'That's it, but I think it's a bit of a pose. He plays classical music when he's at home.'

'Has he got a studio at the house?' said Libby.

'Oh, yes. The attic – well, where an attic would be – the whole of the roof space. I believe he makes all the Fludde albums there.'

'Goodness, are they still recording?' asked Cassandra. 'They're a bunch of old hippies, aren't they?'

'Fran tells me they still perform at festivals and things,' said Libby. 'So I suppose there's still a market for new records.'

'They're not records anymore, Lib,' her cousin informed her.

'I know, I know. Anyway, so he and Vernon knew each other. Before they came here presumably.'

'I don't know about that,' said Mike.

'Well, they've got the same houses, built by the same builder …'

'But the builder might have built them on spec,' said Cassandra.

'No, Vernon's was commissioned,' said Mike.

'So did the builder just use the same plans to build a replica just down the road? On spec? How would Ron have heard of it?' Libby argued. 'No, they knew one another before. Perhaps Vernon was a Jonah Fludde fan. There must have been an age gap, though?'

Mike shook his head. 'Not much. They were both young in the late sixties, early seventies.'

'Oh, I suppose so.' Libby frowned. 'I wonder if their friendship went back that far?'

'Why are you trying to find a connection between them, Lib?' asked Cassandra. 'They knew one another. Isn't that enough?'

'No,' said Libby. 'I want to know if there's a reason for

50

murder in their – um – association.' She turned to Mike. 'Did Vernon seem to be friendly with anyone else in the group?'

'He was friendly with everybody,' said Mike. 'Quiet, but friendly. We usually have a drink after meetings. I didn't go the other night, thank God, because of the drive back here.'

'Where do you usually rehearse?'

'Oh, it's not so much a rehearsal, just a get together. The group meet every other Monday in the back of The Poacher. This is the first time we've actually rehearsed for anything.'

'Oh.' Libby looked disappointed. 'So you don't know anything more about any of the members?'

'Not really. There's Derek Chandler, he's a solicitor, Lewis, of course ...'

'Do you know Lewis?'

Mike looked surprised. 'Of course! I'm his garden supplier – I introduced him to the group. Or rather, I was telling Edie about it one day when I was over there and she was very keen, so when she told Lewis he decided they'd both join.'

'Oh,' said Libby. 'Then you might have met my son. He and his boss do a lot over at Creekmarsh.'

'Adam? He's your son? Well, what a small world!' Mike beamed at her. 'They're good you know, him and his boss. But he doesn't look the type to be a gardener.'

'Well, he wasn't. He got his degree and couldn't get a job – you know, the usual – and then Mog offered him some temporary work. And he's still there. He loves it. Occasionally he helps out at our friend's restaurant as well.'

'Well, he's happy, and he obviously loves plants. Are you a gardener?'

'Libby is to gardens as a snowstorm in summer,' said Cassandra. 'Disaster.'

'Oh, I'm not that bad,' protested Libby. 'My little patch isn't bad.'

'No, but all you've got is the cherry tree and a few shrubs.'

'Well, it's a small garden,' said Libby, on the defensive.

'I bet there's more you could do with it,' said Mike.

'Of course there is. I'm going to have a go at it while I'm

51

here,' said Cassandra.

'I'll help, if you like,' said Mike, looking at her.

'Oi! I'm still here, you know.' Libby glared. 'And I might not *want* anything done to it.'

Mike looked abashed, but Cassandra sat up straight and fixed Libby with her headmistress stare. 'Nonsense. I'll just pretty it up a bit. Pots. You can move them about.'

'We-ell,' said Libby, 'I suppose …'

'Good that's settled, then,' said Cassandra. 'When do you have some time, Mike?'

'I can leave the shop in charge of the boys – we don't do that much at this time of year, and we don't sell trees or holly or mistletoe, so I could come over tomorrow if that's all right. How long are you down here for?'

'I don't really know,' said Cassandra, glancing at Libby. 'I only meant to come for the weekend, really …'

'Stay as long as you like,' said Libby. 'Harry won't turn you out of the flat.'

'Flat? I thought you were staying with –?' he gestured at Libby.

'I forgot she was coming, so our friend Harry is putting her up in the flat over his restaurant.'

'The same restaurant your son works in?'

'That's the one. So she can come and go as she pleases,' Libby said pointedly, and Cassandra glared at her.

'Ah,' said Mike, and looked at his hands.

'Well, we'll see you tomorrow,' said Libby, standing up, 'but before I forget, what about this Dr Robinson?'

'I don't know much about him. He started the original group in Canterbury, I think, but this one's taken him over, especially with the concert coming up.'

'Is he medical?'

'Eh?'

'You know – a medical doctor, or a doctor of philosophy or something?'

'I've no idea!' Mike looked startled. 'I always assumed he was a medical doctor, but perhaps not. He's just Eric.'

'Right, Lib, that's enough questions. Poor Mike must feel he's been hit with a battering ram.' Cassandra stood up and held out her hand. 'See you tomorrow, Mike, and thanks for the coffee.'

Libby followed them out of the shed noting the easy manner in which they conversed as they walked, their loose strides matching. Cassandra would certainly *not* be going home at the end of the weekend.

'Was that worthwhile?' asked Cassandra as they drove away.

'I don't know, was it?' Libby glanced sideways at her cousin.

'What do you mean? We went there for you to ask questions.'

'And for you to check Mike out.'

'Libby! He's a very good – plantsman. We've got quite friendly over the years.'

'It's a wonder you've not been down before, then.'

'Well, I'm here now,' snapped Cassandra, and turned her head pointedly towards the side window. Libby grinned.

She dropped Cassandra outside The Pink Geranium and drove home. The answerphone light was blinking when she let herself in.

'Fran? You left a message?' Libby tucked the phone between chin and shoulder while she manoeuvred herself out of her cape.

'Yes, and on your mobile, as well.'

'I was driving. I told you – Cass and I went over to Mike Farthing's. I asked you to come.'

'I know you did. I was going to tell you I've met another member of the ukulele group.'

'You have? How?' Libby sat down by the table in the window and pulled her laptop towards her.

'He came into the gallery this morning to buy Christmas cards.'

'How do you know he was in the group? Did he tell you?'

'Oh, yes. The first thing he said was, were you and I investigating the murder? He knows who we are, you see. Then he said he was a member, so I asked him about Vernon Bowling. He got a bit tight-lipped, but said he didn't know him well. I got the feeling he didn't like him much.'

'So you've seen him before?'

'He's quite a regular. He used to live in Steeple Martin and retired down here some years ago with his wife, but she died. He's always seemed a bit sad and lonely to me.'

'Perhaps that's why he joined the group.'

'Yes, that's what he said. And then he – well, it was a bit odd. He started to say something else, like "I wouldn't if …" and then he hesitated and said, "If I'd known there would be a murder", but I'm sure that wasn't what he started saying.'

'Like – "If I'd known Vernon Bowling was a member", do you think?'

'It did cross my mind,' said Fran, 'as he'd been a bit odd when I asked about Bowling.'

'Would he talk to you again, do you think?'

'I doubt it. When he asked if we were investigating and I said no, he said "Good. Leave it to the police".'

'But people are always saying that to us,' said Libby. 'What's his name?'

'Bob Alton, but honestly, Lib, I don't think you'd get anything out of him. And after all, you've got no connection with the thing, so no right to barge in.'

'I know, I know. But don't you want to hear how we got on this morning?'

Libby repeated all the details of the conversation with Mike Farthing. 'And Cassandra had the cheek to say she was going to have a go at my garden and Mike's going to help her. Starting tomorrow.'

'But it's midwinter! Not exactly the time to start redesigning a garden.'

'She said pots. Can she do pots in midwinter?'

'She could plant some up ready for spring I suppose. You'd have to keep them in the conservatory.'

'I knew it. It's just an excuse for her to see Mike Farthing again. Honestly, Fran, it was like watching a couple of grey-haired teenagers. If we have that conversation again about her moving down here I don't think we'd have to do much persuading.'

'Hold on,' laughed Fran, 'they've only just met.'

'No, they haven't. They've known one another for years, apparently, through his nursery. They've emailed and talked on the phone – it's just like internet dating.'

'Hmm. I remember when Rosie tried that,' said Fran.

'Rosie was a different kettle of fish. She really wanted to meet a man, even though she must be the same age as Cass. Cass and Mike have a common interest, that's what's brought them together.'

'I suppose so,' said Fran. 'Anyway, what are you going to do now?'

'Put something in the slow cooker for dinner and think about tonight's rehearsal,' said Libby. 'Why?'

'I meant about the murder.'

'Nothing. You just said yourself, no reason to barge in.' Libby eyes strayed to the laptop screen, where the first page of search results for Vernon Bowling was showing.

'That's never stopped you yet.'

'Well, it'll have to, now. Unless Lewis or Edie get arrested and I have to rescue them.'

'Ha! Let me know if that happens.'

Libby switched off the phone and clicked on the top result for Vernon Bowling, which turned out to be a report of his murder. The next result was his wiki entry which contained the bare facts about the Dellington experiments, and details of his subsequent career as a research scientist of no particular note. She sighed and closed the laptop. It really wasn't her business. On impulse, she stood up and put her cape back on. She would go and ask Cass to come out to lunch, and dinner could wait.

She was almost level with Bob the butcher's shop when she became aware of a slight commotion ahead of her and saw a mobility scooter bearing down on her from across the road. Driving it grim-faced and malignant, was Monica Turner, terror of Maltby Close, her white hair tightly curled, her bright red coat at odds with her glowering face. And she was heading straight for Libby.

Libby stopped. Surely the old bat wasn't going to run her over? She passed under review anything she might have done recently to incur the old lady's displeasure. She soon found out.

'You!' said Monica Turner. 'It's always your fault! And now, on top of that fornicating racket every Monday night so a person can't sleep, it's murder. So what are you going to do about it?'

Chapter Nine

Libby stared. 'I beg your pardon? What are you talking about?'

Monica Turner moved her vehicle a threatening yard closer to Libby and poked her head forward.

'Those banjos. In the church hall – it's sacrilege. And desecrating the graveyard,' her lip trembled, 'with the murder of that – that – *man*. And you brought them here. Disturbing the peace. As if you couldn't be satisfied with your so-called theatre – that Hetty Wilde should be ashamed of herself.'

Libby watched fascinated as spittle formed at the corners of Monica Turner's improbably fuchsia lips.

'Mrs Turner, I'm sorry you feel like that, but the vicar is surely the one you should talk to. She let the ukulele group hire the hall, and I don't think she could be accused of conniving at a murder.'

'Vicar! That woman's no more a vicar than I am. I have to go all the way to Canterbury every Sunday now.' The head poked even further forward, like an aggressive turtle.

'You do? Why?'

'Only place with a proper vicar.' The spittle flew. 'I shall write to the bishop.' Monica Turner swung her vehicle abruptly round to cross the road and nearly knocked the postman off his bike.

'Blimey!' he said, watching the mobility scooter streak across towards Maltby Close. 'What's up with her?'

Bob the butcher appeared from the doorway of his shop. 'She was just blaming our little local murder on Libby here.' He shook his head. 'Among other things. Needs her bloody eyes tested. Blind as a bat she is.'

'Can't understand why it wasn't her who was murdered,' said the postman, mounting his bike. 'See yer.'

As he departed, so Libby saw Flo Carpenter hurrying across the road towards her.

'What did the old bat want?' she yelled. 'She stirrin' it again?'

Libby grinned. Flo was the queen of Maltby Close, and Hetty's closest friend. Her late husband Frank had owned the barn which had formed the basis for the select Over Fifty-fives development of bungalows, and the community hall at its heart was named after him. Sadly, not all the residents, leaseholders all, were cut from quite the same cloth as Flo, who now arrived, panting.

'She's bin goin' on at everybody about that uke group for weeks, and now she's sayin' it's the devil's work and serves 'em right one of 'em's got himself done in. That what she's bin sayin'?' Flo's accent reverted wholly to that of her East End upbringing in times of stress.

'And blaming Libby for it,' said Bob with a grin.

'Silly ol' cow.' Flo patted her chest. 'Cor, she do make me mad! If she's goin' round stirrin' up trouble fer you, gal, she'd better watch out. I'll 'ave the 'ole Close boycott 'er!'

'How?" asked Libby, amused.

'Send 'er to Coventry, that's 'ow. Cor. I need something to settle me, now.'

Libby looked at her watch. 'Come on, let's go and get Harry to give us a glass of wine. Won't be as good as yours, of course.'

'Come on, then.' Flo linked her arm through Libby's. 'Cheer-ho, Bob.'

'You haven't got your coat on,' said Libby, as they made their way to The Pink Geranium.

'Nah. Saw that old bat outa me winder and just run out the 'ouse.'

'So it's unlocked?'

'Yeah. Don't matter – no crime in the Close.'

'Except murder.'

'Weren't in the Close, were it? Behind church.'

Libby opened the door of the restaurant and grinned at a surprised Harry.

'We need stabilising glasses of wine, please, Hal. We've had an upset.'

'That weren't no upset. I'll upset 'er,' said Flo, sinking down onto the sofa in the left-hand window.

'I'll pop over and lock the door, shall I?' said Libby. 'You can tell Harry all about it.'

'All right, gal. Key's on the mantelpiece.'

By the time Libby got back, Hal was sitting opposite Flo, a bottle of wine and three glasses on the low table between them.

'Old cow,' he said, as Libby sat down next to Flo. 'She had the cheek to complain about Pete and me to the parish council once, did you know?'

'About what?' Libby asked.

'She didn't think "the likes of us" should be living in the village, and certainly shouldn't be serving it meals. What she thought the parish council could do, I'm not sure.'

'She was complaining about the vicar, too,' said Libby. 'Apparently she has to go all the way to Canterbury to get a proper male vicar.'

'Yeah,' said Flo. 'She made a point of goin' to the first service the poor gal held and getting up in the middle of the first prayers shoutin' "abomination". Well, not getting' up, y'know. Then she turns that bloody machine round in the aisle and leaves. Rest of us didn't know where to put ourselves.'

'Poor vicar,' said Libby. 'I've not met her yet. Is she nice?'

'She's a good gal. I wasn't sure at first, but I met your Patti, an' I thought, "Well, she's not so bad", then young Bethany arrived. We all call her Beth.'

'How do the rest of the Close like her?' asked Libby.

'Fine. She don't badger us.'

'She's all right,' said Harry surprisingly. 'Comes in here with her husband.'

'Oh, she's married?'

'Any reason why she shouldn't be?'

'None at all. All vicars used to be married, didn't they? But the only ones I've met recently haven't been.'

'John's all right, an' all,' said Flo. 'Some kinda businessman.

'E come round and mended my kettle last week.'

'Mended your kettle?' Libby repeated.

'The fuse, or whatever it is.' Flo shook her head impatiently. 'I dunno. They 'ave these closed plugs these days. He did it, anyway. My Lenny's no use.'

'So Bethany and John have the approval of Maltby Close, all except Monica Turner,' said Libby. 'Has she got any friends?'

'Oh, that Vi Little. She's so mousy she just agrees with everything. And she plays bridge or whist or something somewhere every week. Dunno where.' Flo's accent was returning to its pre-upset normality.

'Well, at least if she complains to the police about anything they won't take it seriously,' said Libby. 'They know how to deal with people like that.'

'They might suspect her for the murder, though!' said Harry. 'Serve her right.'

'I can't see her luring someone to the churchyard and beating him to death with her handbag, can you?' said Libby, with a laugh.

With Flo restored to good temper, Libby went into Harry's little courtyard and called up the spiral staircase to the flat above.

'Cass? Fancy a pub lunch?'

'What's wrong with my lunch?' muttered Harry from behind.

'Nothing, but you won't charge us.'

'I will, if you want?'

Libby looked over her shoulder and grinned. 'OK, then.' She turned back. 'Where is she? Have you seen her go out?'

'I didn't even see her come in,' said Harry. 'Shall I go up and knock?'

But there was no need. Cass appeared at the top of the steps.

'Libby,' she said, and stopped.

'What?' Libby went up a few steps. 'Cass, what is it?'

'The police. They're questioning Mike.'

Libby held out a hand and pulled Cassandra down the rest of the steps and into the restaurant.

'Now,' she said, as they sat down on the old sofa again and

Harry fetched a fresh glass. 'How do you know?'

'I rang to arrange a time for tomorrow. He answered and said he couldn't talk, the police were there.'

'Well, that's nothing to be worried about,' said Libby. 'They'll be talking to all the uke group members.'

'But they've already done that, on Wednesday. He told me.' Cass looked at the wine. 'Hal, could I have white, please?'

Harry raised his eyebrows. 'White? Of course.'

'I'll pay,' Cass said.

'Don't be silly,' said Harry, disappearing into the kitchen.

'Told you so,' Libby called after him.

'Told him what?' asked Cassandra.

'Nothing. Go on, so what else did he say?'

'That was it. He answered the phone saying "Mike Farthing" – it was his mobile, you see – and when all I'd said was "Mike", he just said "I can't talk now. The police are here." And he hung up.'

Harry returned with a bottle of dry sémillon.

Libby frowned. 'Bit abrupt.'

'That's what I thought. It must be serious. What on earth can they want to talk to Mike about?'

Harry poured wine. 'You don't know him very well,' he said. 'Not personally.'

'No, and he did know Vernon Bowling. He did his garden, didn't he?' Libby topped her own glass up with red.

'I suppose so.' Cassandra gnawed her lip. 'But he *can't* be a murderer. He'd no reason …'

'You can't possibly know that,' said Libby. 'But don't worry. Unless they haul him off to the station, I expect he'll ring you to apologise'

Cassandra smiled weakly. 'What an idiot, I am. Behaving like a teenager.'

'I thought that, too,' said Libby, with a grin.

'But you've never been close to murder before, have you,' said Harry, sitting astride a chair and resting his arms along the back. 'Whereas we have plenty of experience.'

'Well, don't boast about it,' said Libby. 'He's right though,

Cass. It comes as a bit of a shock. And if he does ring, if there's anything I can do …'

'What she means is she's dying for a legitimate reason to poke her nose in,' said Harry with a grin.

'No,' said Libby, trying to look shocked. 'Just trying to help.'

'Yeah, right.' Harry swung himself off his chair and ruffled Libby's wiry locks. 'Now I've got to get back to work. Are you staying for lunch?'

'No thanks, Hal. Cass, how about a trip to the seaside?'

'To see Fran?'

'Yes – and we can have lunch overlooking the harbour.'

'Yes, that would be lovely,' said Cass. She drained her wine and stood up. 'Thanks, Harry. You must let me pay for the wine.'

'And break the habit of a lifetime? Get away.' Harry removed both bottles and looked dubiously at Libby. 'You've had two – should you be driving?'

'We'll go in my car,' said Cassandra. 'I've only had one.'

While Cassandra went up to the flat to fetch her coat and car keys, Libby called Fran to apprise her of their imminent arrival.

'She's fallen for that Mike, then,' said Harry, as she put her phone away.

'Mad, isn't it? She only met him yesterday. She's been emailing him for years, though.'

'Why?'

'She's a mad keen gardener and he owns a nursery.'

'Oh, Farthing's Plants. That one. Yeah, Pete told me last night.'

Cassandra appeared at the door. 'Come on, then, Lib. Thanks again, Harry.'

Libby directed Cassandra out of the village and towards Nethergate, pointing out the Tyne Chapel where black masses had supposedly been held, and the road to Bishop's Bottom which led ultimately to the Willoughby Oak, scene of more Satanic activity only a couple of years ago.

'Why is there so much of that sort of thing round here?' Cassandra asked, as they began to descend the hill towards

Nethergate.

'No more than anywhere else,' said Libby. 'Anywhere where there are old stories of witches or ancient murders is bound to attract modern-day witches. The Willoughby Oak was where they hanged a wise woman called Cunning Mary, and every year there are supposed to be carryings-on on the anniversary of her death by a black magic coven. Well, there were until a couple of years ago.'

'Were you involved?'

'Er – a bit. Look, we're coming up to the square. Turn left there, and we'll see how near to Coastguard Cottage we can park.'

Harbour Street glowed weakly under a pale November sun. Halfway along, past Guy's gallery and shop and Lizzie's ice cream booth, now shut until April, Coastguard Cottage stood, its white walls and blue paintwork looking rather smug among the duller grey and flint of the other cottages.

'Looks like a postcard,' said Cassandra, as she parked just beyond the cottage.

'It is, now,' said Libby. 'I've painted it for Guy, and one of the best sellers in his gallery is the view from the front room window. I had a picture exactly like that on my bedroom wall when I was a child, and I just keep replicating it.'

'Couldn't you just do prints of it?' said Cassandra curiously. 'Seems an awful lot of work.'

Libby shook her head. 'No. Guy's customers like original work. I've now become known as a "local artist" and the prices have gone up exponentially.'

'Good for you.' Cassandra got out and locked the car. 'Come on. I want to see what your friend Fran has to say about Mike.'

'She doesn't know him,' said Libby, leading the way across the road.

'Does she have to? I'm relying on her psychic power!'

Chapter Ten

'No, Cass, you can't!' Libby turned on her cousin, elbows planted firmly on her hips.

'Why not?' Cassandra raised her eyebrows. 'That's what she does, isn't it?'

'No, it isn't. Fran gets pictures in her head which her children used to call "Mother's Moments". That's all. And when anyone's tried to harness it, it tends not to work.'

'It used to. You told me she was employed by Goodall and Smythe to check out houses for nervous buyers. And she's been consulted by the police.'

'But she always had something to relate to. She's not even met Mike, or even seen a picture of him.'

'That's easy. We'll call up his website.' Cassandra strode past Libby and knocked on the blue door.

Fran peered out of the front window looking surprised. 'It's open. You know it's always open.'

'Not me,' said Libby, making a face. She reached past Cassandra and opened the door.

Cassandra, looking chastened, stepped back. 'Sorry. Can never seem to forget I was a headmistress.'

'No, I'd noticed,' said Libby. 'It's all right, in you go.'

Fran was sitting in the window seat.

'So what did you want to ask me, Cassandra?'

Cassandra gaped and Libby hid a grin. 'About Mike Farthing,' she said. 'She suggested you could look at his photograph on his website.'

Cassandra glowered and Fran laughed.

'Come on, then,' she said, and led them to the table on the other side of the room where her laptop stood, already open.

'What were you doing?' asked Libby, as a picture sprang up

on the screen.

'Looking up Dellington.' Fran typed "Mike Farthing" into the search engine.

'Farthing's Plants?'

'That's it.' Cassandra bent over Fran's shoulder. 'And that's him.'

'Hmm. Looks nice,' said Fran.

'He is.' Cassandra cleared her throat and looked the other way.

'But,' said Libby, 'he appears to be being questioned by the police.'

'If he's a member of the ukulele group that's natural. They'll all be questioned.'

'Yes, but they already have been, on Wednesday,' said Cassandra. 'And he sounded–'

'Bothered,' suggested Libby.

Fran peered at the screen. 'Well, nothing's coming to mind,' she said apologetically. 'But it rarely does.'

Cassandra sighed and sat down abruptly on the arm of Fran's sofa. 'I'm behaving like a teenager, and I'm sorry.'

'Don't worry about it.' Fran stood up and patted her on the shoulder. 'This sort of thing coming on – ah – later in life, as it were, can be pretty hard. Libby and I have both had to deal with it.'

'But you're both younger than I am. I haven't had any sort of relationship with a man since my husband died.'

'Not even a flutter of interest?' asked Libby.

'No. I tried. I even went out with a couple of people a year or so after Colin died, but I just felt uncomfortable, and there was no … um …'

'Physical attraction,' supplied Libby. 'Right, and you've got to have that.'

'What, even at my age?' Cassandra laughed shakily. 'That's why I feel so foolish.'

'Because you do feel that for Mike,' said Fran shrewdly.

'And I'd take a bet that he feels the same for you,' said Libby. 'So he'd better not be guilty of something. Come on, we're going to have a very late lunch.'

'But how can I feel like this at my age?' Cassandra returned to the subject as they walked along Harbour Street towards The Sloop. 'And how could he? Look at me. I've got grey hair –'

'So has he,' put in Libby.

'And I'm not exactly glamorous, am I?'

'I don't think Mike would go for glamorous,' said Libby.

'Stop analysing,' said Fran. 'I know it's difficult – I did the same thing when I met Guy.'

'And Ian,' said Libby.

'Your policeman friend?'

'The same. He was very angry the first time Fran met him, but the next time, when he asked for her help, well, that was different.'

'I nearly made the biggest mistake of my life,' said Fran.

'But Ian is – was – gorgeous.' Libby said.

'*Is* gorgeous,' said Fran, opening the door of The Sloop. 'And I know you've always secretly fancied him.'

'Does Ben know?' asked Cassandra, looking horrified.

'Oh, I expect so,' said Libby. 'But he also knows I'd never do anything about it.'

Settled at a table in the window overlooking the tiny harbour, Fran returned to the subject of the murder.

'Now think. Is there any reason you can think of that the police would be interested in Mike?'

'We saw him this morning and asked him some questions,' said Libby.

'*You* asked him questions,' corrected Cassandra.

'And the only thing he said was that he'd helped with his garden. And with Ron Stewart's. Oh – and Vernon lived in the first of those new Georgian houses and Ron Stewart lives in the second one, that we saw yesterday. I told you that on the phone.'

'So they're all friends?'

Libby looked at Cassandra. 'I didn't get that impression, did you?'

'You said Mike said Vernon and Stewart were friends and shared lifts. And that they usually went for a drink after rehearsals.'

'Meetings, he said they were. Held in a back room at The Poacher. Vernon would have been able to walk there. I expect he meant shared lifts to Steeple Martin.'

'Only not last Tuesday,' said Fran, frowning.

'Is that significant?' asked Cassandra.

'Well, it could be, if it's a break from the norm.'

'But that's nothing to do with Mike.'

'No. It's plants, though.'

Libby and Cassandra looked at each other.

'Eh?'

'What?'

Fran looked up. 'Sorry. It just popped in. Plants.'

'Well, yes, that's what Mike is – a plantsman.'

'Yes.' Fran sighed. 'I'm sorry. I don't suppose that's got anything to do with it.'

'No.' Cassandra was frowning at her. 'I don't understand how it works.'

'Fran's moments?' said Libby. 'There's nothing to understand. I tried to explain – things just pop into Fran's head as though she's always known them. And sometimes she's had quite unpleasant experiences.'

'Which I do not want to experience again, I can assure you,' said Fran. 'Which is why I try and suppress it these days.'

'But if it's been so helpful –?'

'It isn't always, and it can be very uncomfortable.' Fran wriggled in her chair. 'I promise, if anything does happen to strike me, I'll let you know.'

Cassandra sat back, obviously dissatisfied, and Libby kicked her under the table.

Their ham sandwiches arrived, garnished with crisps, which Cassandra poked at distastefully. Libby sighed.

'Cass, if you're going to be difficult, we'll go home now.'

'What?' Cassandra looked up, surprised.

'You're not happy with Fran or the sandwiches, and I'm getting cross with you.'

Fran laughed. 'And you're never difficult, are you, Lib?

Leave her alone. She's suffering from the pangs of – well, something – for the first time in years, and under not particularly nice circumstances.'

Cassandra reached for Libby's hand. 'No, you're right, Lib, I am being difficult.' She turned to Fran. 'Sorry, Fran.'

'That's all right,' said Fran. 'Eat your crisps.'

When they'd finished lunch, Fran took them to see Guy in his gallery, where Cassandra was shown some of Libby's pictures, including one of the back of Dragon Island, the lump of rock that sat in the middle of Nethergate Bay, with Harbour Street, Victoria Place, and Cliff Terrace showing faintly in the background.

'I like that one,' she said. 'Sort of vaguely impressionistic.'

'Sheer laziness, I expect,' said Guy with a grin. 'She's supposed to make sure I've got a selection, but she falls behind rather.'

'I'm just a carthorse,' grumbled Libby.

'Workhorse,' said Fran, 'and you're not. You hardly do any until Guy's sold out.'

'By the way,' said Guy, 'that old boy you were talking about came back while you were out.'

'Bob Alton?' said Fran. 'You remember, Lib, I told you earlier. What did he want?'

'You, actually,' said Guy. 'I asked if I could give you a message, but he said no, he'd come back another time.'

Fran and Libby looked at one another.

'We'll Google him,' said Libby.'

'Or ask Mike,' said Cassandra.

'But we can't – at least, not yet. I think you ought to get in touch with the organiser of the group,' said Fran. 'You can easily do so to see what's happening about the concert.'

'Yes, but they had a meeting last night,' demurred Libby. 'I was there.'

'But he might have heard from people who weren't there,' said Fran. 'It's a legitimate question. And you can always give the impression you're asking on behalf of Andrew.'

'Andrew?' said Guy. 'What's he got to do with it?'

'Not Andrew Wylie, Andrew McColl.' Libby turned to Fran. 'See there's another one who thought it was our Andrew.'

'That would be a good idea, though, Lib,' said Cassandra.

'Yes, but Dr Robinson isn't going to know why one of his members wanted to speak to Fran, is he?'

'No, that's true,' said Fran. 'Oh, well, I don't suppose it's important.'

'The fact that he's been in twice to see you?' said Libby. 'I would suspect *he* thinks it's important.'

'He'll come back, then, won't he?' said Fran. 'And if I'm at home, Guy can call me.'

'Suppose so,' said Libby. 'Anyway, Cass and I had better be getting back. I've got to cook before rehearsal tonight. I was going to put something in the slow cooker earlier, and I forgot.'

'You're hopeless,' said Fran. 'Have you got anything in?'

'Oh, loads,' said Libby. 'We won't starve.'

'And I'll take you all to dinner tomorrow at Harry's,' said Cassandra.

'And we all have to go to Hetty's for lunch on Sunday,' said Libby. 'No getting out of that.'

Cassandra checked her phone all the way home, despite Libby's nervousness.

'Leave it, Cass. You'd hear it if it rang. Keep your eyes on the road.'

Cassandra's mouth was set in a thin line as she nodded. Libby sighed.

'Drop me off when you park,' said Libby. 'I'm going to pop into the eight-til-late on the way home. Dinner at six thirty all right? It has to be early on rehearsal nights.'

'Fine,' said Cassandra, as she drew in to a parking space on the opposite of the road from The Pink Geranium. 'Do you think I should risk ringing again?'

Libby considered. 'I think that would be OK, actually. After all, he might have thought it would be pushy to ring you back.' She didn't really think this, but Cassandra looked in need of reassurance.

'Right.' Cassandra got out of the car. 'I'll do it as soon as I get indoors. And I'll see you at half past six.'

Libby crossed the road to Ali and Ahmed's eight-til-late shop hoping they had some vegetables as Joe and Nella's farm shop was closed. A bag of stir-fry mushrooms and beansprouts was all that seemed to be on offer, so she bought those and a small French stick, before rushing into Bob the butcher's shop just as he was beginning to close up, and asking for chicken.

'Why didn't you buy it this morning?' he asked, reluctantly going into the back of the shop.

'I didn't think of it then, and I've just told everyone I've got loads at home.'

'Which you haven't,' said Bob, coming back with some chicken thighs. 'Here – better flavour than breasts. Want some of my Chinese spice to go with them?'

'Oh, yes, you're a lifesaver, Bob. See you later?'

'Yes, eight forty-five on the dot, Madam Director.' Bob handed over the package and took Libby's money.

As Libby let herself into number seventeen the phone was ringing.

'Libby!' said Cassandra's breathless voice. 'Mike rang. You'll never believe what happened.'

'Calm down,' said Libby, sitting down on the stairs. 'I thought you were going to ring him?'

'I did, and there was no reply. Then after I'd hung up, or whatever you do these days, he rang back. Said he'd been busy in the glasshouses.'

'Well, that would be the normal state of affairs, I suppose.'

'No, listen! He had to be in there because the police had spent all day searching them. The place is a mess.'

'Searching the greenhouses? What on earth for?'

'Marijuana.'

Chapter Eleven

'*What?*'

'I know. I couldn't believe it. He couldn't stay long, because he had to close up – although he'd been closed all day – but said he was still happy to come over tomorrow and tell us all about it.'

'Did they find any? Marijuana, I mean.'

'Of course not! Well, I don't know, actually, he didn't say. But if they had, he'd have been arrested, wouldn't he?'

'I suppose he would,' said Libby doubtfully. 'Is he sure about coming over tomorrow? I mean, I'm in no hurry.'

'But I won't be here for ever,' said Cassandra, 'so it has to be now.'

'Hmm,' said Libby.

'So, anyway, I said ten thirty – is that all right?'

'It's a bit early,' said Libby.

'Ten thirty? Early?'

'Oh, well, I suppose it depends on your point of view. But I might not be dressed, I'm warning you!'

All Cassandra could talk about over dinner that evening was Mike Farthing and why he should have come under suspicion. Libby was secretly glad she had rehearsal that evening, rather than having to sit and listen to her cousin all evening, however, she invited Cassandra to come and watch if she wanted to, rather than spend the evening in the flat on her own.

'I'd love to, if you wouldn't mind,' said Cassandra, pleased. 'I haven't seen any of the stuff you do here. And I thought yesterday what an impressive theatre it was.'

'OK. I go up about seven thirty to open up, so you can follow me when you're ready.'

'Do you go up, too, Ben?'

'I'm in it,' he grinned, 'so, yes. And I keep an eye on any backstage work, too, as I'm the set designer.'

'So we'd better get a move on, then?' said Cassandra, standing up and picking up plates.'

'Thanks, yes,' said Libby. 'Stick those in the dishwasher while I go and clean my teeth, will you?'

At the theatre Ben disappeared backstage and Libby went round turning on lights while Cassandra prowled round investigating.

'It's just like a real theatre,' she said meeting Libby on the edge of the stage.

Libby bridled. 'It *is* a real theatre,' she said.

Cassandra went faintly pink. 'Of course, sorry, I only meant …'

'That we're just a piddling little amateur theatre in the middle of nowhere?'

'No!' Cass made a face. 'I admit that's what I thought when you started on this project, and I thought it was a waste of your talent.'

'Did you think that when I did amateur theatre when I was still married?'

'No, I suppose not …'

'We have higher standards and state of the art facilities,' said Libby, 'and we are pro-am. There are quite a few theatres like us up and down the country. I'm ex-pro, so is Ben, actually –'

'I didn't know that.'

'Yes. He used to be a flyman in his youth, and he's toured with TIE productions.'

'Ah!' said Cassandra. 'I *do* know what TIE is.'

'I should hope so, you being a headmistress!'

'What is it, then?' said a voice behind them.

'Theatre In Education,' said Libby, turning round. 'Good lord, Mike! What are you doing here?'

'I couldn't stand my own company,' he said with a doleful grin. 'I was going to see if anyone wanted to come for a drink.'

As he was looking straight at Cassandra when he said this, Libby hid a grin.

74

'Good idea,' she said. 'You can save Cass from a boring evening watching us rehearse.'

'Oh, I –' Cassandra began.

'No, I mean it. Then I shall make you come down after Christmas to see the finished product without having spoilt it by seeing the shambles it is now!'

Libby watched as they left the auditorium, obviously very conscious of each other, and then turned to Ben, who had come up behind her. 'And why did he come all the way over here to find someone to have a drink with?' she said. 'We have it on his own say-so that he often uses The Poacher in his own village.'

'Perhaps he feels embarrassed having had the police all over his place today.'

'Maybe … I think it's young love, though.'

'Young?' Ben raised his eyebrows.

'I'll bet that's what it feels like to them.' Libby tucked her arm through her beloved's. 'That's how I felt when we started seeing each other. I didn't know quite how to behave.'

'No, I know,' said Ben. 'And you thought I was the area's prime Lothario.'

'Well, you were.'

'Just because I took a few people out to the theatre …'

'Go on with you!' Libby gave him a nudge that nearly sent him off the edge of the stage.

'Stop fighting, children.' Peter came through the doors from the foyer.

'Did you pass Cass and Mike Farthing on the way here?' asked Libby.

'I did. Many a good tune played on an old fiddle,' said Peter.

'Oh, Pete, really!'

'What happens if the fiddle's out of tune, though?' said Ben.

'Mmm.' Libby sighed. 'Oh, well, no use us worrying about it. Lorraine's coming in to work out where her dancers are going to fit in tonight, so we ought to get cracking.'

At ten o'clock, an exhausted and grumpy cast staggered out of the theatre doors on its way to the pub, followed shortly afterwards by Libby, Ben and Peter.

'Susannah's working them hard,' said Peter.

'Yes, but aren't they sounding good?' said Libby.

'She'd get more out of them if she stopped treating them like children,' said Ben.

'That's true,' Libby mused. 'I'll have a word, but I don't want to upset her.'

'You might upset the cast otherwise,' said Peter. 'There were some very mutinous looks tonight.'

Libby sighed. 'Which is worse? Losing a cast member or a musical director?'

'Which is rarer?'

'Depends which cast member,' said Libby.

'Bob,' said Ben. 'And, potentially, me.'

'Oh, dear.' Libby looked at him and shook her head. 'I'll ring her in the morning.'

Cassandra and Mike Farthing were still in the pub when they arrived, in the corner of the lounge bar, while the cast members were round the corner. Libby decided to leave her cast to their grumblings.

Mike stood up as she approached the table. 'Coming to join us?'

'Yes, please, I've had enough of the luvvies for tonight.' Libby sat down. 'Ben and Pete are getting drinks.'

Mike looked at Cassandra. 'I've been telling Cass about my run-in with the forces of law and order. She thinks I ought to tell you, too.'

'You don't have to,' said Libby, who was nearly dying from curiosity. 'And do you want Ben and Peter to hear?'

'I don't mind,' said Mike. 'I don't want to talk about it in the village, but I must talk to somebody.'

Well, that answered that question, thought Libby, as Ben and Peter arrived with drinks. 'Go ahead, then, Mike.'

'They arrived at the nursery at about eight,' Mike began, 'and of course, the place was locked up.'

'You don't live on site, then?' asked Peter.

'No. I live just down the road. So they rang me and told me to get down there and open up.'

'Why didn't they come and collect you? If you'd been guilty of anything you'd have done a runner,' said Libby.

'Actually, they said they were sending a car, but I told them I was on my way anyway. Which I was, almost. So I met the police car at the end of the nursery drive.'

'And then what?' prompted Ben, when Mike seemed to have dried up.

'Then they asked me to unlock the office and started asking me questions about Vernon's garden.' Mike sighed and pushed his hand through his already untidy grey hair. 'I couldn't understand it at all. Then they asked me about his greenhouse, and I said I'd had nothing to do with that, so they asked me about his attic.'

'His attic?' repeated Libby.

'Yes. I couldn't understand that, either, so then they asked if they could look in the greenhouses, and told me they'd got a search warrant. And then the dogs arrived.'

'Sniffer dogs?' asked Peter.

'Yes. So I unlocked all the doors and off they went. Eventually I asked what they were looking for, and made the rather stupid mistake of suggesting marijuana. So, of course, that started them in on me again. Had I smoked it, had I ever been a user, was I supplier – the lot. They even took me back to the house and searched that.' He shook his head and Cassandra laid a hand on his arm. He smiled briefly and continued. 'Eventually they seemed to be convinced that there were no marijuana plants in the nursery or my house and never had been, and disclosed the fact – which by now I'd guessed – that the whole roof space of Vernon Bowling's house had been turned into a marijuana factory.'

Ben whistled.

'Good God,' said Peter.

'Blimey,' said Libby. 'The same area that Ron Stewart has his studio in his house.'

'I told them I'd only ever been in the garden and knew nothing about the house. I was never invited in. I've been in Ron's house, but he's a different kettle of fish.' Mike looked at

Cassandra. 'I was quite a Jonah Fludde fan in my youth.'

'But they shared an architect – or a builder, didn't they?' said Cassandra. 'I wonder …?'

They must have done,' said Libby. 'We were talking about that yesterday, but you didn't know, did you, Mike?'

'I still don't. The police didn't mention Ron this morning.'

'I wonder if they've tumbled to the coincidence of the duplicate houses yet?' said Libby. 'Do you think we ought to mention it?'

'I don't want to set them on to Ron,' said Mike, shaking his head.

'So presumably they came after you this morning thinking you'd helped Bowling to set up his cannabis factory?' said Peter. 'What about his wife? Did she know about it?'

'I've no idea,' said Mike. 'I don't know much about the cannabis factory, either. I expect that'll be on the news, don't you? The police love showing things like that.'

'Couldn't you smell it when you were in the garden?' asked Ben. 'I always thought you could.'

'If it was in the attic he'd have had venting systems of some sort and it would have dispersed quickly in the air,' said Mike. 'I looked it up after the police had gone.'

'Do you think he had the house actually designed for it?' asked Cassandra. 'They'll be after the builder, if so, won't they?'

'Bound to be, I would have thought,' said Ben. 'And the architect.' His mouth turned down at the corners. 'I wonder who that was.'

Libby patted his hand. 'He used to be an architect, you see,' she said to Mike.

'But it might not have been designed for it,' said Peter. 'It could just as easily have been set up afterwards. Perhaps he was going to have a studio up there like Ron Stewart.'

Libby was frowning. 'What puzzles me is why they came after you. I mean, I know you helped him set up the garden, but why should they assume you helped with the marijuana?'

'I suppose because I grow plants.' Mike shrugged helplessly.

'I don't know.'

'I wouldn't have thought that was enough to sick them on to you,' said Ben, 'they must have had a lead from somewhere.'

'But where? I've never had anything to do with cannabis or any drugs, except for once at college and it made me ill.' Mike took a morose gulp of coffee. 'I could do with a real drink.'

Ben stood up. 'Let me …'

'No.' Mike shook his head and smiled. 'I daren't. I need my licence.'

'You'll have to come over and have dinner and stay overnight,' said Libby.

'How about tomorrow?' suggested Cassandra. 'I'm taking Ben and Libby to Peter's restaurant –'

'Harry's,' corrected Peter.

'Harry's, then. Why don't you join us?'

'You could stay in our spare room,' said Libby.

'Ours is almost next door,' said Peter, sending Cassandra a wicked look.

'Well …' Mike looked round the group, looking bewildered. 'It's awfully nice of you …'

'But you've got other things to do on a Saturday night, I bet,' said Libby.

'No.' Mike sat up straight and grinned. 'I'd love to, actually.' He shook his head. 'I only met you a couple of days ago and suddenly you've become friends. Things like that don't happen to me.'

'It's the Libby effect,' said Peter. 'I think you've just been gathered into the select bunch of Libby's Loonies.'

Chapter Twelve

'It never occurred to me to ask last night,' said Libby, curling herself round Ben under the duvet, 'if Mike was still coming over this morning.'

'Oh, Lord,' groaned Ben. 'I know he said we were all his new friends, but enough is enough.'

'Shall I ring Cass? She could perhaps put him off. I'm sure the original suggestion was only a ploy to get them together, and now that he's coming tonight ...'

'I must say,' said Ben, struggling into a sitting position, 'I've never seen a relationship develop so quickly.'

'Not since we were teenagers, anyway,' said Libby. 'Although we don't know there's a relationship yet. He drove away last night, and the only time they've spent alone together was in the pub.'

'It's pretty obvious,' said Ben. 'I just hope your cousin isn't throwing her cap over the windmill too soon.'

'Well, she can't get up to much tonight, he's staying with Pete and Harry.'

'She could still invite him up to the flat for coffee.'

'That *would* be obvious,' said Libby. 'She'd be too embarrassed.'

The phone rang beside the bed.

'Talk of the devil,' said Libby. 'We were just wondering if you and Mike were still coming over this morning, because we're still in bed.'

'I don't need to know that,' said Cassandra crisply. 'I was ringing to say we aren't. Mike has a lot of clearing up to do, and as he's coming over this evening ...' Her voice trailed off.

'You've spoken to him this morning, then?'

'He rang to say he wasn't coming.' Cassandra cleared her

throat. 'And that he was looking forward to this evening.'

'Sounds as if he doesn't get out much,' said Libby wickedly.

'He admitted that, didn't he? That's why he joined the ukulele group.'

'All right, all right.' Libby grinned at Ben. 'So my garden's safe for now. We'll see you at The Pink Geranium later, or would you like to do something today? Go and see something?'

'I was thinking of driving into Canterbury, actually. Would you like to come?'

'Sightseeing?'

'Well, yes. I haven't been to the Cathedral for years.'

'There's a Wagamama there,' said Libby. 'We could have lunch.'

'Do you never think of anything but food and drink, Libby?'

'Um ...'

'I was going to see the Cathedral, walk through Dane John Gardens, and go and see the new Beaney Gallery.'

'Right,' said Libby. 'Would you like company or would you prefer to go on your own?'

'Actually, I would quite like company,' said Cassandra, her voice thawing a little. 'What time? I'll drive.'

At eleven o'clock Libby walked down Allhallow's Lane and met Cassandra on the corner by the vicarage.

'I must meet the new vicar,' she said as she climbed in to the car. 'Flo tells me her name is Bethany.'

'Apropos of what?' asked Cassandra, swinging the car round to the right and the Canterbury road. 'And who's Flo?'

'That house behind the wall where you picked me up is the vicarage, and Flo is Ben's mum Hetty's best friend. They both came down here hop picking during the war, and ended up marrying locals. Ben's father was the heir to the estate (that's the Manor) and Flo's husband was a farmer with a great taste in wine. That's the short version, anyway.'

'Didn't you open the theatre with a play about it?' Cassandra glanced curiously at her cousin.

Libby shuddered. 'Yes. Peter wrote it, and someone was murdered. Then when he wrote another play, someone else was murdered, so now he's got a bit of a phobia about it.'

'Ah.' Cassandra slowed down behind a tractor. 'One of the hazards of living in the country.'

'You get used to it,' said Libby.

'So what about the pantomime? What is it?'

'It's one of mine,' said Libby. 'You remember I used to write them in the bad old days when I was still in the job?'

'Vaguely, but that sounds as though you were in the police!'

'All right, when I was a pro actor. We revive them now and then, and sometimes other people use them, too, although that isn't always a pleasant experience.'

'Oh, don't tell me – not another murder.'

Libby looked surprised. 'Well, yes, actually, but that wasn't what I meant.'

Cassandra sighed. 'Good God.'

Libby trailed after her cousin through the Cathedral, the Beaney Art Gallery and Museum, and finally persuaded her to sit in Dane John Gardens and eat a sandwich.

'Do you want to do any shopping?' she asked hopefully.

'No, thanks. We might as well get back now.' Cassandra looked at her watch. 'It's getting on for three.'

'OK.' Libby brushed crumbs off her coat. 'We can have a cup of tea at home.'

'Is tea your answer to everything?'

'No, sometimes wine or whisky will do,' said Libby with a grin. 'Sorry, am I a bad influence?'

'Yes.' Cassandra gave her an affectionate hug. 'Sorry if I'm still doing the headmistressy thing.'

'That's all right, you can't help it, but don't expect me not to answer back.'

Cassandra smiled ruefully. 'I deserved that.'

On the way home, the conversation turned somewhat inevitably to the murder.

'I wonder if Fran's heard any more from that chap who was asking for her yesterday?' said Libby. 'What was his name?'

'I don't remember.'

'Alton – that's it. Bob Alton. I never looked him up after all.'

'Why don't you ask your friend Lewis about the other members?'

'He wouldn't know. He's the celebrity feather in the group's cap, but he doesn't always go to the meetings, which is why I went once with Edie to keep her company. We know he knows Mike, but I don't know that he knows anyone else.'

'I'll ask – er – you can ask Mike about that.' Cassandra glared through the windscreen.

'Cass, give it up. You've already admitted you like Mike. Stop trying to hide it.'

'I'm just not used to this, Lib. I was married for thirty-three years, and I never had so much as a flirtation with anyone but my husband, and I've never had a flicker of interest in anyone since he died.'

'What about the dates you went on?'

'I did that because I felt I ought to. They were people I already knew, and it felt wrong, somehow.' Cassandra sighed. 'So where this has come from, I've no idea. I mean, neither of us are strikingly attractive, are we?'

'Mutual interest and the fact that you'd built up a relationship over the phone and online gave it a healthy start, I imagine.'

'That's what internet dating is supposed to do, isn't it?'

'Supposed to,' said Libby, 'but a friend of ours got into rather hot water trying it out a couple of years ago.'

Cassandra turned her head to look at Libby briefly and smiled. 'And which murder was that?'

Libby laughed. 'One of the black magic ones, actually!'

'Mike's meeting us at the restaurant,' said Cassandra as she dropped Libby at the end of Allhallow's Lane.'

'You can have a drink in the flat first, then,' said Libby, with a wink.

Cassandra laughed. 'You're incorrigible, young Lib!'

The sky was already darkening as Libby hurried up the lane, and there was a definite nip in the air. Well, she thought to herself, it is just about turning into December, and before they knew it, Andrew's Christmas Concert and then the pantomime would be upon them. And tonight, Harry would have decorated

The Pink Geranium with his less than tasteful swags of lights.

In fact, when Libby and Ben arrived, they found Cassandra and Mike seated together on the sofa in the left-hand window, beneath quite tasteful bowers of pink and silver lights and vegetation.

'I thought I'd stick with signature pink,' said Harry coming up with menus and a bottle.

'It looks very nice,' said Cassandra. 'When did you do it?'

'Between lunch and dinner today,' said Peter, arriving along with a rush of cold air. 'We've been spraying twigs silver for days.'

'You should have let me know,' said Mike. 'I've got some in the shop. We don't sell much of it, as we're not known for this sort of thing, but I keep a small stock.'

'Well, I didn't know that, did I?' said Harry. 'But I'll know next year. Now, here's a bottle of red to be going on with. Anyone want anything else? And Adam will be over to take your orders when you're ready.'

'I didn't know Ad was working here tonight,' said Libby.

'He doesn't have to tell you everything he does,' said Ben. 'He's all grown-up now!'

Adam, in his long white apron, appeared at that moment with the white wine Cassandra had requested.

'Hello,' said Mike, standing up and holding out a hand. 'You look different from the last time I saw you.'

Adam, surprised, shook his hand, 'What are you doing here' obviously hovering on his lips.

'Mike's an old acquaintance of Cassandra's,' said Libby, hoping neither Mike nor Cassandra would dispute this. After all, they had known one another for a long time, just not in person.

'And I'm in this ukulele group,' added Mike.

'Oh!' Adam's face cleared. 'The murder. Bet Mum's involved, aren't you Ma?'

'No,' said Libby, feeling her face growing warm. 'Just … well, no, not really.'

Adam smiled knowingly. 'Right.' He looked round the table. 'You aren't ready to order yet, are you? I'll come back in a bit.'

'Your family and friends obviously expect you to be in on this,' said Mike as Adam went back to the kitchen.

'Oh, she always is,' said Ben.

'Even when she isn't supposed to be,' said Peter.

'Do you think Fran will be asked about anything?' Cassandra looked at Mike. 'I've told you about Fran, haven't I?'

'Er …' Mike was looking confused again.

'Fran's psychic,' said Libby. 'If you don't believe that, it doesn't matter. But she has these insights, or "moments" as we call them, where she can sometimes pick things up which help the police.'

'The police? I didn't think they did that sort of thing in this country.'

'Not often, but Ian – DCI Connell – has found it very useful at times. She's actually saved lives. Anyway, nothing's popped into her head yet.'

'Yes, it did,' Cassandra interrupted. 'When we had lunch yesterday and we were wondering why the police were with Mike. She just said "Plants".'

'But I'm a plantsman. My business is called Farthing's Plants. That's obvious, surely?'

'What the *police* wanted you about. You're involved in a murder investigation, it could have been anything, not plants at all,' said Libby.

'I suppose so,' said Mike, still sounding doubtful.

'They could have been looking for a murder weapon,' put in Peter.

Mike blanched. 'God, really?'

'Which,' said Libby thoughtfully, 'could have been plants.'

Mike's mouth dropped open.

'Well, you know, poisonous plants. Foxgloves, or laburnum, or deadly nightshade.'

'Nicotiana,' suggested Cassandra.

Mike looked from one cousin to the other. 'I don't know which of you is worse.'

Ben and Peter laughed.

'Cass is only just learning,' said Libby, 'but she's getting the hang of it.'

'I don't want to rush you,' said Adam appearing in front of them again, 'but it is Saturday night, and we are getting busy.'

This effectively put a stop to any further discussions of the murder, but when the coffee stage arrived and Harry elected to join them, still in his chef's whites, slinging a leg across a chair to sit astride it and lean on the back, the subject bubbled up again.

'How far have you got?' he asked?

'With what?' asked Peter. 'The coffee pot?'

'The murder,' said Harry, stealing a sip of Peter's wine.

'We haven't talked about it since we first arrived,' said Libby. 'It didn't seem appropriate.'

'Well, I think you might have to re-think that,' said Harry, 'because I've just taken a phone call from that new Chief Detective Inspector Connell, who is on his way right now to have a word with you.'

Chapter Thirteen

'Don't look so worried, Mike,' said Ben. 'That means he's tried the house, and tried Harry to see if we were here. It won't be formal.'

'At least he didn't call the mobile,' said Libby. 'He was being discreet.'

Harry grinned. 'And here he is.' He stood up and turned the chair round. 'Hello, Ian. I'll go and make you some more coffee.'

Ian took the chair and raised his eyebrows at Mike and Cassandra.

'Mr Farthing,' he said. 'Libby didn't say she knew you.'

'She didn't,' Cassandra said quickly. 'I'm here visiting – she's my cousin, you know – and Mike and I are old acquaintances.'

Ian cast Libby a suspicious glance.

'Quite, quite true, Ian. I only found out because I took Cass to Sir Andrew's meeting in the theatre on Thursday and she dragged Mike over to meet me.' Libby smiled. 'Honestly, I know it sounds like too much of a coincidence, but there it is.'

Ian sighed. 'I'm pleased to meet you, Mrs …'

'Oh, just call me Cassandra. Pleased to meet you, too.'

Ian looked at Mike doubtfully. 'However, nice though it is to see you in a different setting, Mr Farthing, I think I'd better be off.' He stood up. 'I'll call you in the morning, Libby.'

Cassandra stood up so hurriedly she nearly knocked her chair over. 'No, no, please don't do that. I understand you want to talk to Libby, and not in front of Mike, so we'll take our coffee upstairs, shall we, Mike?'

Harry arrived with the fresh pot of coffee.

'Top your cups up, then, and go up through the kitchen,' he

said.

Cassandra topped up the cups and led a bemused Mike away through the kitchen, while Harry took over Mike's seat and Ian sat down again.

'Your cousin?' he said to Libby. 'She made me feel like my old headmistress.'

'That's exactly what she was until she retired. I think she's going to manage Mike within an inch of his life.'

'Really? I thought she said acquaintance …?'

'Yes, but I think it's becoming more than that.'

'She's become protective of him,' said Ben. 'I just hope her faith isn't misplaced.'

'I hope so, too,' said Ian. 'You see, we got a tip-off about his nursery.'

A shocked silence fell around the table.

'But – but he said nothing was found,' said Libby, finding her voice.

'Nothing was, but that didn't mean there hadn't been something there,' said Ian.

'There would have been forensic traces,' said Peter. 'Wouldn't there?'

'But we hadn't really got the grounds to dig everything up, or the resources at the time,' said Ian. 'And there was no evidence of anything having been got rid of. No burning material, or evidence of recent burial.'

'Compost heap?' said Harry.

'Dogs would have smelt it, and they got absolutely nothing.'

'Well, there then,' said Libby. 'He's in the clear.'

Ian frowned. 'We have to find out why we were given a tip-off.'

'Who told you? You can ask them.'

'That's just it. It was anonymous.'

'And you still had to look into it?' Peter raised his eyebrows in his unintentionally superior manner.

'Of course. I'm afraid I can't go into the details with you.' Ian poured himself coffee. 'But what I really wanted to ask you was –' he looked at Libby '– if anything has been said about the ukulele group to you or in your hearing.'

'Gossip,' said Libby.

'Unofficial gossip?' said Ben.

'Obviously.' Ian gave a deprecating smile. 'These chats are always unofficial.'

'But often useful,' said Libby. 'Well, no, I haven't. Except what Mike's told us, and I expect he's told you all that, too.'

'Tell me what it is, then.'

'Just how he was the one who brought Lewis into the group. Mike works with Adam and Mog and is Lewis's plant supplier. He was talking about the group to Edie one day when he was over there, and she wanted to join, so Lewis came too.' Libby thought for a moment. 'Then there was the fact that Vernon Bowling and Ron Stewart had identical houses, both with large attics –' she glanced at Ian '– and must have used the same builder, but he didn't know how long they'd been friends.'

'They had the same builder?' Ian frowned. 'Identical houses?'

'Yes. Didn't you know?'

'I haven't been to Mr Stewart's house, only Mr Bowling's. Are you sure about this, Libby?'

'Yes. I've seen them both. It's very obvious. Of course, Ron Stewart uses his attic as a studio. Recording, you know.'

Ian looked thoughtful. 'That's interesting.'

'I said Mike should tell you, but he said he didn't want to get Ron into trouble.'

Ian looked up sharply. 'And what did he mean by that?'

'Well …' Libby looked confused. 'I guess it meant he didn't want to involve Ron unnecessarily. I mean, look what's happened to Mike himself. Someone's said something about him and his plants and brought the mighty force of the law down on his head.'

Ian nodded. 'But this is exactly why I wanted to talk to you. You hear things we don't.'

'So now I'm your snitch.' Libby sniffed.

Ian, Peter, Harry, and Ben laughed.

'Or snout,' said Ben.

'Stool pigeon,' added Peter.

'Look, Libby, you want this cleared up, don't you? If it isn't, it could mean your Sir Andrew's concert could be in jeopardy.' Ian leant his elbows on the table and stared at her.

'And he wouldn't be pleased,' said Harry, letting the chair he'd been leaning back in crash to the floor. 'Especially as they approached him and he altered the concept to include them.'

'And what happened to nosy Libby trying to solve murders?' said Peter. 'What happened to her.'

Libby's colour was becoming alarmingly high. 'So I'm only useful because I'm a nosy cow?'

The four men sighed in unison.

'It wouldn't be much use if policemen weren't nosy, would it?' said Ian. 'Come on, Libby, I'm not asking anything illegal.'

'But very unorthodox,' countered Libby.

'Yes,' conceded Ian, 'but my consulting – or helping – you and Fran over the years has always been unorthodox. I don't exactly broadcast it.'

'But Fran and I have managed to get into the papers.'

'Yes, but not always for the right reasons,' said Ben.

'And you're lucky to have media contacts,' said Harry.

'If you mean Jane Baker on *The Mercury*, she's hardly national broadsheet, is she?'

'And that Campbell person from Kent and Coast TV,' added Peter.

Libby let out a huge sigh. 'Oh, all right. But I've told you everything now, anyway. Except about Monica Turner.' She giggled. 'I'd love to see you question her as a suspect.'

'Monica Turner?' Ian frowned.

'She's an old battleaxe who lives in Maltby Lane,' explained Ben. 'And she accused Libby of bringing down murderers and ukulele players on the community.'

'And she hates gays and lady vicars,' said Harry.

Ian looked amused. 'Perhaps I'll have to question her myself.'

'I wonder who'd come off best?' said Harry. 'She thinks Pete and I are an abomination.'

'I suppose there weren't any signs of homophobia among the members of the group?' asked Libby suddenly. 'I was thinking of Lewis. He can provoke people badly if he feels like it.'

Ian looked wary. 'I couldn't say.'

'That,' said Libby triumphantly, 'means there is! Although if Bowling was homophobic, I can't see Lewis killing him because of it.'

'There, you see?' Peter turned to the other men, spreading his hands. 'After all her protestations, she's off again.'

'I only wondered.' Libby finished her coffee. 'Was there anything else, Ian, or can we rescue Mike?'

'Not unless you've got any more revelations.' Ian stood up. 'You've given me something to think about, anyway. And don't go investigating on your own.' He turned to the other three men. 'As if she would.'

They all nodded sagely.

'And,' he said to Libby, 'you could just ask Fran ...'

'Nothing yet,' said Libby, and blushed again. 'Not that ...'

'Keep in touch,' said Ian, and lifting a hand in farewell, vanished through the front door.

Libby went out through the kitchen and called up the spiral staircase. Cassandra appeared after a moment or two.

'He's gone,' said Libby. 'You can come down now.'

When Mike and Cassandra rejoined the group round the table, Harry had provided a bottle of brandy, a fresh coffee pot, and a new bottle of wine.

After they had all chosen their preferred beverages, Libby sat back in her chair and looked at Mike.

'I'm afraid I told him about Ron and Bowling having the same houses. I thought he would already know, but he didn't.'

'He would have found out anyway,' said Mike. 'You didn't find out why they'd picked on me?'

'He wouldn't tell us,' said Ben. 'Just that they'd had a tip-off.'

Mike shook his head. 'I still don't understand it.'

Libby let out another gusty sigh. 'I know, but I've just told him about Ron's house, and he'll be bound to go and look at that – that's a tip-off, too. And none of it actually might mean anything.'

'Did you tell him anything else, Libby?' Cassandra had on her headmistress look, fixing her cousin with a gimlet eye.

'Only about Monica Turner,' said Harry with a grin.

'Monica …?'

'I told you about the mad old woman on the mobility scooter who thinks Pete and Harry are – what did she call it, Hal?'

'An abomination,' said Harry.

'Well, he wouldn't take that seriously, would he,' said Cassandra sharply. 'Be sensible, Libby.

Five pairs of eyes turned to her in surprise.

'I don't think that's fair, you know,' said Mike gently, and Cassandra went bright crimson.

'I'm doing it again, aren't I?' she said. 'Sorry, Lib.'

'Hmm.' Libby didn't look at her cousin. 'Anyway, as Ian's asked me, I shall be taking notes on anything I hear from now on.'

Peter opened his mouth and closed it again, Ben looked at the ceiling and Harry snorted into his brandy glass.

'Well,' said Mike carefully, 'I think you ought to tell him there was homophobic element in the ukulele group, too.'

Chapter Fourteen

This time the brandy went up Harry's nose and he had to be patted on the back by Peter.

'What do you mean?' asked Libby, leaning forward. 'Against Lewis?'

Mike nodded. 'I'm afraid so. And your friend Edie made it very clear that she was very unhappy about it.'

'Oh, no,' groaned Libby.

'What happened?' asked Ben.

'Do I have to say?' Mike looked shifty.

'Someone has to,' said Peter. 'There could be something in this, and Libby could hardly go to the police with hearsay.'

'If you didn't want me to ask questions,' said Libby firmly, 'you shouldn't have made the suggestion.'

'I thought you could just tell the police what I said.'

'I could. And they'd want to know a) how I knew and b) who was involved.'

'Couldn't you speak to Lewis?'

'Adam,' Libby called, and her son's head poked out of the kitchen. 'Is Lewis at home at the moment?'

'Until Monday.' Adam's head withdrew, no doubt to continue his conversation with the PhD student he was so taken with, who was also one of Harry's casual staff.

'I'll call him tomorrow then,' said Libby. 'And I'll probably take Fran with me if he's up for a visit.'

Cassandra looked hopeful. 'Can I –'

'No. And don't forget we go to Hetty's for lunch tomorrow.' Libby finished her wine and coffee and stood up. 'Well, I'm tired. Lovely meal as usual, Hal. See you tomorrow, Cass. Mike, nice to meet you in a civilised manner.' She gave Peter a kiss on the cheek. 'Come on, Ben.'

'Mike, are you coming with me?' asked Peter. 'Hal's just got to make sure everything's OK in the kitchen.'

'Oh, the lovebirds can lock up,' said Harry. 'See you tomorrow, everybody.'

On their way along the high street, Libby looked round and saw Mike being escorted out of The Pink Geranium between Peter and Harry.

'No hanky-panky for Mike and Cass tonight, then!' she said.

'Don't be disgusting,' said her beloved, giving her a suggestive squeeze. 'At least, not here.'

A phone call on Sunday morning assured her that Lewis and Edie would be in all morning, and Libby called Fran to ask if she'd like to meet her at Creekmarsh.

'I can't, Lib. Sophie's coming for lunch and I've got to slave over a hot stove. Tell me about it afterwards.'

'Bother,' said Libby, turning to Ben. 'Now I've got to go on my own – and *don't* suggest I take Cass.'

'I wasn't going to,' said Ben with a grin, 'but Hetty is at this moment ringing Edie to suggest they come to lunch with her.'

'Oh.' Libby was taken aback. 'So I don't have to go to Creekmarsh?'

'If they say yes, no,' said Ben. 'If you see what I mean.'

A few minutes later, Lewis was on the phone.

'We're coming to Hetty's, lovie, so if we come early we'll come down to you before we go to the Manor. OK?'

'Well, that solves that problem,' said Libby. 'Will Hetty have enough of everything?'

'When have you ever known my mother do a small roast?' Ben laughed. 'She'll probably ask Flo and Lenny, too, just to make up the numbers.'

Lenny was Hetty's brother, who had been sweet on Flo in his youth, and, now in their twilight years, as Flo put it, they had found each other again.

Lewis and Edie arrived at twelve o'clock, and Libby offered coffee.

'Only a little drop for me, ducks,' said Edie. 'I don't want to spoil one of Hetty's lunches.'

'So, Libby. Come on. This is about Vernon Bowling the homophobe, I suppose?' said Lewis.

Libby and Ben were stunned into silence.

'He was, you know, dear,' said Edie. 'Made me so cross, he did.'

'What did he do?' said Libby, finding her voice at last.

'Oh, it started the first time we went,' said Lewis, sounding amused. 'Eric Robinson introduced us to the group – you knew Mike was the one who told us about it?'

Libby and Ben nodded.

'Well, Robinson said something like: "We're very pleased to have Lewis Osbourne-Walker from the TV and his mother joining us," and Vernon Bowling said, in one of those voices that pretend to be a whisper but everyone can hear, "We don't need that jumped up faggot." Everyone pretended not to hear him, but of course, they did.'

'And then he took every opportunity to be rude to us.' Edie bridled. 'Nasty man.'

'Did anyone else agree with him?' asked Ben.

'Dunno.' Lewis shrugged. 'His mates were Ron Stewart and that solicitor, Derek Chandler. He seemed perfectly friendly with everyone else. They used to stay on for a drink at The Poacher after meetings, but I never did.'

'Mike said he was friendly but quiet,' said Libby, 'but it was Mike who suggested there might be homophobia in the group.'

'Well, ta, Mike!' said Lewis. 'All that does is give me a motive.'

'Don't be a silly bugger,' said Edie. 'You was in sight of me the whole time last Tuesday.'

'I think they might not see it like that,' said Libby. 'You're his mum, after all.'

'Have you told your mate Ian?' asked Lewis.

'That Mike said there was homophobia in the group? No. As I said, they'd want to know how I knew, and they'd then regard it as hearsay.'

'They might follow it up, though,' said Ben.

'The I'd better go and tell him meself,' said Lewis, with a

grin. 'Just in case.'

'Lewis!' Edie was horrified.

'Safer that way, Mum.' Lewis finished his mug of coffee. 'Got his number, Lib?'

Reluctantly, Libby read out Ian's numbers. Lewis elected to try the official one first. He left a message, then looked at Libby.

'I won't disturb the poor bugger on his day off, if it is a day off.'

'I doubt it. He never seems to have days off when he's on a murder case.' Libby shook her head. 'But maybe not. Time enough tomorrow.'

But Ian called back as they were starting on Hetty's pre-lunch sherry. Lewis excused himself and wandered out in to the hall. Hetty shook her head at Edie.

'Every bloody mealtime when there's bin a murder,' she said. 'Don't know 'ow that Ian keeps body and soul together.'

Cassandra looked at Libby. 'Really?'

'Seems to be. The police don't take much notice of a Sunday lunchtime.'

Lewis came back into the room.

'He knew,' he said simply.

'He what?' said Libby.

'About Bowling's homophobia.' Lewis sat down next to his mother. 'And didn't seem bothered.'

'So it hasn't made you suspect number one, then,' said Ben. 'That's a relief.'

'He did say he'd like to talk to me, though.' Lewis frowned. 'He's coming over this evening, Mum. You don't mind, do you?'

'No, ducks, course I don't. Him coming to us is better than you having to go to the police station, isn't it?'

'Of course it is,' said Libby. 'It's more informal. You know how he always likes to come and chat with us …'

'Not quite the same,' said Lewis. 'Still, I'm glad it's him and not that awful woman we had before.'

'Big Bertha, wasn't it?' said Ben. 'All of five feet two, if I remember rightly.'

'And she really didn't like us, did she?' said Libby with a grin.

'You taunted her, that's why,' said Ben. 'If she could have found a reason to lock you up, she would have.'

After lunch, Edie and Hetty retired to Hetty's sitting room for a chat and a doze, and Libby led the way down the Manor drive to the pub.

'So what do you know about the other members of the uke group, then Lewis?' asked Libby, when they were settled at a table by the fire. 'I didn't think you'd know anything. I mean, when I went with Edie that time it was because she said the rest of them weren't very friendly, but they didn't seem too bad the other night.'

'Well, you know now why they weren't friendly – or why she thought they weren't friendly.'

'But why keep going? There must be other ukulele groups in the area,' said Peter.

'She's an old lady,' said Lewis. 'She wouldn't cope with trying to find another group, especially as I'm not with her a lot of the time. At least Libby's been with her once, and she knows Mike. And she enjoys it. It's got her fingers working again, and she's well made up with that.'

'She doesn't know anything about any of the other members either, then?' said Ben.

'Nah. Once she heard what Bowling said, that was it. More a question of *her* not being friendly, not the rest of 'em.'

'Ah.' Libby nodded. 'Now, what do you think about Mike's nursery being searched?'

'Eh?' Lewis looked startled. 'Mike – what?'

Between them, Libby and Cassandra explained.

'I've no idea.' Lewis looked from to the other. 'And you're saying Bowling had a *cannabis* factory?'

Cassandra nodded. 'I'm surprised it hasn't got into the media already. And the police had a tip-off about Mike having been Bowling's garden designer, so they put two and two together.'

Libby frowned. 'It was more a tip-off that Mike had something to do with the cannabis, as I understood it.'

'Mike?' Lewis threw back his head and laughed. 'He's the last person in the world to have anything to do with drugs.'

'Yes, we thought so,' said Libby. 'And he told us he'd only tried it once, in college, and it made him ill.'

'And he's a moral sort of bloke,' said Lewis. 'Wouldn't be mixed up in anything dodgy.'

'But the police don't know that,' said Peter. 'They have to take everything at face value.'

The pub door opened, letting in a blast of cold air and Harry.

'What have I missed?' He swung a chair back to front and took up his usual position astride it.

'Not much,' said Ben.

'Vernon Bowling was homophobic,' said Libby. 'And Ian knew.'

'And Edie was hostile,' added Peter. 'Do you want a brandy?'

'Yes, please, dear.' Harry patted Peter's hand. 'So are you both chief suspects?' he asked Lewis.

'I don't think so. The dishy inspector's coming to see Mum and me tonight, though.'

'With handcuffs in his back pocket, no doubt.' Harry grinned round the table. 'Well, the world's well rid of Mr Bowling, then.'

Cassandra frowned. 'I don't think anyone deserves to be murdered.'

Harry smiled at her. 'Strangely enough, neither do I.'

Cassandra looked confused.

'Don't worry, Cass, you get used to him,' said Libby.

'What you need to do,' said Harry, accepting a brandy goblet from Peter, 'is find out who else had a grudge against Vernon Bowling.'

'Who needs to?' asked Ben.

'Well, Libby and Cassandra, obviously. Libby because she's nosy and doesn't want Lewis or Edie arrested, and Cassandra because she doesn't want Mike Farthing arrested. And me, actually, because I don't want Andrew's concert to flop.'

There was a short silence. Then Cassandra turned to Libby.

'Is this what it's always like?'

'What what's always like?'

'When a murder happens. You all sit and talk about it.'

Libby looked round at her friends. 'Yes, I suppose so.'

'And drink a lot?'

'Well ...' Libby made a face. 'I suppose so. Most of our talking seems to take place over a drink of some sort – alcohol or tea.'

'Or coffee,' said Peter.

'Or soup,' added Harry.

Cassandra shook her head. 'I don't understand it.'

'What don't you understand?' asked Libby. 'Look, think about it. If someone comes round unexpectedly, unless you throw them out, you invite them in for a cup of tea or coffee, don't you?'

'No.' Cassandra shook her head.

There were exclamations of surprise from the others round the table. Cassandra went faintly pink.

'Right, you don't do that. So you don't take anyone for a drink either? You wouldn't get together in a pub?'

'No, of course not! I wouldn't go into a pub on my own!' Cassandra looked shocked.

'In that case, you don't live the same sort of life that we do.' Libby looked faintly dissatisfied.

Cassandra was silent.

'But that doesn't mean she doesn't want us to find out about the murder for her Mike's sake,' said Harry.

Libby regarded her cousin thoughtfully. 'But she's got to help.'

'She can help without having to have a drink,' said Ben. 'If she wants to.'

Chapter Fifteen

'Of course I want to.' Cassandra sat up straighter in her chair.

Libby noticed she hadn't corrected Harry's statement referring to "her" Mike. 'OK, just don't question our methods, Watson.'

'You mean stop being a headmistress,' Cassandra said with a wry smile. 'I'll try.'

'Didn't work on me anyway,' said Harry, raising his brandy glass. 'Cheers.'

'So,' said Lewis, 'the suspects. So far: me and Mum because of the homophobia, Mike Farthing because of the cannabis, who else?'

'Our Monica,' said Harry, with a grin.

Libby and Peter laughed.

'Who?' asked Lewis.

'An old battleaxe who lives in Maltby Close, over there,' Libby gestured. 'She's anti everything, including the ukulele group and the female vicar, and rabidly homophobic. She accused me of bringing the whole world crashing down round her because I was involved with the theatre.'

'However,' said Ben, 'she does rely on a mobility scooter to get around.'

'Oh, deadly, then,' said Lewis. 'Not a serious contender.'

'Sadly, no,' said Libby. 'I don't think she'd get her scooter into the graveyard.'

'Right, who else?' said Lewis. 'I suppose any member of the uke group.'

'If they had a motive,' said Libby. 'But we don't know who could have had a motive.'

'There's the obvious one,' said Ben, 'that you actually discussed with Ian.'

'You mean the Dellington business?' said Harry. He turned to Lewis. 'You remember that?'

Lewis didn't, so Harry explained.

'So you think someone might want revenge on him for something that happened then?'

'It's possible. Ian was looking into it,' said Libby. 'Then there's the old boy who wanted to talk to Fran. He's a member. Bob something,'

'Bob Alton? But what motive could he have?' asked Lewis.

'No idea, but he asked Fran if we were investigating the murder, because he was a member of the group, then came back to talk to her but we were out. I don't know if she's seen him since. But it looks as though he knows something.'

'So that's it?' Lewis looked round the table. 'Nobody else?'

'Screwball Stewart,' said Peter. 'I'd be taking a close look at him.'

'Why?'

'He and Bowling had identical houses,' said Libby.

'So?' Lewis frowned. 'Yours is identical to the other houses in your street.'

'No, these were both commissioned,' Cassandra suddenly came to life. 'By the same builder. With huge attic spaces.'

'Bowling's was his cannabis farm, Stewart's is supposed to be his studio,' explained Libby.

'And that makes him a suspect?' asked Lewis.

'Well,' said Libby. 'Ian didn't know.'

'He does now,' said Peter. 'And really you should be letting him do his job.'

'Without interference,' said Ben mildly.

Harry snorted with laughter.

'All right,' said Libby meekly. 'But if Mike or Lewis need help ...'

Lewis patted her arm. 'I know, Sherlock.'

Ben and Libby wandered home after Lewis announced he had to go and pick up Edie.

'Cass doesn't really fit in, does she?' said Libby.

'Too straight-laced?' asked Ben with amusement.

'A bit. The only reason she's interested in the murder is because Mike Farthing's involved. And that's because she's fallen for him like a ton of bricks and doesn't know how to deal with it.'

'You don't think he's guilty, do you?'

'I don't think so,' said Libby, 'because I like him, but then I've liked murderers in the past. They aren't always evil through and through, are they?'

'No, a lot are just panicking because they can't deal with a situation,' said Ben. 'And that looks a bit like this one. An unprovoked attack in the graveyard.'

'I suppose he could have arranged to meet someone after the rehearsal? Someone unconnected to the group?'

'Unlikely, surely? If it was someone from outside the group it would have been better to meet them on neutral territory. No, it's got to be someone from the group,' said Ben.

Libby sighed. 'And we aren't going to get any more from Ian, are we? I suppose we'll just have to hope something falls into our laps.'

Ben laughed. 'Honestly, Lib! You're incorrigible. But don't forget Ian did ask you to let him know if you heard anything.'

The next morning Libby was dying to call Lewis to find out what Ian had said the previous evening when she was pre-empted by a phone call from Fran.

'Bob Alton came to see me yesterday.'

'Why didn't you call me?'

'Because I knew you had been to Hetty's and had Cassandra with you. You couldn't have come over.'

'But I would have wanted to know what he said.'

Fran sighed impatiently. 'And that's what I'm going to tell you now. Bob Alton's son was killed at Dellington.'

'No!' Libby gasped. 'So he has a motive, too?'

'I suppose he does,' said Fran reluctantly, 'but I'd hate to believe it. He's such a nice old boy, and so lonely.'

'We were only saying yesterday how we'd met and liked a few murderers,' said Libby. 'It could be him.'

'It could, but his son's death is a matter of record, so I'm sure

105

the police know about it. After all, we know Ian was going to look into the Dellington angle.'

'What was his name?' Libby pulled her laptop towards her.

'Roland Alton. Are you looking it up?'

'Yes,' said Libby. 'And ugh!' She read a little more of the entry. 'What a way to die. And how angry their relatives must have been.'

'Bob says they were. But the MOD just closed ranks and the whole thing sank without trace until that Operation Antler brought it out into the open again.'

'So what did Bob Alton have to say about the murder?'

'Not much. He said he found out who Bowling was some time after he'd joined the group. He was introduced to people by their first names, and it wasn't until there was a list sent round of the people who were going to be in the Christmas concert he saw the surnames. He didn't even know Eric Robinson was a Doctor. Or that Stewart was a rock musician.'

'Come to think of it, we still don't know what Robinson is a doctor of,' said Libby. 'So was he there on Tuesday night?'

'Robinson?'

'No, silly, Bob Alton.'

'Yes. He didn't go to the meeting on Thursday, though. He felt as if he was being a hypocrite.'

'Poor bloke,' said Libby. 'So what next?'

'What do you mean, what next?'

'What are we going to do?'

'Do?' Surprise sounded in Fran's voice. 'Nothing. We aren't investigating this.'

'No, that's what the others said yesterday. So I said unless Lewis or Edie, or, of course, Cass's Mike are involved ...'

'Lewis or Edie?'

Libby explained. 'And I was just going to ring Lewis to see how they got on last night when you rang.'

'And it's already "Cass's Mike", is it?'

'Seems to be. But I was saying to Ben, she doesn't really fit in, does she? With us.'

'You were all for her moving down here last week.'

'I know – and I think it would do her good. But perhaps not too close to us.'

'She could move in with Mike.'

'Bit early for that,' laughed Libby. 'I think she'd be horrified.'

When Fran rang off, Libby rang Lewis's mobile.

'Where are you?'

'In the back of a car being driven somewhere for a shoot,' said Lewis. 'If you want an update, why don't you ring Edie. No handcuffs, you'll be pleased to know.'

Libby rang the Creekmarsh landline.

'No ducks, he were lovely. Well, he is a nice man, isn't he? Why don't you pop over? I've got a lovely lemon drizzle cake I made for yesterday, but after we'd been to Hetty's we couldn't manage it. The Inspector had a slice. And what about your friend Fran?'

Libby called Fran back.

'All right, but I mustn't be long,' she said. 'You do realise we're now into December and trade is picking up? I don't want to leave Guy here all on his own too long.'

The road to Creekmarsh led out of Nethergate along the coast, twisting and turning, alternately hiding and revealing glimpses of the sea. Banks that in spring were clothed thickly in cow parsley and campion now had bare, bent, and windblown hawthorn and elder crowding in on either side, until the road widened and turned sharply to the right. A pub stood on the right-hand side, and a heavily wooded lane led off to the left, with an old signpost pointing to "The Church" and a small wooden finger post announced "Creekmarsh Place".

The bare trees overhung the lane, before opening out to show the little church on the left. Finally the lane began to slope down and she could see the sea. Now there was a lawn to her right, an old wall and the gateposts.

Libby drove up to the house, where Edie stood waving.

'Fran's coming on her own,' she said getting out of the car. 'You all right?'

'I'm fine, lovie,' said Edie. 'You come along in out of the cold. We'll leave the door open for Fran.'

In the kitchen a kettle sang on the hob and on the big scrubbed table sat a huge lemon drizzle cake on an old-fashioned cake stand. As Libby sat down, they heard the crunch of wheels on gravel, and in a moment Fran blew in through the door.

'Now,' said Edie, when they were all seated, with tea and cake. 'You'll want to know about that nice inspector. Ian, isn't it?'

'Yes. What did he want to ask you?' said Fran.

'Well, he just wanted to know what that Bowling man had said about my Lewis and if there was anyone else who'd said the same thing.' Edie drew herself up and folded her arms. 'I told him, I didn't listen to anything any of 'em said. Didn't hold with it.'

'But you kept on going to the group?' said Libby.

'Well, I enjoyed the playing. And the company, when Lewis was there. And I know Mike. Nice boy.'

Libby suppressed a smile at Mike Farthing, sixty-five if he was a day, being referred to as a boy.

'But nobody else was nasty about Lewis?' asked Fran.

'Nobody I heard, but you can't never tell, can you?' Edie shook her head. 'There was that Stewart person, some sort of pop star, dunno what he was doing there, but he was thick with that Bowling, so I never had nothing to do with him. And that Doctor Whatsisname. He was the leader. Not sure about him.'

'You didn't speak to Bob Alton?' asked Fran.

'Bob …? Oh, I know. Old boy from Nethergate. Always looked sad. Yes, I spoke to him. Quiet, but lovely.'

'He used to go for the company, he said,' Libby put in. 'He's been to see Fran.'

'About the murder?' Edie's eyes sparkled. 'I could ask him round here, couldn't I? He might like a chat.'

'He might,' said Libby, failing to suppress another smile. 'What about the solicitor?' She turned to Fran. 'What was his name?'

'No idea,' said Fran.

'Derek Chandler.' There was scorn in Edie's voice. 'You won't want to have nothing to do with him. I told you. He was another one thick with that Bowling and Stewart. I wouldn't trust him as far as I could throw him.'

'Why's that?' asked Libby.

'He's the one that tried to swindle that woman out of her savings. Lives in your village. Vi Little.'

Chapter Sixteen

The stunned silence that followed this statement was obviously a surprise to Edie.

'You didn't know about that?' She looked from one shocked face to the other. 'Thought she'd told everybody.'

'How do you know?' asked Libby, recovering. 'I thought you didn't know anyone in Steeple Martin except Hetty.'

'And Flo,' said Edie. 'That woman with the mobility scooter was going round telling everybody in her close about it. Dunno why she didn't hire the town crier.'

'What, she even told Flo? I thought they were daggers drawn.'

'Nobody likes her, but she wanted the world to know about her mate's troubles. Don't know what good she thought it'd do. Only made her look barmy.'

'What happened, then?' asked Fran. 'How did he swindle her?'

'Well,' Edie looked away evasively, 'actually, turned out he didn't have nothing to do with it. So he said.'

'But what *happened*, Edie!' Libby leant forward and fixed her eyes on the older woman's face.

'Oh, she made some kind of investment through him – or his firm – and it lost money.'

Libby sat back, looking puzzled. 'Well, that happens, sometimes.'

'Yes, but turned out it was on their paper, like, but not really from them. And when they looked, the money wasn't there. And he said he'd never told her about it, and didn't know nothing about the company, neither.'

'So somebody was pretending to be from the solicitors and she believed them?' said Fran.

'Something like that. But we was all sure he had something to do with it. Shifty, 'e is.'

'Who's we?' asked Libby.

'Flo and Hetty and a couple of others from Maltby Close, and Dolly Webley from New Barton Lane. Oh, and Una, up Steeple Lane.'

'Goodness! I didn't realise. Why haven't you been to see me?'

'We're all old biddies,' chuckled Edie. 'Flo lets us meet in the room they've got named after her old man. We have a good gossip and a cuppa. Dunno why Hetty hasn't mentioned it.'

'I've met Dolly and Una,' said Libby. 'You remember, Fran? Auntie Dolly, and Freddy's grandma Una?'

Fran nodded. 'So you've all talked about Vi Little's problem?'

'That woman –' Edie turned to Libby. 'What's 'er name? Mobility scooter?'

'Monica Turner.'

'Yes – 'er. Well, she comes in when we're there – can't very well stop 'er, can we? – and tells us all about it. Then the next time we see 'er, we ask what's 'appened. And she says this Chandler's denyin' it. Was in the paper.'

'The local?' asked Libby.

'Yeah – your mate's paper – the *Mercury*.'

'Well, thank you, Edie, that's really useful,' said Libby. 'Do you mind if we tell Ian?'

'Your nice inspector? No, you go ahead, lovie. Would'a told 'im meself if I thought it was useful.'

Half an hour later, they left Edie's warm kitchen.

'Shall I tell Ian, or will you?' asked Libby, as they stood outside on the gravel drive.

'It's really nothing to do with me,' said Fran. 'But if I were you, I'd check with Jane about the piece in the paper. It might be completely irrelevant.'

'Well, of course it is,' said Libby, much struck. 'It's nothing to do with Vernon Bowling, is it?'

'Unless he was scammed as well, but it sounds to me like one of those that are used on the elderly and vulnerable, not on an astute cannabis grower.'

'True.' Libby sighed. 'Oh, well, maybe I won't tell Ian. I might ask Flo, though. And Jane.'

On impulse, when Libby reached Steeple Martin, instead of going straight through the village and home, she turned left up Steeple Lane. Past Steeple Farm she drove, and on to the row of cottages where Una lived.

She got out of the car and looked over the road to where she could see the dewpond, half surrounded by bare trees, the little river Wytch dribbling sluggishly into it. Below that, the village lay spread out like a whimsical painting. Libby turned and knocked on the farthest green front door.

'Well, my duck! Haven't seen you for a bit.' Una pulled the door wide.

'Hello, Una.' Libby stooped to kiss the little woman's cheek. 'How are you?'

'Just dandy, I am, you ask your Auntie Flo.'

'Yes, I've just been hearing how you all meet for tea and a chat. Why didn't anyone tell me?'

Una looked surprised. 'You don't want to know about us oldies, duck. Now, tea?' Libby knew she'd never get away with a refusal, so nodded and followed her hostess into the sitting room. Una, wearing her usual thick hand-knitted jumper and comfy slippers tottered through to the kitchen and soon came back with a tray. Libby jumped up to take it from her.

'How's Sandra?' she asked, referring to Una's next door neighbour. 'I haven't seen anything of her for ages.'

'Didn't you hear, duck? She went and got married again. Very quiet it was. Lives over to Shott, now.'

Shott, again. 'No, I didn't know. Who's in next door now?'

'No one, dear. They let people use it now and again, but her husband, he says they'll have to do it up before they sell it, and he's worried it might disturb me.' She twinkled at Libby. 'So let 'em have mine it when I go, I reckon.'

Libby laughed.

'So what is it you want to know, then?' asked Una, handing

over a proper cup and saucer.

Libby looked up in surprise. 'Nothing, actually. Edie was just talking about you this morning and I realised I hadn't seen you for – oh, must be a year, now.'

'Oh, I thought it must be about this 'ere murder.' Una appeared unconcerned.

'Why – what on earth would you know about that?'

'Sandra's new husband and her. They're in that banjo group.'

Libby's mouth fell open for the second time that morning. Una gave a nod of satisfaction.

'Very pally with that Vernon Bowling's missis, she is. Phoned me to tell me all about it last Wednesday. They didn't know, see. They'd been away to see her husband's son's new baby.'

'Well!' Libby sat back in her chair and regarded the other woman in awe. 'How is it you always seem to have so much information?'

'Just an older version of yourself, duck.' Una chuckled. 'Nosy, I am. I'll tell her you asked after her.'

Ten minutes later, Libby excused herself.

'How's Freddy, by the way? Is he still enjoying himself over in Maidstone?' she asked as she left.

'He says so. Seems to come back a lot, though. Wouldn't be surprised if he didn't come home. Now you come in again, my duck. Don't be a stranger.'

Libby drove back down Steeple Lane, on into the high street and parked almost outside The Pink Geranium. Harry waved, but Libby indicated that she was going up to see Cassandra. Harry opened the door.

'Mike's there,' he said. 'Come in here for a minute.'

'What are you doing here, anyway?' asked Libby, as she followed him inside. 'It's Monday, you're closed.'

Harry sighed. 'How many times do I have to tell you I have to come in to sort out the books and the ordering? Pete works all morning, and, let's face it, we live practically next door. It's no hardship.'

'So why have you stopped me from going up to see Cass?'

Harry grinned evilly. 'I thought you might walk in on a scene of debauchery.'

'I was going to knock, not barge in.'

'Anyway, he's only been there half an hour, I thought they ought to have a bit of time alone.'

'Thoughtful.'

'It was, wasn't it? And now you can yell up the back stairs and ask them if they would like coffee.'

'I expect she's already given him coffee.'

'Don't make difficulties. We want to know what they're talking about, don't we?'

Libby eyed him suspiciously. 'What's all this about?'

Harry patted her arm. 'I'm getting as nosy as you, petal, that's what.'

'All right. I've got stuff to tell Cass, anyway.'

'What?'

'I'll call them down and you can hear.'

Libby went into the back yard and called up the spiral staircase. Cassandra appeared at the top.

'Harry's got the coffee on and I've got something to tell you. Do you and Mike want to come down?'

Cassandra looked over her shoulder and Mike came out behind her. They both started down the stairs.

'Well,' began Libby, when they were settled at the big table in the window, 'Cass will have told you, Mike, what Lewis said yesterday.'

'Yes,' said Mike doubtfully. 'I don't see what help it is.'

'You were the one who suggested homophobia as a motive,' said Libby.

'The reverse, actually dear,' said Harry. 'Someone killing Batty Bowling *because* he was homophobic.'

'Same thing.' Libby brushed it away. 'And then Edie confirmed it this morning. And told me that the solicitor, Derek Chandler, apparently tried to swindle Vi Little out of some money. You know, the friend of the Turner battleaxe. And then I saw someone else who told me that a mutual acquaintance has moved to Shott and is a bosom buddy of Mrs Bowling. And her husband's in the ukulele group.'

Harry regarded his friend with amusement, Mike and Cassandra with bewilderment.

'So you've found all this out,' said Harry, 'and what are you going to do with it?'

'Er …' Libby looked round at the three faces. 'Actually, I don't know.'

Mike turned to Cassandra. 'How does she do it?'

Cassandra shook her head. 'I've no idea. I've never been around before when she's been mixed up in murder.'

Harry gave a theatrical shudder. 'How awful. Sounds like a murder mystery.'

'It is – oh, I see what you mean. A book.' Cassandra was now looking even more confused.

Harry grinned at her, then turned back to Libby. 'So, dear heart, what are you going to do?'

Libby's face fell. 'Well, nothing I suppose.'

A silence fell.

'Unless,' said Cassandra suddenly, 'Mike is arrested.'

'What?' Mike started to get up, but Libby flapped a hand at him.

'What she means is that then I would be compelled to investigate on your behalf.'

'I'd rather you didn't,' said Mike, looking nervous.

'Oh, she'd never make things worse for you,' said Harry. 'In fact, she's been known to make things better. If she believes in you, of course.'

'Oi!' said Libby. 'I am still here, you know.'

'All right, petal, all right.' Harry patted her arm. 'Drink your nice coffee.'

'I'm awash with tea. Elderly ladies always ply one with tea.'

'Who was the acquaintance who knew the Bowlings?' asked Cassandra.

'She used to be Sandra Brown, and lived up Steeple Lane. Then she remarried and moved to Shott. I should think she's about your age, Cass.'

Cassandra's eyes slid sideways to Mike and quickly back to

Libby. 'You don't know her name now?'

'I think I do,' said Mike. 'One of our members married a widow called Sandra a couple of years ago. Very smart woman with silver hair.'

'That's Sandra!' said Libby. 'What's her husband's name?'

'Alan Farrow, and actually, they don't live in Shott, but Itching. In Perseverance Row.'

'What does he do? Was he a particular friend of Bowling's?'

'I didn't think so, and I think he's retired.' said Mike. 'I didn't know his wife was a friend of Bowling's wife.'

'And are you suddenly going to discover a reason to stage a reunion with the lovely Sandra?' asked Harry.

'No.' Libby glared at him. 'As I said before, only if there's a threat to someone I know.'

'And it's not really surprising that people should know each other in small communities like ours,' said Mike. 'I bet there are lots of people with friends in all the villages.'

'Well, yes,' said Libby, 'but when Ian showed us the list of people in your group none of us knew any of the names except Patti. Now I come to think of it, I'm surprised she only recognised Ron Stewart, as she's vicar of the church in Shott.'

'She's in charge of several parishes, isn't she?' said Mike. 'And not many of us go to church.'

'True. She didn't even know the Bowlings until her churchwarden told her.'

'And what's this about old Vi Little being swindled?' asked Harry. 'Mind you, she's such a wet weekend, anyone could do it.'

'You know her?' said Libby.

'Course I do. She won't come in here, because Monica Turner told her not to, but I see her around the village.'

'That's not a motive for murder, though,' said Cassandra. 'It wasn't the solicitor who was murdered.'

'No.' Libby let out a sigh. 'In fact, the only one who's got a real motive is poor old Bob Alton.'

'Unless, of course, there's someone else who had a son who died at Dellington,' said Harry.

Chapter Seventeen

'What?' Cassandra and Mike stared at Harry.

'Yes, said Libby, annoyed. 'How did you know? I haven't told you yet what Fran said.'

'You're not the only one who Googles, dear. His name came up when I was looking our Vernon up.'

'Oh.' Libby turned to Mike and Cassandra. 'You see, this nice Bob Alton went to see Fran. His son was one of the victims of the tests at Dellington. He said he didn't connect Vernon with them until he saw his name in a list of the people appearing in the concert.'

Mike nodded. 'That's true. I only know the names of some of the members. The others are just Bill, or Jim, or something. I only knew Vernon because of his house and garden.'

Harry was regarding him curiously. 'Exactly how long had Bowling lived in Shott? It was a new house, as Ron Stewart's was, Libby says.'

'Not that new. Ron's been there longer, about five years. Vernon – oh, about three years.'

'Did they live in the area before that?' asked Libby.

'No, or not that I knew.' Mike looked faintly surprised. 'I never asked.'

'And it never came up in conversation? That's unusual,' said Libby.

'Not everyone swaps life stories as soon as they've met, petal.'

'No, but you say things like "I had a plant like that in my old garden in … in …" oh, I don't know, Manchester, say.'

'No, nothing like that,' said Mike. 'I don't know where Ron Stewart was either.'

'I still think it's really odd for him to be in this group, you know,' said Libby thoughtfully.

'Perhaps Batty Bowling blackmailed him into it,' suggested Harry.

'More likely to be Eric,' said Mike. 'He was the leader of the group. *I* don't know how he got Stewart on board, either.'

'Well,' said Harry, standing up, 'there we all are, still discussing it, even though our pet snufflehound can't do anything about it.'

'No.' Libby sighed. 'I would like to know, though.'

'What? How Eric got Screwball Stewart to join his group?'

'And everything else. Why have he and Bowling got the same house. Who suggested that Mike had a connection with the cannabis factory. What happened with the swindling solicitor. Was anyone else the relative of a Dellington victim.'

'How many beans make five?' Harry gave her a friendly squeeze. 'Go on home, you old trout, and concentrate on your pantomime. Plenty of mysteries to solve there – like why the dame hasn't learnt her lines and why the principal girl can't sing.'

Libby accepted the inevitable and over the next two days tried to forget about the little local murder and concentrate on the pantomime, her painting, and her cousin. Cassandra had decided to stay on for a few more days, but although Libby offered to take her out, or at least cook for her, Cassandra seemed to be perfectly content on her own, or, as Libby suspected, driving herself over to Farthing's Plants. Fran was busy helping Guy in the shop, and Ben was spending a lot of time in the estate timber yard, a busy place in the run-up to Christmas.

The Wednesday evening rehearsal went as smoothly as it could with several key cast members off with the inevitable winter bugs, and Libby found herself reading the parts, alternating between Fairy Godmother and Principal Boy.

'I've had enough!' she said to Ben, after dismissing a grateful cast fifteen minutes early. 'Is it worth rehearsing with so many not here?'

'You've got to keep up momentum, dear heart.' Peter

appeared through the auditorium doors. 'Come on. Time for a restorative drink. Your reverend friend will be in the pub by now.'

Sure enough, Patti and Anne were already in the snug by the fire. Libby looked round for Cassandra and Mike, but they were nowhere to be seen.

'Harry said she'd gone out about five,' said Patti.

'Over to Mike's,' said Ben. 'I think they might be serious.'

'Oh, how nice! That's your cousin, isn't it, Lib?' Anne moved her wheelchair closer to the table.

'Yes. He owns Farthing's Plants,' said Libby. 'Oh, and Patti, several of these people are your parishioners.'

'So I gather,' said Patti. 'The trouble is, they don't all come to church, and as I've got four parishes to look after, I just don't know them all. I told you, I had no idea Mrs Bowling was an occasional member of the congregation in Shott.'

'But you know Ron Stewart?'

'Well, yes, because he's a personality, and it was suggested that he become a patron of the joint parishes show. Can't say I know him well, though.'

'What about Alan Farrow in Itching. Would you know him?'

'Farrow? Is that Sandra Farrow's husband?' Patti looked surprised.

'Libby let out a breath. 'That's what I was coming to. I knew Sandra when she lived here.'

'She did? I didn't know that. I only know here because Mrs Bowling – what did I say her name was, Anne?'

'Denise.'

'Oh, yes, well, Denise Bowling had asked this Sandra Farrow to keep her company when I went to see her. I told you I'd have to, didn't I?'

'And what was she like?' asked Libby.

'Sandra or Denise?'

'Both, really.'

'Is she still at it?' Ben and Peter returned to the table with drinks.

'At what?'

'Asking questions,' said Ben. 'She can't stop.'

'It's natural.' Patti shrugged. 'It's an unusual and horrible thing to happen on your own doorstep, as I know. Naturally, Libby's curious about it. We all are.'

'That told you, poppet.' Peter patted his cousin on the shoulder. 'Take the word of a vicar.'

Patti blushed. 'Sorry.'

'No, wise words,' said Ben, 'and absolutely right. No wonder you're a rev.'

Libby was still looking smug when Ian brought a flurry of snow through the door with him.

'Snow?' the word floated round the bar as the flakes melted.

'Just started,' said Ian. 'I don't think it'll settle.'

Ben got up to fetch Ian's coffee.

'So, no Harry tonight?' Ian looked round.

'Not finished yet,' said Anne. 'He was very busy.'

'Pre-Christmas rush,' said Libby. 'He'll be in if he can.'

Ben returned with the coffee.

'Your cousin gone home?'

'No, we assume she's gone over to see Mike Farthing,' said Peter. 'It's becoming quite a love story.'

'Really.' Ian frowned. 'We still haven't let him off the hook you know.'

'You can't suspect him of having anything to do with that cannabis factory, surely?' said Libby.

'You know I can't tell you that, Libby.'

'What can you tell us, then?'

Ian cocked an eyebrow at her. 'And there was I, hoping for a nice quiet chat at the end of the day.'

'But …' began Libby.

'Leave him alone, Libby,' said Patti, laughing. 'He doesn't always come here on a Wednesday to consult you.'

'Oh.' Libby felt the tell-tale colour coming up her neck. 'Sorry. Just on your way home, then, were you?'

'I was actually.'

Anne leant forward, elbows on the table. 'So where do you live, then? Is Steeple Martin on your way home from

Canterbury?'

'Sorry about these nosy women, Ian,' said Peter. 'But you know them by now.'

'It's a question I've been waiting for you to ask for years, now,' said Ian. 'Thanks for the coffee, Ben.'

'I never thought of it,' said Libby slowly, 'but I suppose, yes, it is odd, the way you come here late on a Wednesday ...'

'Odd?' Ian laughed. 'Well, perhaps I won't, then.'

'No, no!' said Libby hastily. 'We look forward to seeing you.'

'And picking my brains.'

'Oh, hell,' said Libby.

'Don't worry, you've been very helpful in the past, as you know. And, as it happens, you might be now.'

Everyone sat forward and Ian laughed again. 'Here go – what was it? – Libby's Loonies – again.'

'All right, you may mock,' said Libby. 'What can we do?'

Ian looked round the table. 'I just wondered if any of you knew, or could find out anything about other members of the ukulele group. We can only go so far, and in-depth screening of every member is going to take resources we don't really have.'

Ben, Peter, Patti, and Anne all looked at Libby.

'Well, go on, then. Tell him,' said Peter.

With a grin of triumph, Libby launched into the tale of her investigations.

'And tell me,' said Ian, when she had come to a breathless finish, 'why *were* you asking all these questions?'

'Er ...' said Libby, and the others laughed.

'Sheer nosiness,' said Ben.

'Well, I can't pretend it hasn't helped,' said Ian, 'but I'd be shot if anyone at the station found out.'

'Oh, your Sergeant Maiden knows,' said Libby.

'And is sensible enough not to mention it,' said Ian. 'So, tell me again about Derek Chandler. That's definitely something we can look into.'

Libby told him.

'And Robert Alton – we did know about his son, but maybe

123

we'll dig a bit deeper.'

'But he didn't know Vernon Bowling was who he was until he saw his name on a list,' said Libby. 'And what about Ron Stewart's house?'

'Yes, we're looking into that. We've tracked down the architect.'

'And the homophobic angle?' asked Peter.

'Lewis called me on Sunday, if you remember. We didn't know all the details, but it had already emerged. Mrs Bowling said her husband was quite upset about it.'

'So was anyone else in the group homophobic?' asked Libby.

'It isn't quite the sort of question you ask,' said Ben.

'Actually, it is,' said Ian, 'when phrased correctly. "Were you aware of Mr Bowling's homophobic attitude?" quite easily leads on to "and do you think someone might have felt strongly enough ..." and you're almost sure to get a sense of whether the person agrees or disagrees.'

'And have you?' asked Libby.

'Not yet. We're going to have to go back over all the statements and ask some more questions.'

'Oh, dear, they won't like that,' said Patti.

'No, but this will be "In the light of new evidence". We don't have to tell them what evidence.'

'So, is there anything I can do?' Libby asked brightly.

'No, Libby.' Ian was laughing again. 'Just keep your ears and eyes open – though I hardly need to ask you to do that, do I?'

'And her nose twitching,' added Ben.

'And ask Fran if she's seen anything.'

'Cassandra asked her that when we first heard you were talking to Mike,' said Libby. 'And she said "Plants" – which I suppose was fairly obvious.'

'Not necessarily. We could have been asking for his alibi.'

The door opened and Harry came in with a flurry of long scarves.

'Ah! The traditional Wednesday night police interrogation.' He flung off coat and scarves and threw them in the general direction of the coat stand. 'Can I get anybody a drink?'

A general shuffling of position made room for Harry while he went to the bar with his order.

'So, what's new?' he asked when he came back to sit astride his favourite chair.

They told him. He regarded Libby seriously.

'Actually, petal, wouldn't it be better if you got your cousin to back off a little bit? She's just assumed Mike's innocent, and while I like him – hell, we gave the bloke a bed for the night! – we don't really know anything about him.'

'He's right, Libby,' said Ian.

'But you don't have anything against Mike,' Libby protested. 'Except that he's a plantsman and helped Bowling design his garden.'

'And who better than a plant and nursery man to design a cannabis factory?' said Peter. Libby scowled at him.

Ian stood up. 'I must be off. Any more titbits you hear please pass them on. Goodnight all, and, Libby, be careful.'

Anne broke the short silence which followed his departure.

'Do you realise he still managed not to answer our question?'

'What question?' said Patti.

'Where does he live?'

Chapter Eighteen

Libby relayed the results of her visits and Ian's comments to Fran the following morning.

'So you see, he would like to hear anything you – er – see.'

'And you consider you've got carte blanche to continue ferreting around?'

'Well, he didn't say *not* to.' Libby wandered out into the kitchen with the phone.

'Honestly, Lib!' Fran laughed. 'You're incorrigible. Which angle are you going after now?'

'I can't see I've got any angle, really. I can't pretend to be crusading on to prevent a miscarriage of justice against Mike, not after everyone warned me off last night.'

There was a short silence.

'What?' said Libby.

'I don't think Mike has anything to do with the murder.'

'But …?'

'Plants.'

'You said that before,' said Libby with a sigh.

'It's just all I can see. And I know that given his job, it's self-evident, but there's something …'

Libby let another beat go by.

'So what shall we do? Shall we go and see him? You've never been there.'

'What about your cousin?'

'What about her?'

'Should we take her with us?'

'Good lord, no! I suppose I should tell her we're going, though.'

'If you do,' said Fran, 'she'll either insist on going with us, or go over on her own. Or has she gone back to London?'

'Not as far as I know. She wasn't in last night, and if she got back before we left the pub, she certainly didn't come looking for us. Harry thought she'd gone to Mike's.'

'See? She'll insist on protecting him.'

'OK. I won't tell her. When are we going? Shall I meet you in Shott?'

'Yes, we can meet in car park of The Poacher. Then we can have lunch there after we've seen Mike.'

Pausing only to ring Ben's mobile to tell him she was going out with Fran, Libby flung on her latest cape and strode out to the car.

On the way through Itching, she looked out for Perseverance Row, but didn't spot it. In The Poacher's empty car park, she prepared to wait for Fran.

'Your mate not with you?' Sid Best was leaning down looking in the window. Libby let it down.

'Waiting for her, actually. Then we thought we'd come and have lunch with you.'

'Bit early for lunch.'

'No, we've got to go somewhere first.'

'Ah.' Sid tapped the side of his nose. 'Investigating.'

Libby's face began to heat up. 'Sort of.'

Just then, the little black and cream Smart car turned into the car park and Sid stepped back.

'I'll see you later, then,' he said. 'Good hunting.'

'We're committed to lunch here now,' said Libby as she approached Fran.

'Let's hope we're not thrown out of Mike's nursery and end up having morning coffee instead,' said Fran, preparing to drive out of the car park. 'Which way?'

'You know,' said Libby pensively, as they drove round the green and into Rogues Lane, 'we haven't decided what we're going to say.'

'No. Tell him what you found out yesterday?'

'He knows. I told him and Cass yesterday lunchtime. He told me Sandra's new name.'

'Right. So – what?'

'My pots? He and Cass were going to come round last Saturday to sort them out, then they didn't.'

'It was only an excuse, you said so.'

'Still, I could ask, couldn't I? And – I know!' Libby was struck with sudden inspiration. 'Floral decorations for the theatre for the concert – you know, holly and mistletoe and ivy and stuff.'

'I suppose so,' said Fran doubtfully, 'but you always go to Joe and Nella for those sort of things.'

'I still will. This is An Excuse.' Libby pointed. 'Look – there's the turning.'

But when they drew up on the forecourt of Farthing's Plants, they found they didn't need an excuse after all, as Cassandra came rushing out of the office.

'Oh, Libby, they're here again!' she wailed.

'What?' Libby climbed out of the car, realising as she did so that two sleek dark cars were parked unobtrusively to the side of the forecourt. Unmarked police cars.

'They're talking to him in the office, and two others are in the glasshouses. They won't let me or the boys leave, either.' Cassandra took a deep breath and Libby interrupted.

'Who are the boys and who's here?'

'The boys?' Cassandra looked confused.

'Yes. You said "the boys".'

'Oh, Gary and Patrick. They work here. They're in the shop.' Cassandra gestured vaguely behind her.

'When did you get here?' asked Fran, joining them.

Cassandra looked from Fran to Libby. 'I – er –'

'I think,' said Libby to Fran drily, 'that means she was here all night.'

'Um.' Cassandra's face glowed pink.

'Where can we go to sit down?' asked Fran. 'There's not room for us all in my car.'

'Mine's over there.' Cassandra jerked her head. 'I – I think I've got my keys.'

'If they won't let you leave, they aren't likely to have let you keep the keys,' said Libby. 'We'll just have to stay here. Now, I asked you before, who's here?'

'Policemen, who do you think?'

'It's not Ian?'

'No, I'd have told you. It's a different branch or something.'

'Ah.' Libby's eyes wandered to the glass houses. 'Drugs squad.'

'How do you know?' Cassandra gasped.

'It's an obvious inference,' said Fran, 'under the circumstances.'

'And I hate to tell you,' said Libby, 'but I think you're about to come under the spotlight.'

Cassandra turned to see the purposeful approach of a stocky officer.

'Mrs – er – Freeman? Would you come with me, please?'

Cassandra opened her mouth, but nothing came out.

'Go on, Cass. Might as well get it over with,' said Libby. 'Call if you need me.'

'And you are?' The officer turned to Libby with a frown.

'Mrs Sarjeant, Mrs Freeman's cousin.'

'Do you know Mr Farthing?'

'Only as a member of the ukelele group.'

'Ah! You're a member?'

'No.' Libby shut her mouth like a trap.

'Now, look –' the officer began to bluster and Libby drew herself up to her full five feet and two inches.

'I suggest you apply to Detective Chief Inspector Connell for any further information.' She turned to get in to Fran's car. 'Good day.'

Fran hastily climbed into the driver's seat and began to turn back towards the drive.

'Was that wise? You've probably antagonised that officer, and he'll make it worse for Cass.'

'No, he'll ask Cass about me, and she'll explain. Oh, God, I wish she hadn't met up with Mike now!'

Fran glanced at her. 'Have you changed your mind about him, then?'

'No, I haven't, but if she hadn't recognised him in the first place she wouldn't be under the microscope, would she? I'm going to call Ian.'

'I doubt if he'll appreciate that.'

'I don't care. I'm not having my cousin interrogated like a common criminal.'

Both of Ian's numbers went to voice mail, so Libby left 'call me back' messages on both of them.

'What now?' asked Fran, as she drove back through Shott.

'How about Itching? Perseverance Row? See if we can find Sheila Brown as was.'

'You can't knock at every door asking for her.'

'We could see if there's a shop.'

Fran snorted. 'Itching's even smaller than Shott. It won't have a shop. I didn't even notice a pub.'

'Hmm.' Libby peered out of the window as they climbed the small hill out of the village. 'Church?'

'Shares the one in Shott, didn't Patti say?'

Libby sighed. 'Oh, well, we'll have to go home I suppose. Let's go back to The Poacher.'

Fran found a place to turn the car and drove back to the pub.

'Find what you were looking for?' asked Sid, as they went into the bar.

'Not really,' said Libby. 'Can we have coffee, please?'

'What sort?' Sid's hand hovered over the smart coffee machine.

'Black,' said Fran.

'White,' said Libby. 'We're the despair of the baristas.'

Sid grinned.

'Do you know all the members of the ukulele group, Sid?' asked Fran, hitching herself on to a stool.

'Most of 'em. Why?'

'Do you know Alan Farrow? Only he married a friend of mine from Steeple Martin, Sandra Brown,' said Libby.

'Course I know Alan and Sandra, they're regulars. Fancy you knowing Sandra.'

'Not so surprising, really,' said Fran. 'It's a very small part of the world.'

'That's so.' Sid pushed their mugs towards them. 'Sandra and Alan met at a darts match over your way, I seem to remember.'

'Darts? Sandra doesn't play darts, does she?'

'Captain of our ladies team,' said Sid. 'Do you 180 soon as look at you.'

'Really? I never knew,' said Libby, shaking her head. 'I must tell Una.'

'Then there's poor Mike,' said Fran, glancing up under her eyebrows. 'Shame about him.'

'Shame? What do you mean? Mike Farthing?'

'He's got the police round again,' said Libby with a theatrical sigh.

'Mike?' Sid sounded incredulous. 'The most law-abiding bloke there is.'

'But you'd have said that about Vernon Bowling, wouldn't you?' said Libby.

Fran kicked her. 'And then he got murdered,' she said.

Sid frowned. 'Yeah. Never can tell. Derek Chandler, now. Lives in Itching. Know him, do you?'

'The solicitor? Yes.' Libby glanced warily at Fran. 'We – er – know a bit about him.'

'Not surprised. That old biddy lives in your village – she said he was trying to con her, didn't she?'

'But I thought he was cleared?'

Sid tapped his nose. 'Mud sticks.'

'Oh, dear,' said Libby. 'Poor Mr Chandler.'

Sid sniffed. 'Not my type. Doesn't stop for a drink, ever. He was a bit chummy with Bowling, like.'

'Oh?' Fran moved her coffee mug with a forefinger. 'Did he act for him when he bought the house?'

Sid looked startled. 'I – I don't know. Quite likely, I suppose. But Bowling had that house built.'

'Yes, we know,' said Libby. 'It's the same as Ron Stewart's, isn't it?'

'Look, I told you before –'

'It's all right Sid, the police know all about that. They've had to talk to Stewart, obviously. Now,' said Fran, 'what have you got on the lunch menu?'

Mollified, Sid fetched a menu which consisted mainly of toasted or untoasted sandwiches.

'That was an inspired guess about Chandler,' said Libby when they were seated at a table in the window overlooking the green.

'That's all it is, a guess,' said Fran, 'but it makes sense.'

'So Chandler would know who the architect is.'

'I should imagine the police do now,' said Fran. 'And they'll have spoken to Ron Stewart again.'

'They do. I told you, Ian said so last night. I was just linking people up.'

'And it's obvious that the whole cannabis factory thing hasn't leaked out yet. That's why I had to shut you up.

'Oh?' Libby raised her eyebrows. 'So why mention Ron Stewart's house and the joint architect?'

'That's just a connection between Stewart and Bowling.'

Sid came over with two plates of sandwiches and crisps. 'Enjoy.'

'Thanks,' said Libby with a bright smile. Then quietly to Fran, 'Should we try and call Cass? Let her know where we are?'

Fran shrugged. 'You can try, but if the police are still questioning her she won't be able to answer.'

'They can't still be talking to her! She's only known Mike a few days.'

'There will be records of their online communications for – how long did she say?'

'Oh, I don't know – years. And phone.'

'There you are. They won't believe they've only just met. Especially as it looks as though she spent the night with him. They aren't youngsters who jump into bed on the first date.'

'I still don't know what they think they're going to find at Mike's place. It's already been searched.' Libby pushed moodily at a crisp.

'Not by the drugs squad. I expect they'll bring in dogs.'

'They already did. Oh, dear.' Libby took out her phone. 'Still, I'm going to try.' She keyed in Cassandra's number, but after a moment, she shook her head. 'No, you were right. It's gone to voicemail.' She put the phone away. 'Do you suppose that officer will have spoken to Ian?'

'Maybe. Or he'll have asked Cass to explain.'

They ate their sandwiches in silence, and were just about to leave, when the door crashed open and Cassandra burst in.

'Libby! Do something! They've arrested Mike!'

Chapter Nineteen

The only other customer in the bar peered over the top of his newspaper and shook his grey head. Sid came hurrying out from behind the bar.

'Mike? They've arrested Mike? What for?'

'I don't know. They questioned me for ages and then sent me outside. That's when I saw the dogs.'

Libby nodded. 'Told you they would. Did that officer get in touch with Ian?'

'I don't know. He asked me about you.' Cassandra sank down on a chair. 'Could I have a drink, please?'

'Are you driving?' asked Sid.

'No,' said Libby. 'If she can leave her car here, I'll take her home with me. What do you want, Cass?'

'Brandy,' said Sid. 'You two want anything?'

'Another coffee?' said Fran. 'I'll fetch them.'

'So who's that?' asked Sid, as she followed him to the bar.

'Libby's cousin Cassandra,' said Fran. 'Friend of Mike's.'

'Close friend, if you ask me,' said Sid. 'I've never seen her.'

'No, she lives in London. But I think she's thinking of – er – moving down …'

'Be good for Mike if she did,' said Sid, loading mugs and a brandy goblet on to a tray. 'Not if he's …'

'Going to prison,' Fran finished for him. 'Let's hope it doesn't come to that.'

'He couldn't have murdered Bowling,' said Sid. 'Just not possible.'

Fran smiled, but said nothing, and carried the tray back to where Libby and Cassandra were now sitting in silence.

'Libby says she can't do anything.' Cassandra appealed to Fran. 'She can, can't she?'

'I'm afraid not,' said Fran in a low voice. 'Our only inside contact with the police is Ian, and this is an arrest by the drugs squad by the look of things. The whole case will have been referred to them because of the cannabis factory. Nobody would take any notice of us.'

'But why? I don't understand it. He hadn't got any cannabis plants – they searched before.'

'There must be something,' said Libby, 'they wouldn't arrest him without a good reason.'

'But you hear of people being arrested for the daftest of reasons these days.' Cassandra was obviously desperate. 'Somebody must be able to get him out.'

'He'll be asked if he wants a solicitor,' said Fran.

'Let's just hope it isn't Derek Chandler,' said Libby.

'If it's part of the whole Bowling case, then Chandler is a possible witness, even if he isn't a suspect, so he wouldn't be allowed to attend,' said Fran.

Cassandra sipped her brandy and coughed. 'How can we find out, then?'

Fran and Libby exchanged glances.

'We can't,' said Libby. 'None of us are related to Mike. And I called Ian to tell him they were questioning you, so he knows there's something going on.'

'What did he say?'

'He didn't. I left messages on both his phones.'

Cassandra banged her brandy goblet on to the table with a hiss of frustration.

'I've got to go,' said Fran. 'I promised Guy I'd be back to shop-sit.'

'And I'm driving myself home,' said Cassandra, standing up. 'One brandy isn't going to affect me.'

Libby cast a despairing look at Sid behind the bar, who shrugged. 'All right, I'll follow you,' she said. 'Hold on while I pay Sid.'

Sid waved his hands and shook his head. 'On the house. Keep me informed.'

Libby smiled gratefully. 'We will, Sid, thanks.'

'Aren't publicans nice?' she said, as they stood outside in the car park.

'Mostly,' said Fran.

Cassandra was getting into her car.

'I'd better go,' said Libby. 'I don't know what I could do if she crashed, but I'd be there …'

Cassandra appeared in complete control of her car, however. She took the sharp, narrow corners in Itching carefully and drove sedately along the Canterbury road back to Steeple Martin, where, instead of parking in the high street as near to The Pink Geranium as possible, she turned into Allhallow's Lane and parked opposite number seventeen.

'Sorry, Libby,' she said, as Libby got out of her own car. 'I don't want to just sit in that flat on my own, waiting for news.'

'No, all right, come in.' Libby opened the door and fell over Sidney. 'Watch the cat.'

Cassandra took off her coat and sat on the chair by the empty fireplace.

'Hold on a mo and I'll light the fire,' said Libby. 'Do you want tea or anything?'

Cassandra shook her head. 'Not yet. Maybe later.'

Libby bustled about fetching kindling and keeping up an inconsequential flow of chatter.

'It's all right, Lib. You don't have to try and keep my mind off things.' Cassandra cut into a wandering diatribe against the iniquities of the local council.

Libby sat back on her heels and watched the kindling catch. 'OK. How about telling me how you and Mike have got to this stage of a relationship so quickly? And how much you actually know about him?'

Cassandra bristled. 'Are you saying he might be guilty?'

'Of what? I have no idea. Neither do you.'

Cassandra looked confused.

'So go on. How come this rush of lust swept you both off your feet?'

'Don't speak of it like that.' Cassandra scowled at her cousin. 'And you don't know how it felt.'

'No, I don't. Ben and I had a rocky time at the beginning because we were both over fifty and not sure how to manage a proper relationship. It did take a murder to bring us together, though.'

Cassandra sighed. 'I suppose the murder has accelerated it for us, too. But I can't tell you what I felt when I first spoke to him last Thursday. It was like the room lighting up.'

'It looked like it,' said Libby.

'And I found myself watching for any little signs – you know, his eyes catching mine, or an accidental touch – just like a bloody teenager.'

'Cass! I've never heard you swear!'

'And he felt the same. All the way through that meeting on Friday morning, I could tell. And then when he came over on Friday evening ...'

'Weren't you tempted to ask him to stay at the flat on Saturday after we'd had dinner?'

'No. Everyone would have known.' Cassandra's colour was creeping up her neck. 'I didn't think anyone would notice last night.'

'How did that happen, then? Did he ask you over?'

'No.' Now the colour had crept right up to Cassandra's hairline. 'I just turned up.'

'Did he mind?'

'No.' Cassandra held out her hands to the fire. Libby put a log on and gave it a poke.

'So?'

'Not the details, Lib. Sorry.'

'OK. So now you've slept together and he's been arrested. And he said nothing to you about Vernon Bowling, or the murder or anything?'

'No. We weren't really thinking about anything but ourselves.' Cassandra shook her head as if to clear it. 'It comes as such a shock after being on your own for years and having no interest in the opposite sex to suddenly feel – well, like a teenager, as I said. And to find out that you haven't ...' She ground to a halt.

'Lost the ability,' suggested Libby. 'Or capacity.'

Cassandra nodded and Libby stood up.

'Are you ready for that tea now?'

Libby's phone began to burble. She fished it out of her bag.

'Ian!'

'What were you telling me, Libby? Your cousin's been arrested?'

'No, no. She was questioned. Mike's been arrested, by the drugs squad, I think.'

'Yes, so I've just been informed.' Ian's voice was grim. 'There's rather a lot of inter-departmental wrangling going on right now. What about your cousin?'

Libby explained. Cassandra was on her feet, her hands gripped together.

'Is she with you now? Can I speak to her?'

Libby handed over the phone and went back to the kitchen. Just as she was putting mugs on the table Cassandra came in and handed back the phone.

'He says he'll let us know what's happened if he can.' Cassandra pulled out a chair and sat down at the table. 'And he said he'll tell the drugs squad about me. And you, actually.'

'Well, that's all we can hope for, isn't it?' Libby poured tea. 'Wouldn't you rather go back to London and your normal life? Keep your mind off it all?'

'No. I might pop back and fetch more clothes, if Harry doesn't mind me staying in the flat a bit longer. I've offered him rent.'

'Oh, he won't accept that. Fran and Adam have both had fights with him about rent.'

'But I'm using the heating and hot water. He ought to take a contribution to those.'

'Don't worry about it. When will you go?'

Cassandra frowned. 'I could go now, couldn't I? I won't be able to see Mike until he's released – when will that be?'

'No idea. It depends on what they're holding him for, and what his solicitor can do to get him out. I wouldn't bank on today.'

'I'll go in a bit, then. Shall I phone Harry?'

'No, I'll do it,' said Libby. 'Drink your tea, then you can go. Unless you want to pick anything up from the flat?'

'No, I've got my keys with me. I'll probably stay overnight and come back in the morning.' Cassandra put her hand over Libby's. 'You will call me if anything happens, won't you?'

'If I hear anything, of course.' Libby patted Cassandra's hand in turn. 'I'm now going to utter one of the most useless phrases in the English language. Try not to worry.'

When Cassandra had gone, Libby called Harry.

'Course she can stay. So it's a real love match between her and Mike, then, is it?'

'Seems to have taken them both by surprise,' said Libby. 'I just hope this whole arrest thing is a mistake, that's all. Ian didn't sound too happy about it.'

'Well, he was issuing a warning last night, wasn't he?'

'Yes, but this is the drugs squad. I don't know how they got involved.'

'Oh, come on, Lib! Ian could hardly have kept the cannabis factory quiet. I expect his superintendent got a request from the drugs people and couldn't refuse.'

'But what could they find that Ian's crowd didn't? There were no cannabis plants in the greenhouses.'

'Equipment? Letters? Emails? Phone calls? Could be anything, not just actual plants.'

'You're a comfort.'

'I know. Little ray of sunshine, me.'

Unable to settle to anything, Libby put her cape back on and set off for Maltby Close.

'Come in, gal.' Flo held the door open on to a fug of cigarette smoke. Lenny, dapper in white shirt and cravat, rose from his chair by the electric fire.

'What can we do for you?' Flo sat down in her own chair and waved Libby to a seat. 'Got more trouble with that Monica Turner?'

'No, Flo, actually, I wanted to ask if you knew anything about her friend, Vi Little. And Derek Chandler, the solicitor

140

who apparently tried to swindle her.'

Flo's eyes twinkled. 'I should say so, gal! Bugger tried it on me, too!'

Chapter Twenty

'He *what*?'

'Course, 'e didn't get anywhere, stands to reason. And it was me told Vi Little. And that Turner then tried to blame me. Cor! Takes the biscuit, that woman.'

'So, what exactly happened?'

Lenny moved towards the tiny kitchen. 'Shall I make us a cuppa, then?'

'Not for me, thanks, Lenny,' said Libby. 'I'm awash with coffee and tea.'

'Nice droppa Merlot, then?' offered Flo.

'No thanks, Flo. Bit early for me.'

Flo eyed her guest dubiously. 'Not like you, gal.'

'I'm not that bad!' laughed Libby. 'So come on, Flo. Tell me what happened with Derek Chandler.'

'I got this email, see.'

'Email? I didn't know you were online!'

'Course I am, gal. Got to be these days, ain'tcher? Anyway, I got this email from this Chandler, looked all official, like, sayin' that I got this inheritance comin' from a distant relative, and wantin' me details to confirm I was 'oo I said I was.'

'Did you have a distant relative?'

'If I 'ad, it'd be pretty bloody distant! Nah – it was a scam. Just wanted me bank details. So I phoned 'em. And this Chandler, they said 'e wasn't there, but they'd take a message. So I told 'em just what I thought of 'em. They was shocked. All flustered and "Sorry, madam, don't know anything about it," you know.'

'So what about Vi? She's not online, surely?'

'Nah. First I 'eard about Vi was when we was all in the 'all fer something or other and she was complaining about being swindled. So I listened, and she'd 'ad a phone call. And she, poor mug, gave all 'er details and the money disappears from 'er bank. And she says it was this Derek Chandler. So I says did she bother to call back, and o' course, she says she didn't take the number. So I says, leave it with me, and I phones again and tells 'em what's what.'

'What happened next?'

'Oh, then I calls the police. No, I didn't bother your Ian. I just called the nick in Canterbury and told 'em all about it. And they sends round this nice lady officer to talk to me and Vi. And they 'auled ol' Chandler in. Accordin' to 'im, it was a scam, someone usin' 'is name. It's a well-known one, accordin' to the solicitors' society, or 'ooever they are. Anyway, Vi got 'er money back – don't ask me 'ow, and that was the end of it.'

'Wow!' said Libby, as Lenny came back with a tray. 'I didn't know anything about this.'

'No reason why yer should. Told Het, but she don't gossip.'

'No, she just always seems to know things when we need them,' said Libby. 'How did Monica Turner blame you?'

'I couldn't follow it. If I hadn't turned this bloke down 'e wouldn't't've gone after Vi or something. Didn't matter that 'e'd gone after Vi before me.' Flo shook her head and reached for a dainty Spode teacup. 'Silly cow.'

'He didn't go after her, then?'

'If 'e did, she wasn't sayin'. Make 'er look a fool, wouldn't it?'

'Has she got email?'

'I dunno. Why?'

'Just wondered. And did the police manage to trace the scam emails?'

'No idea, duck. I wasn't a victim, see, only Vi, and she wouldn't say anythin' to me after, would she?'

'Scared of what Monica would say?'

'Yeah. Not so much as a thank you, I didn't get.'

'I wonder how he got on to you in the first place?' said Libby. 'Sticking a pin in the directory?'

Flo was scornful. 'Use yer brain, gal. What's this place?

144

Gracious livin' fer the over fifty-fives. Over sixty-fives, more like. All owner-occupied. Not cheap. Stands to reason occupiers got a bit stashed away, and old – so they've lost their marbles.'

'Except they haven't,' grinned Libby.

'No – most of us are all right. Some a bit – well, like Vi. Not up to the minute.'

'And that's why she looks up to Monica Turner. Is she up to the minute?'

Flo shrugged. 'No idea. Gets most of 'er opinions from the gutter press, I reckon.'

Libby was thoughtful. 'She knew who the victim was. She got that from the press, I suppose.' Libby glimpsed the corner of *The Independent* tucked down by Flo's chair.

'Well, o'course she did, we all did.'

'But when she said "that *man*", it was almost as though it was personal. Do you think she had a relative at Dellington? Perhaps who's buried in the churchyard?'

'We'd 'a heard about it, I reckon. Any grievance she had against the world she told everybody.'

'Well, that's most helpful, Flo.' Libby stood up.

'Now you're not pokin' yer nose in again, are yer? No good'll come of it.'

'It has in the past, though, hasn't it?' said Libby, bending to kiss Flo's cheek. 'I'm going to see your vicar, now.'

'What for?'

'As a member of her flock I'm entitled to,' said Libby, with a grin. 'Bye, Lenny.'

In fact, the idea of seeing Bethany Cole had only just occurred to Libby. Although Monica Turner and Vi Little both attended church in Canterbury and Flo was at the very least agnostic, Libby reckoned most of the other residents of Maltby Close would attend their local church, and Libby wondered if anyone else had been targeted by the spurious Derek Chandler.

The vicarage stood on the corner of her own lane, the lilac tree overhanging the wall, now bare. Libby had never opened the high painted gate in all the years she had lived here, and felt as if she was entering the Secret Garden.

The path, overgrown with weeds, led indeterminately between what had once been flower borders, to a wide front door under a weather-beaten porch. Not finding a bell, Libby rapped sharply on the door..

After a while, the sound of bolts being drawn increased Libby's feeling that she had stepped into a fairy tale, a feeling that the face that peered out quickly dispelled.

'Hello? Goodness, we haven't had anyone come to this door since we've lived here! Did you want me? I'm Bethany Cole.'

Libby sighed with relief. Bethany's round, pretty face was surmounted by abundant light brown hair drawn back into a thick and untidy plait. She looked far too young to be a vicar.

'Hello, yes,' began Libby. 'I'm –'

Bethany laughed. 'Oh, I know who you are! You're Libby Sarjeant and you live just down the road here. If I didn't already know about you, Patti would have filled me in. Come in, come in.'

Libby followed her into a dark hall, along a passage and into what was almost a different house. Light, airy, and welcoming, the big kitchen looked out on to a wide terrace and a drive.

'Oh, I see! People come in this way,' said Libby, realising that the drive came out in the high street. 'I didn't know.'

'That's all right,' said Bethany cheerfully. 'You found me anyway. Sit down, do. Tea?'

'Do you mind if I don't? I keep being fed coffee and tea!'

'Oh, so do I!' said Bethany sitting down on the opposite side of the huge table. 'I'm afraid "More tea, vicar" has come to mean more than a cliché to me. Now, what did you want to talk to me about? The murder? Or that man who tried to prey on my parishioners?'

'Goodness!' said Libby. 'Are you a mind-reader? Or has Patti been talking to you? She didn't mention she knew you.'

'We all know each other, at least vaguely. We're in the same diocese, and women priests tend to stick together. I gather you're quite close friends?'

'Yes, I suppose we are. We see one another once a week, anyway.'

'Oh, yes, when she comes over to see Anne on a Wednesday. She sometimes pops in here if she's early.'

'Oh, I didn't realise. She's sometimes been to see me before Anne gets home. She never told me.'

'Well, I haven't been here that long, and I take it you aren't likely to be a member of my congregation!'

'No, sorry.' Libby made a face. 'But you're the one the ukulele group approached about using the church hall, aren't you?'

'Actually, it was my churchwarden, Tom. I don't know whether you know him?'

'Tom? No, I don't think so.'

'He's a friend of Lenny and Flo's,' said Bethany.

'No, I don't know him,' said Libby, 'but it was Flo who told me about you.'

'Oh?'

'Yes,' said Libby uncomfortably. 'When she was talking to me about Monica Turner.'

'Ah! Yes, I heard you had a bit of an altercation with her the other day.'

'Do you hear everything?' asked Libby.

'Most things filter through.' Bethany grinned. 'Gossip becomes sanctified when told to a vicar. And it's often so very righteous.'

'Oh, I bet it is.' Libby laughed, deciding she liked Bethany Cole. 'Did the leader of the group get in touch with you?'

'I've got no idea. I've had very little to do with it. Tom's is the name on the board outside – he's the caretaker as well as my churchwarden.'

'Oh, well, perhaps I'll ask Flo to introduce me. Although she'll think I'm making use of her again.' Libby sighed. 'I do seem to get in touch with people just because I think they can tell me something.'

'But at least you get in touch. That's important, especially to older people.'

'Most of the older people I know get out and about more than I do,' said Libby.

147

'I doubt that,' said Bethany, with a smile. 'Now, how can I help you?'

Libby was startled. 'I don't know …'

'If I tell you that several of the ladies in Maltby Close were targeted by Derek Chandler, will that help?'

Libby gasped. 'They were? How do you know?'

'For a start, Monica Turner wasn't keeping quiet about Vi Little's brush with him.'

'No, that's when Flo got on to the police.'

'Ah, you know about that. Well, it turned out that it had happened to several of them, and they were too ashamed to tell anyone about it. It appeared, after the police had investigated, that someone was using Mr Chandler's name and company to run a scam. The money was recovered.'

'But how? How would they have discovered a hidden bank account? None of the victims knew the bank details, did they?'

'No, they were merely asked to give *their* bank details. I believe the trail wasn't very well hidden. They looked into who had taken the money from each of the victims, and although there were different names, eventually they were all tracked to one account, although the owner of the account has never been found. The banks, on the authority of the police, removed the money and gave it back to the victims. But if Flo hadn't raised the alarm, whoever it was would have got away with it.'

'I suppose it couldn't have really been Derek Chandler?'

'I expect the police would have looked at him very carefully, don't you?' Bethany stood up and went to fill a kettle. 'I've decided I do want tea, now. Want a cup?'

'Yes, please.' Libby shrugged off her cape. 'This is a lovely kitchen.'

'It is, isn't it? It was pretty awful when we moved in, but they let us modernise. At our own expense, of course.'

'Do you have another house elsewhere?' Libby knew Patti didn't but assumed when she retired she would move in with Anne, so the question didn't arise.

'We kept our old flat. Well, I say ours, it was John's really. We rent it out, and when I retire we'll sell it and buy a hovel in the country.'

'Do you still get moved around a lot?'

'There aren't enough vicars to do that!' laughed Bethany. 'I'm lucky, I've only got this one and Steeple Mount, but Patti's got – how many? – four? Poor woman gets so stressed. She'd be lost without her churchwardens.'

'Yes, she was saying she didn't even know that the widow of the murder victim was a parishioner in Shott until her churchwarden told her.'

'Was she?' Bethany sat down again, pushing a mug towards Libby. 'I didn't know that. In fact, I don't know much about the murder at all, except that it was in my churchyard and the bishop wants to do some sort of blessing and cleansing on the place. I told him he couldn't until the police have finished.'

'They talked to you, then? The police?'

'They had to, didn't they? I think the nice police inspector who came to see me was a bit shocked that I was a woman.'

'If it was DCI Connell, he'll more than likely have been thinking "Not another one". He knows Patti quite well.'

'Tall, very dark hair, and an intense face?'

'That's Ian. He's a friend, actually, and he investigated Patti's murder.'

'Oh – the one in her church? That was horrible, wasn't it? And you investigated, too, didn't you?'

'Well – sort of.'

'And now you're investigating this one? Oh, that's good. Patti says you always get your man.'

'Oh, dear,' said Libby with a groan. 'I'm not really an investigator, you know. It's more that I get involved despite myself – and then there's Fran, of course, but you wouldn't be interested in that side of things.'

Bethany put her head on one side. 'Oh, don't be so sure. Patti's told me all about Fran. And she's actually saved lives, hasn't she? Well, as the man said, "There are more things in heaven and earth, Horatio".'

'I didn't believe in anything like that,' said Libby, 'but I've seen the evidence with my own eyes, and Ian has, too. Which is why he asks her to look at things, sometimes. Which is how I come to get involved.'

'Patti said that you get involved without Fran, too.'

'Because I'm incurably nosy,' said Libby, burying her nose in her mug. 'Which is a sin, I'm sure.'

Bethany laughed. 'A new commandment – "thou shalt not be nosy." It'd never take off.'

'Anyway,' said Libby, 'You aren't nosy. I barged in on you for no good reason and all I've done is pick your brains.'

'Such as they are to pick, and anyway, I'm just as nosy. Just that the dog collar –' Libby had noticed she wasn't wearing one 'rather inhibits one.'

'It didn't inhibit Father Brown,' said Libby.

'Different times,' said Bethany.

'Well, thank you, anyway. I've got something to work on.'

'You didn't say why you're investigating this one. Apart from it being in your own village, of course.'

'Nosiness at first, but now someone we know has been arrested and it's got a bit personal.'

Now it was Bethany's turn to gasp. 'How dreadful! Is he local? Do I know him? I'm assuming it's a man.'

'He lives in Shott, the same as the victim. His name is Mike Farthing.'

'Farthing's Plants! No! He's such a nice man. We've been asking his advice on the garden. He was going to come over and look at it, to see what was worth saving. You know, where you came in.'

'He is a nice man, and rather a special friend of my cousin's.' Libby saw no need to say that the special friendship had only started last week. 'And your front garden looks as if it could have been idyllic once. Very Secret Garden.'

'That's exactly what I thought when I first saw it,' said Bethany. 'But tell me, why has Mike Farthing been arrested?'

'Oh, that's a bit complicated, and we're not supposed to know,' said Libby. 'Sorry.'

'That's all right,' said Bethany. 'I'm a priest, remember? But if I can help in any way, please let me know. I'm loving this

village and the church, but my parishioners are all on the well –
elderly side. It would be nice to get to know some younger
people.'

'Thanks for classing me as younger,' said Libby with a grin.
'But why don't you come down to the pub on a Wednesday
evening when we meet Patti and Anne? You and your husband,
of course.'

'Could we? You wouldn't mind?' Bethany looked delighted.

'Of course not. It would be nice for Patti and Anne, too.'

With expressions of mutual esteem, Libby and Beth parted at
the gate of the Secret Garden, and Libby trudged the few yards
to her front door. It was fully dark now. She heard a slight noise,
but she completely missed the shadow which detached itself
from the alley beside the end of terrace cottage.

Chapter Twenty-one

Libby swam into consciousness, wondering why Ben was looming over her, and why she felt so dreadfully sick.

'I've rung for an ambulance,' Ben was saying. 'They said don't move you.'

'What?' Libby became aware of little pinpricks of cold on her face and other shapes moving behind Ben.

Harry was suddenly beside Ben.

'Don't move, you silly old trout. Someone hit you.'

'Hit …?' Oh, that was the thumping, nerve-shattering pain in her head, then. She closed her eyes.

'No, Lib – darling? Stay with us.' That was Ben. She made an effort to open her eyes and suddenly there was a blue light and someone else bending over her. And, thankfully, she slid back into blackness.

She awoke to the white slickness of a hospital room. Someone moved beside her, but it wasn't Ben, it was Ian.

He smiled. 'You're back. I'll fetch Ben.'

'Just a minute.' Libby tried to clear her throat and Ian immediately held a glass of water to her lips. 'What happened?'

'Ben came back from the Manor to find you lying outside your house in the snow. He realised someone had hit you and called the ambulance. Someone saw the call and relayed it to me, recognising the name and address, and I arrived just as you were being loaded into the ambulance. At the same time as the vicar, too. She said you'd been to see her.'

Libby tried to concentrate. 'Yes. I only had to walk about a hundred yards. I didn't see anything. Did I?'

'We don't know. It's unlikely that you would remember anyway. Remember when Harry got hit on the head? And Ben, come to that.'

'But why? I'd been to tea with the vicar. Why would anyone …?'

'Don't worry about it for now.' Ian stood up. 'I'll send Ben in. They're keeping you in overnight –'

'How long have I been here?'

'Since about six. It's nearly midnight.'

'I can't even remember what day it is.'

'Nearly Friday.' He stooped and kissed her cheek. 'Now stop thinking.'

Ben appeared as soon as Ian left, and Libby found herself crying. He said nothing, but enfolded her in as much of a hug as he could.

'Silly,' she croaked after a while. 'I'm all right, aren't I?'

'No permanent damage,' smiled Ben, sitting back on the chair at the side of the bed. 'If it was the same person who hit Vernon Bowling, their aim was off.'

'The snow,' said Libby. 'It was snowing.'

'It had just started.'

'I slipped.' Libby's eyes opened wide. 'I remember. As I got level with the house – I slipped. Perhaps nobody hit me after all.'

'No, love. You were face down with a lump the size of a cricket ball on the back on your head.'

'But when I came round I was facing upwards. There was snow on my face.'

'Yes, because I turned you over as soon as I found you. After that we didn't dare move you.'

'We?'

'I called Harry and Pete to see if they knew where you'd been, and they came rushing over, naturally.' Ben grinned. 'I called Fran and Cass, too, but neither of them knew what you'd been up to after you came home with Cass. Why did she go back to London?'

Libby frowned. 'I don't know. Did she?'

'Sorry, love.' Ben leant forward and put his cheek against hers. 'No more talking. I'll let you get back to sleep.'

'Not quite yet, I'm afraid!' said a cheerful voice. 'A few

154

checks now she's back with us. All right, Libby?'

Libby scowled. 'Mrs Sarjeant.'

The nurse looked startled and turned to Ben. 'It's usually only the old ones who say that.'

He smiled. 'Old-fashioned, our Mrs Sarjeant.' He bent to kiss Libby's cheek. 'I'll be outside.'

'No, go home. Get some sleep.'

'Good idea, Mr Sarjeant,' said the nurse. Ben smiled.

'Thank you. I'll see you in the morning, love.'

It wasn't until the following afternoon, after an MRI scan and various pokings and proddings that Libby was allowed to go home. She still felt woozy and disinclined to eat, but assured everyone she was fine. She and Ben arrived to find number seventeen under siege.

'Let's get her inside, first,' said Ben. 'Can you walk, love?'

'I thought it was her head?' said Flo from the back of the small crowd.

'It was, but my legs won't behave,' said Libby. 'Why are you all here?'

'Heard you was comin' home.' Hetty had pushed her way to the front. 'Give me the key, Ben.'

Inside, Sidney took one look at all the people invading his home and made a dash for the conservatory.

'Thank you all,' said Libby, after Ben had laid her carefully on the sofa. 'But I don't think I'm up to a press conference yet.'

'Come on, Hal,' said Peter. 'We'll speak to you later, Lib.'

'No –' Libby held out her hand. 'Just you two and Hetty. I need to talk about it, just not with everyone.'

When Flo, Lenny and the neighbours had been politely sent on their way, Libby told Peter, Harry and Ben as much as she could remember of yesterday's events. Hetty appeared as she finished, bearing a tray of tea.

'I've put a chicken casserole in yer oven, gal,' she said. 'And I'm goin' up now to change yer bed. All right, all right,' she said as Ben got up as if to stop her. 'Least I can do.'

'She's the best mother-in-law,' said Libby, accepting a steaming mug from Peter. 'And the tea in hospital was awful.'

'Well,' said Harry, leaning back in his chair and stretching long legs out in front of him, 'you can hardly blame her for getting herself into trouble this time, Ben.'

'Hardly. A hundred yard walk from tea with the vicar to your own front door,' said Peter.

'I don't think it was my having tea with the vicar that caused this.' Libby gestured to her bandaged head.

'What was it, then? Something to do with Mike Farthing?' suggested Ben.

'I wouldn't have thought so,' said Libby, starting to shake her head and deciding not to. 'Someone who's been bothered about who I've been talking to. And I haven't spoken to Mike. Has Ian been in touch?'

'Yes. He says he'll speak to you when you're ready.'

'It ought to be soon,' said Libby, fretting.

'I'll give him a ring, then,' said Ben, exchanging glances with Peter and Harry.

'Don't you think you ought to rest a bit more before you talk to him?' said Harry, as Ben hesitated in the doorway, phone in hand.

'No. I need to talk about this. I know I've got myself into trouble in the past, but this was completely unprovoked. I'm very angry.' Libby tried to look fierce under her bandage.

Ben nodded and moved into the kitchen.

'Why has he done that? So that I can't hear what he says?' Libby picked pettishly at the cover Hetty had placed over her.

'No,' said Ben, returning from the kitchen. 'Just so I could hear above the noise in here.'

'We weren't being noisy!' said three voices together.

'No reply. I've left a message.' Ben came and sat on the floor next to Libby. 'Do you want to go up to bed when Mum's finished?'

'Ben, dear, she's not up for that quite yet,' said Harry, smirking.

'No,' said Libby with a pale smile. 'Not yet. I want to speak to Ian first.'

'But he might not get the message for hours,' said Peter. 'I'd

156

take the opportunity of a rest. Besides, the bathroom's upstairs.'

'Ever practical, Pete,' said Ben, while Harry and Libby laughed.

Ben's phone warbled.

'Ian's coming round now.' Ben ended the call. 'As long as you're all right, he said.'

'In that case,' said Libby, 'you can help me upstairs first, or I won't be able to concentrate.'

Three bewildered faces stared at her.

'The bathroom,' she said wearily. 'You put it into my head.'

By the time Ian arrived ten minutes later, complete with a young detective constable in tow, Libby was back on the sofa with fresh tea, and Hetty had gone back to the Manor.

'Are you sure you're up to this?' said Ian, taking the chair Peter had vacated for him. Harry courteously pulled a chair forward for the constable, who looked a little bemused.

'Do you want us to go, Ian?' asked Ben.

'No, you're fine. I imagine you all know all about it anyway.'

'Right. Do you and …?'

'DC Fielding,' supplied Ian.

'Want coffee? Or tea?' finished Ben.

'No, thanks, Ben. Now, Libby. Describe exactly what happened yesterday. From yesterday morning when you went to see Mike Farthing.'

Libby patiently recounted the visit to Farthing's Plants, Cassandra's appearance and subsequent arrival at The Poacher.

'And what happened after that?'

Libby described her visit to Flo and her call on the vicar, and what she'd discovered about Derek Chandler.

'But nobody would have known I was going to see Bethany – I didn't know myself until I was at Flo's.'

'When did you first hear about Derek Chandler?'

'I told you that – when I went to see Edie at Creekmarsh. And then when I went to see Una and she told me about Sandra Brown marrying and moving to Shott. Although Sid at The Poacher told us that she actually lives in Itching, and is a crack shot at darts. Or whatever you are at darts.'

'And Chandler lives in Itching.' Ian frowned.

'And Sandra Brown – Farrow, sorry – is a friend of Mrs Bowling's.

Ian sat back and glanced at DC Fielding, who was earnestly scribbling in his notebook.

'I thought you'd all have had iPads, now,' said Libby, following his gaze.

DC Fielding looked up. 'Believe it or not, this is easier,' he said.

'So all you've been talking about over the last week is Mike Farthing and his cannabis connection –'

'Which there isn't,' said Libby with a scowl.

'And Derek Chandler and his supposed financial scam,' Ian continued smoothly.

'Well, Mike didn't hit me. He was safely at the station being questioned, wasn't he?'

'He was. And I can't see Derek Chandler lurking in the alleys of Steeple Martin, either, even if he'd heard of you, which I doubt he has.'

'So, who?' Libby frowned. 'I didn't think anyone hated me that much.'

'Someone we've come across before?' suggested Harry. Ian and DC Fielding turned to look at him. 'Sorry to interrupt.'

'No, it's all right Harry.' Ian stretched his back and frowned. 'I must learn to sit properly. No, you could be right. After all, between you you've certainly logged up a few enemies.'

By now DC Fielding was looking more confused than ever. Ian took pity on him.

'These people are actually my friends,' he said, 'and in fact have been – ah – *instrumental* in some of the more spectacular arrests over the last few years.'

'Oh,' said Fielding, enlightened. 'So is Mrs Sarjeant the –'

'No,' put in Mrs Sarjeant quickly. 'I'm not psychic.'

'Mind you,' said Ian, 'I'm surprised she isn't here.'

'She wanted to come over, but I thought the fewer people the better today,' said Ben. 'She'll be here tomorrow.'

'So there's nothing else you can tell me?' Ian turned back to

Libby. 'You did nothing else during the week?'

'No. Well, you saw us on Wednesday, so you know I haven't.'

'Can you tell us what the situation with Mike is?' asked Peter. 'Libby said he was arrested by the drug squad.'

'He was,' said Ian. 'There was rather a heated high-level exchange over that.'

DC Fielding was looking horrified. Ian smiled at him. 'Don't worry, Gerry. I shan't give away any secrets.'

'Talk to Sergeant Maiden,' said Libby. 'He knows what it's all about.'

'He's sitting his inspector's exams soon,' Ian told them. 'Then there'll be no holding him.'

'Anyway,' said Peter, 'getting back to Mike.'

'Something was found on his computer,' said Ian, 'but I can't tell you anything else.'

'Is he still in custody?' asked Harry.

'No, he's back at his business. And I believe your cousin is there with him.'

'Oh, nice!' said Libby. 'I'm knocked on the head and she comes back from London to go straight to the jailbird instead of her poor injured cousin.'

'London? She went to London? When?'

'Almost as soon as we got back here from Shott. She said she wanted to get a few things because she was going to stay down here a bit longer.'

'And you let her go?'

'Let her …?'

'Sorry.' Ian shook his head. 'Of course you couldn't stop her, nor would you have wanted to. It's just my suspicious mind.'

'You thought perhaps she was taking something from Mike to hide?'

'It crossed my mind.'

'She couldn't have done,' asserted Libby. 'Once the police arrived yesterday morning, she and Mike were kept apart. And she didn't have anything with her when she arrived at The Poacher.'

'Handbag?'

'Well, yes …'

'How big is a memory stick?'

'He put something on a memory stick?' said Harry. 'But why? The stuff would still be on the computer.'

'Unless it was wiped,' said Ian.

'But your experts can trace that sort of thing,' said Ben.

'Look, I'm only being the usual nosy policeman,' said Ian. 'Don't worry about it. I shall talk to Mr Farthing, and your cousin, very soon, whatever drugs say.'

Chapter Twenty-two

Libby couldn't settle. After Ian left she allowed Ben to help her up to bed where she fretted until she decided it was time to eat.

'It's no good,' she said, as she sat down at the kitchen table. 'I need to talk about this.'

'You're supposed to be resting.' Ben frowned as he ladled out Hetty's casserole.

'I can't. Anyway, aren't you supposed to keep from dozing off after concussion?'

'I'm not sure that applies after 24 hours.'

'Well, anyway, I don't want to rest. I want to find out who hit me and why.'

'And how do you propose to do that? I'm not letting you go out of this house until we go to Mum's on Sunday, whatever you say. And Peter's running your pantomime rehearsal tonight. He's excused me.'

'I want to talk to Fran. Do you think she'd come over tonight?'

Ben looked dubious. 'It's a bit late …'

'It's only half past six! Go on, let me ask her. You won't talk to me about it.'

'I do!'

'But you don't approve.'

Ben heaved a sigh. 'All right. I'll fetch your phone.'

Fran, naturally, was delighted and said Guy would come too, and take Ben out for a well-deserved pint.

'I don't think I'm allowed alcohol,' said Libby sadly, 'so we'll have to have tea.'

'That works out fine,' said Fran. 'Guy can have a guilt-free drink and I'll drive home.'

By the time Fran and Guy arrived not long after eight

o'clock, Libby was once more ensconced on the sofa, toes stretched towards the fire and Sidney curled up on her lap. Guy whisked Ben straight off to the pub, while Fran made tea for herself and Libby.

'You look better than I expected,' she said, coming back into the sitting room bearing mugs.

'Except for the fetching head-gear.' Libby accepted a mug and grinned. 'I wasn't hit all that hard, actually. I slipped and whoever it was only hit me a glancing blow. In other words – they missed.'

'But who's "they"?'

'That's what we've got to find out. This is no longer just me being nosy – this is personal.'

'I quite agree, but don't you perhaps think you were hit *because* you being nosy?'

'Of course I was. When you think about it, we've had an awful lot of hits on the head over the years, haven't we? But never actually *us*.'

'We've been in a few tight spots, though. And it's always because we've been nosy.'

'Ah! Now you're admitting you're nosy, too.'

'Well, of course. The annoying thing is that I'm getting absolutely nothing from this at all, and you'd think I would, seeing how close we are.'

'Nothing yesterday late afternoon?'

'No, sorry. We were quite busy in the shop – people seem to have developed a great desire to have original art works as Christmas presents.' Fran looked reprovingly at Libby. 'And yours have all gone.'

'Well, I can't paint like this, can I?' Libby asked smugly.

'I bet you could. Keep you occupied.'

'They wouldn't be very good. And don't say "they never are".'

'I wasn't going to. I was going to say you're not creating earth-shattering masterworks. You could do a couple over the next week, couldn't you?'

'Maybe. Ben won't let me go out anyway.'

'There you are then. You can stay here, think, paint and direct operations.'

'What operations?'

'To find out who hit you. Unless we leave it to the police.'

'Well, of course, Ian's going to do his best. He came this afternoon to take a statement with a new DC. Did you know our lovely Sergeant Maiden's sitting his inspector's exams?'

'That seems very quick. I thought they stayed sergeants much longer. Anyway, what did you tell Ian?'

'I'll tell you,' said Libby, and did so.

'So what have you done to make someone hit you? And was it to shut you up permanently or just a warning?'

Libby went to shake her head and stopped. 'I don't know.' She shivered. 'It's scary. But we don't know anything? How can I be a threat?'

'Someone knows you've been asking questions. Who?'

'Well, Una might have told Sandra Brown. The vicar knew all about Derek Chandler and might have talked to Flo, but I'd only just left her house, not two minutes before it happened.'

'Did someone know you were there and wait for you?'

'Only if they saw me go in, and I went in through the back gate into the Secret Garden.'

'The what?'

Libby explained. 'So nobody could know, unless they saw me leave Flo and Lenny's and followed me. I can't see Derek Chandler doing that, or even knowing who I was, can you?'

'You're thinking it points to him?'

'Who else? He's the one who tried on the scam.'

'Only it wasn't him,' pointed out Fran.

'I bet it was,' said Libby darkly.

'But as you said, he wouldn't know who you were.'

'From a bar of soap, no. Who else, then? Vi Little? She was a victim.'

'But she got her money back.'

'And besides, what the hell does it have to do with Vernon Bowling's murder?'

'Bowling found out and was threatening to expose him?'

163

suggested Fran.

'They were friends,' said Libby thoughtfully. 'Bowling could have found out.'

'Or,' said Fran, 'they were in it together and Chandler got mad with Bowling because somehow it was his fault it went wrong?'

'We're grasping at straws, now,' said Libby.

'What else have we got, then?'

'It's got to be something to do with the murder,' said Libby. 'Somehow, someone thinks I've found out something. Which I – we – haven't.'

'Let's look at why he was murdered. Motive. No idea.'

'Means – we don't know. Blunt force trauma, only worse than mine. No weapon found, and he didn't hit his head on a gravestone.'

'Opportunity,' continued Fran. 'Lots. Anyone could have been lurking about in that graveyard. Can you get into it any way other than from the church and the hall?'

'I expect so. You could go through the woods behind Lendle Lane and nobody would see you. We've been assuming it was someone from the ukulele group, but it could be almost anybody.'

'The passing tramp?' said Fran, with a laugh. 'Beloved of detective stories?'

'Of course, but … see, there was no reason for him to be in the churchyard. It's behind the church and the hall, and his car was in the doctor's car park, like everybody else's. Why did he go there?'

'To meet someone,' said Fran slowly. 'But it didn't have to be someone from the group. If it was something to do with the drugs business, it makes sense. A meeting where no one could see you, with an easy means of escape.'

'We need to know if there were any strange cars parked along the Canterbury Road,' said Libby. 'Can we ask Ian?'

'I think Ian would rather you stayed out of it for the time being,' said Fran. 'We have to do this on our own.'

'Right.' Libby's eyes were sparkling now. 'Who do we talk

to?'

'Who do *I* talk to,' corrected Fran. 'Remember you can't go out.'

'Hmm.' Libby frowned. 'And, of course, if you're seen to be asking questions, they might go after you, too.'

'I shall take great care not to be on my own in any dark places.'

'I was walloped outside my own front door having only walked about a hundred yards.'

'In the dark, no street lighting, and a dark alleyway beside the house.'

'Oh, all right. So what do we do?'

'I suggest you ask your cousin what's going on with Mike. Has he been lying to us? And the police? And I'll talk to Patti and see if she can somehow introduce me to Bowling's widow.'

'How do you imagine she can do that?'

'She's a parishioner. I could suddenly become some sort of support worker, grief counsellor sort of thing.'

'Don't be rubbish! Patti wouldn't allow that.'

'No, maybe she wouldn't. I don't know. I'll think on it. Meanwhile, Jane picked it up on the wire –'

'Picked what up?'

'Your accident.'

'Why was it on the wire?'

'It was a vicious attack. Obviously local TV and radio didn't think it was exciting enough, but Jane did. She said could she do a piece for next week?'

'Bit late by then.'

'But it will go straight on to the paper's website. The word will get out there. Somebody will start talking.'

'Ian might not like it.'

'Jane can ask him,' said Fran. 'That's perfectly normal.'

'Oh, OK. He might quite like it, I suppose. He could get an angle across, couldn't he?'

'Exactly. Now, what might be the motive? The cannabis factory?'

'Or Dellington. A parent like Bob Alton.'

'Someone gay who took exception to his homophobia.'

'Or something else we haven't even heard about.' Libby sighed. 'Needle in a haystack.'

'Or Derek Chandler because of the swindle.'

'Oh, yes, I suppose we'd better leave him in.'

'Well, he's the only one who provided a motive for you being attacked.'

'Because that's what I've been talking about in the village for the last few days? But that means it's someone in the village, and nobody here belongs to the group.'

'But we said it needn't be someone in the village.'

'Oh, so we did.' Libby was frowning again.

'You're looking tired, and I bet your head's hurting.' Fran stood up. 'I'll help you upstairs and then I'll fetch Ben. You can call me tomorrow if you've had any blinding revelations during the night.'

Libby allowed herself to be pulled up from the sofa. 'I don't really have to be helped, just watched in case I topple over,' she said. 'But you're right. I'm feeling a bit fragile now.'

To her own surprise, Libby went to sleep and slept soundly until Ben woke her with a cup of tea.

'I feel better,' she said, struggling into a sitting position.

'That's good, because I've already heard from young Jane. She's been given permission to interview you by the police and wants to come today. I gather you'd be up for it?'

'Dead right.' Libby beamed at her other half. 'Fran suggested it yesterday. She thought the police might have an angle.'

Ben sighed. 'I might have guessed the idea was from one of you.'

'Actually, it wasn't. It really was from Jane. She phoned Fran to ask if she thought I'd be able to be interviewed.'

'Oh, well, quite legitimate, then.' He grinned. 'Drink your tea. Shall I help you with the shower?' He waggled his eyebrows suggestively.

At eleven o'clock, as arranged, the doorbell rang. Libby watched from the sofa as Ben went to let Jane in.

'Hello, Jane.' Ben greeted her with a kiss. 'Oh – hello, Ian!'

Chapter Twenty-three

'I couldn't stop him,' said Jane. 'Sorry.'

'That's all right,' said Libby. 'He just wants to make sure we don't give the game away.'

'What game?' said Jane, sitting in the chair opposite Libby.

'No game,' said Ian, pulling forward a chair from beside the table. 'But there are some things we don't want the public to know.'

'Censoring the press, Ian?' Ben came in with the coffee pot and mugs on a tray.

'Just making sure Libby says the right things and Jane reports them in the right way,' said Ian with a grin.

Jane sighed. 'This is a good story, Detective Inspector. Local woman attacked outside her own home.'

'He's called Ian while he's here, Jane.' Ben sat down next to Libby and lifted her feet on to his lap.

'I know it's a good story, which is why I agreed to you doing the interview,' said Ian.

'You don't always have to ask the police, do you, Jane?' said Libby.

'If we've picked the incident up as I did it's advisable. So, shall we get started?' She took out the inevitable pocket recorder. 'When did it happen and where?'

'You know that.' Libby frowned.

'Thursday evening outside here,' said Jane. 'Just confirming. Can we say where you'd been?'

Libby looked at Ian, who nodded.

'I'd been to tea with the vicar,' said Libby, and suddenly snorted with laughter.

'Really?' Jane looked disbelieving for a moment. 'Oh – you mean your friend over at St Aldeberge's?'

'No, our vicar here. She lives on the corner of Allhallow's Lane.'

Jane looked from Ian to Libby and back. 'Is this connected to the murder in the churchyard?'

'No idea,' said Libby quickly.

'So apart from saying you'd been to tea with the vicar, had walked a hundred yards back home, and someone hit you on the head, that's all I can say?'

'Not at all,' said Ian. 'After all, you can state that this is the second violent attack in less than two weeks –'

'Is it the same MO?' interrupted Jane.

Ian raised his eyebrows at her. 'How would we know? But you can emphasise the fact of the similarity of the attacks, and Libby's connection with the theatre and therefore with the ukulele group who will be performing in the Christmas Concert.'

'Sure you wouldn't like to write it for me?' asked Jane.

Ian grinned. 'No, I'm sure your journalese is better than mine.'

Jane snorted.

Libby began an account of her 'incident', and went on to speculate about it being the second in less than a fortnight, all along the lines indicated by Ian. Jane interjected with a few leading questions and finally asked if she could take a photograph.

'You've got pictures of me on file,' Libby objected. 'I don't exactly look my best.'

'That's the whole point.' Jane was getting out a very professional-looking camera. 'We need the sympathy vote.'

Libby asked for Ben to be in the picture, to which Jane agreed.

'And don't you dare put in our ages,' said Libby, when Jane was packing up. 'I do so hate being defined by my age.'

'Good job you're not a grandmother yet,' said Jane with a grin. 'Then I could have led in with "Grandmother Libby Sarjeant …".'

'You wouldn't dare.'

'No, I wouldn't. We're friends, not enemies.' Jane turned to Ian. 'Do you want to see the copy?'

'I'm sure I can trust you, Jane. And you can speculate all you like.'

'Really?' Jane looked at him narrowly. 'Are you sure?'

'Only around what Libby's told you, of course.'

'Of course.' Jane finished her almost cold coffee. 'I must go.'

'Have another cup of coffee?' suggested Ben.

'Better not. Terry's at work and my mum's got Imogen.'

'Thanks for coming, Jane.' Libby started to get up.

'No stay there, Lib. I'll email you the link before I put it on the website later, and you can check it.' Jane looked at Ian. 'And I'll send it to you, too.'

'A very intelligent young woman,' said Ian after Jane had left.

'Don't sound so patronising,' said Libby. 'And you needn't have to come to check up on her. She's always been very good with Fran and me.'

'Sorry.' Ian stood up and stretched. 'Can you stand another couple of questions?'

'I expect so.' Libby leant across and shook the coffee pot.

'I'll make some more,' said Ben

'You said you went to see Flo yesterday before you went to see the vicar.' Ian sat down in the armchair. 'And that was when you decided to go to see the vicar. Why was that?'

'Because Flo told me about Derek Chandler's supposed scam. He tried it on with her, so she reported it. It was Flo who was instrumental in getting all their money back, really. So then I went to see Bethany, who told me that Flo and Vi Little weren't the only ones.'

'I see. Well, we're looking into it. But tell me why this should be connected to Bowling's murder?'

'Fran and I were wondering about that. It doesn't look as though there's any connection at all, unless it really was Derek Chandler and not someone using his name, and Vernon Bowling knew and threatened to expose him.'

'Nothing concrete, then?'

Libby winced. 'No. And as I said, he wouldn't know who I was.'

'He might. Didn't you go to the meeting in the theatre last week?'

'Yes, but I didn't really meet anyone except Dr Robinson and Mike Farthing.'

'But most of the members of the group would have known who you were?'

'I suppose so, but none of them would know what I've been doing this week. None of them know me personally, or anyone I know.'

Ben returned with the coffee pot. 'But you went to see Una,' he said, 'and she might have told her friend whose husband is in the group. And Mike Farthing knows you now.'

'Yes,' said Libby thoughtfully, 'and Sandra Brown as was is a great friend of Mrs Bowling. If Una told her about me asking, she might have repeated it to Mrs Bowling ...'

'Who might have repeated it to any number of people. I'm sure the members of the ukulele group have been visiting with words of sympathy.'

'Una said Sandra herself is in the group and she knows me. But she wasn't here last week,' said Libby. 'She and her new husband were away.'

'The Farrows.' Ian nodded. 'Anyway, you see how a lot of people could have heard about you – investigating.'

'Poking her nose in,' corrected Ben.

'And, as Jane appreciates, you are a known local – er – character. And you and Fran have clocked up a fair amount of media appearances in one way or another over the years.' Ian accepted a fresh cup of coffee. 'And all the members of the group come from the area, so they would know you by reputation, and of your connection to the theatre.'

'I suppose so, but as Fran and I were saying last night, it might have nothing to do with the group. He could have had enemies we know nothing about – from his cannabis business, for instance.'

'Who would have known he would be in the churchyard at

that very time?'

'He would have made an arrangement to meet them.' Libby warmed to her theme. 'And they could have parked on the Canterbury road, and cut through the woods behind Lendle Lane, and ...'

'Believe it or not, we have been checking, Libby. And nobody saw any cars parked along the Canterbury road that night – and believe me, it would have been noticed. And we've done a proper search of the woods, too.' Ian smiled. 'We do know what we're doing, you know. It's just we don't always tell you.'

'No.' Libby, embarrassed, buried her face in her coffee cup.

'So we're only getting one side of the story,' said Ben. 'You'll be looking at disgruntled relatives of Dellington victims, rival drug lords ...'

Ian laughed. 'That's the sort of thing. This is only one facet. I admit, the attack on Libby seems to be somehow connected, but how I just can't imagine.'

'And why.' Libby scowled. 'It's personal, now.'

'Libby, you must *not* do any more investigating,' said Ian. 'Whether this attack has anything to do with the Bowling murder or not. It's too dangerous.'

Ben raised his eyes to heaven. 'And how many times have we all said that?'

Fran called after lunch.

'Bob Alton came in again. He wanted to know if there was any progress.'

'What did you say?'

'I didn't know. I'm not involved in the case. He's terribly worried about something.'

'Should we go and see him?'

'You're not going anywhere.'

Libby made an impatient sound. 'Only a couple of days. Do you think he's the murderer?'

'I don't know. He's such a nice old boy.'

'Ian was here this morning with Jane. The police are looking into everything we thought of already, including Dellington.'

'I've always told you the police get there before we do – and they usually manage without our help.'

'Not always.'

'That's usually because we – or you – get us into trouble and they have to rescue us.'

'That's not –'

'Yes, it is. By the way, have you seen your cousin yet?'

Libby frowned at the phone. 'No. Most odd. She hasn't even phoned, or been back to the flat. Harry's a bit peeved.'

'I should ring her, then. Did Ian speak to her or Mike again?'

'I don't know. He said he was going to yesterday, but didn't say anything this morning.'

'Give her a ring. At least it will put your mind at rest.'

Libby discovered after this conversation that she wasn't quite as well recovered as she thought, and allowed herself to be persuaded back to bed. Ben unplugged the bedside phone and relieved her of her mobile and drew the curtains.

'There. Now you can get some rest.'

The room was quite dark when he woke her gently with a kiss on the cheek.

'Your cousin called. She wants to know if you want to see her. She's back at the flat.'

Libby stretched and yawned. 'I suppose so. When does she want to come?'

'Soon, I think. Shall I ring and tell her to come now?'

'Yes, please. I'll come down now. Is the kettle on?'

Ben grinned. 'The kettle's always on.'

Libby was sitting beside the newly made up fire with a mug of tea when Ben ushered in Cassandra, who was holding an enormous bouquet.

'Did Mike send those?' asked Libby, staring at the enormous shaggy carnations and poinsettias.

Cassandra bristled. 'No. I chose them for you.'

'Well, thank you.' Libby took the bouquet and sniffed. 'They're beautiful.'

'Yes, well, I felt rather bad about not having phoned or come to see you yesterday.'

'Yes, so did I,' said Libby, not willing to forgive quite yet.

Cassandra's by now familiar blush was flooding her face. 'Mike came home, you see. I had to collect him from the station.'

'I see. Ian didn't know you'd gone to London until I told him.'

Cassandra's eyes slid sideways. 'He told me. He came to see us again.'

Libby nodded. 'He said he would.'

'He wanted to know if I'd taken anything with me.' Cassandra fixed penetrating headmistress eyes on to Libby's amused ones.

'His own idea. Not mine. Not nice, is it, Cassandra? Being suspected of something? How many of your little darlings did you scare to death unnecessarily over the years?'

Now Cassandra looked shocked. 'I didn't come here to argue, Libby. I came to apologise. To explain.'

'Go ahead then. Do both.'

Cassandra sat down in the armchair and eyed Libby's mug.

'Tea?' Ben appeared with another mug, winked at Libby and retired to the kitchen.

Cassandra sighed. 'All right. I'm really sorry. I was still in London when Mike phoned to say they were letting him out, so I just drove straight there. I didn't even look at any texts or messages I'd had. Then last night your Ian came back and told us what had happened to you. I'm so sorry, Lib.'

'Why didn't you ring?'

'I don't know. I felt guilty.'

'Harry wasn't too pleased, either. You didn't tell him you weren't going back to the flat.'

'All right, all right. I know. I've been back this afternoon.'

'So what's going on with Mike?'

'I can't really tell you, because I don't understand it myself, and he won't say much. It's all to do with something they found on his computer – when they came Thursday morning, you know.'

'And they kept him overnight.'

'Until they would have had to apply to a magistrate for permission to keep him longer, I gather. He looks awful.' Cassandra glanced briefly at Libby's bandaged head. 'Not as bad as you, though.'

'Gee, thanks. So are you going to go back and stay with him? It's all progressed rather fast, hasn't it? You only met a week ago.'

'I know.' Cassandra sipped her tea, then looked up with an excited smile. 'I haven't felt like this in forty years, Lib. And he says he hasn't either. It's like an earthquake. I never thought I'd ever –' The blush rose abruptly.

'Have sex again? Yes, I felt like that. And I certainly never thought I could take my clothes off in front of anyone again.'

'Exactly.' Cassandra nodded enthusiastically. 'So I'm going home on Monday, but I'll be back at weekends and for Christmas.'

'What about the kids?'

'They'll understand. And Mike says they can all come down. Although there isn't that much room in the cottage.'

'And what happens,' said Libby, deliberately sounding a cautionary note, 'if Mike ends up in custody?'

Chapter Twenty-four

Cassandra stopped dead, her mug half way to her lips.

'I'm just saying …' Libby began.

'I don't believe you did "just say".' Cassandra looked furious. 'You don't believe him, do you?'

'Believe what? That he didn't kill Vernon Bowling? Or that he's fallen for you?'

Cassandra stood abruptly. 'Any of it. You don't think he's – he's –' She stopped.

'I believe he's fallen for you, yes. I think anyone who's been around the pair of you in the last week couldn't fail to see that, surprising though it is. But whatever you say, you don't really know him, and there must be a reason the drugs squad have been after him. I can't believe in him as blindly as you do. I'm sorry.'

Cassandra sat down again, looking miserable. 'I know. I'm sorry, too. But I've got to try. If I'm wrong, I'll have to put it behind me. I'm not going to do anything stupid like move in with him permanently, or sell my house.' She reached over and touched Libby's hand. 'I really am sorry, Lib. I just haven't been thinking straight. I suppose …' She paused.

'Suppose what?'

'You couldn't – um – see if you could …' She stopped – again.

'Find anything out from our tame policeman?' Libby smiled. 'I've already tried. And I've been forbidden to do any more "investigating".' She touched her head. 'And I'm inclined to agree. Although Fran is keen to carry on.'

'She is?' Cassandra looked surprised.

'She wants to know who did this. So do I. And,' Libby added with a grin, 'at least we know it wasn't Mike.'

Cassandra laughed reluctantly. 'One point in his favour.'

Libby stared into the fire and frowned. 'The police took his computer away – his work computer or his personal one?'

'He's only got one. It's in the office, and the online and mail-order stuff is run from there. And all the accounts – you know, spreadsheets and invoices – they're all there, too.'

'So presumably, the boys – what were their names?'

'Gary and Patrick.'

'They have full access to the computer, do they?'

'Of course they do. They run the shop – although there's very little passing trade, it's mainly mail order. They see to all that.'

'So if there's something on the computer it could have nothing to do with Mike?'

'Yes, but why would they suspect there was something there in the first place?'

'I know. That's the puzzle. Unless it's simply what it seemed to be at first – you know, Mike helping Bowling design his garden and therefore must have helped with the cannabis farm.'

'But …' Cassandra frowned. 'Oh, it's just too ridiculous.' She stood up and bent to kiss Libby. 'I'm off now. I'm going in to see Harry and give back his key, then I'm going back to Mike's. I'll ring you tomorrow.'

'And find out more about Gary and Patrick.'

Cassandra grinned. 'So you aren't going to give up.'

'Just to give me something to do while I'm lying on my bed of pain.'

Libby recounted the conversation over one of Ben's throw-it-all-together stir fries.

'I don't know her well,' he said, forking up rice, 'but she doesn't seem to be the sort to throw her cap over the windmill. I hope she knows what she's doing.'

'That's what I was trying to say to her. I mean, we all liked Mike, but there's got to be something behind this police interest.'

'And don't you try and find out what it is,' warned Ben. 'I prefer my women whole and undamaged.'

'I quite like it that way, too.' Libby grinned. 'But there's nothing to stop me thinking about it, is there?'

'As long as that's all you do.' Ben grinned back. 'And tomorrow you have to be well enough for Sunday lunch, so go and recline on the sofa again.'

On Sunday morning, Libby felt almost normal, although moving fast wasn't an option, as she discovered when she tried to beat Ben to the ringing phone.

'Somebody called Sandra Farrow?' he mouthed.

'Sandra Brown.' Libby nodded, winced and held out her hand for the phone. 'Sandra, hello! I was only asking after you the other day.'

'Hello, Libby, yes, Una told me you'd been to see her. I was wondering, could we possibly meet? I'd like to talk to you.'

Libby raised her eyebrows at Ben, who made a quizzical face in return.

'Actually, that's a bit difficult at the moment. I had a bit of an accident on Thursday and I'm supposed to be taking it easy.'

'Oh, I'm sorry to hear that. Were you much hurt?'

'I hit my head,' said Libby cautiously.

'Oh, nasty! Have you been checked out?'

'Oh, yes, I was in hospital overnight. I just have an interesting bandage round my head.'

'Oh.' There was a short silence. Libby decided to break it.

'Look, I'm not too bad, and I can still talk. You could come and see me at home, if you like.'

Ben scowled.

'Are you sure? It seems a bit insensitive.'

'Only if you want to tell me something that will make me feel worse.'

'Well …' There was another long pause.

'When do you want to come?' Libby's curiosity was getting the better of her.

'Would this afternoon be a good time?'

'No, sorry, we'll be at my mother-in-law's –'

'Hetty?' Sandra's voice lightened. 'Oh, I love Hetty. Say hello to her for me.'

'I will. So, how about tomorrow morning?'

'Yes, thank you. About eleven?'

'That's fine. Do you know where I live?'

'Allhallow's Lane, isn't it? But I don't know the number.'

'Seventeen,' Libby told her. 'I'll see you then.'

'So what was that all about?' send Ben as she ended the call.

'Una's old next door neighbour. I told you she's now a member of the ukulele group.'

'So that was her? And she wants to see you.'

'Yes.' Libby slid a wary glance at Ben. 'Una must have told her she'd seen me.'

He sighed. 'Well, I suppose I can't stop you, but for goodness' sake don't go promising her anything.'

'Like what?'

'That you'll find out who killed Bowling.'

'That might be it, you know,' said Libby. 'She's apparently a friend of his wife.'

'Libby!'

'All right, all right. Just thinking aloud.'

Hetty's lunch was as perfect as ever, and Libby was even allowed a glass of a very nice old Bordeaux.

'Never get much beyond the Australian Shiraz these days,' she said appreciatively, holding the glass up to the light.

'That Sandra Farrow rang me this morning,' said Hetty, and Libby nearly choked on the precious wine. 'Said she'd just spoken to you and were you all right.'

'I didn't know you knew each other. Although now I know about your knitting circle …'

'Don't do no knitting.'

'No, it was just an expression. So did you tell her?'

'Yes. Told 'er 'ow you did it, too.'

'Oh. Did she say she wanted to meet me?'

'Said she was coming over tomorrow.'

'Yes. Did she say why?'

'Didn't ask. Guessed it were to do with this murder.'

Libby sighed. 'I expect it is. But I've been forbidden to do any more investigating.'

'Snoopin',' said Hetty succinctly.

'That, too.'

'Let me know what she wants.' Hetty passed dishes of vegetables. 'Nice woman.'

Ben refused to leave her alone in the house with the nice woman on the Monday morning, and when Sandra arrived, Libby could see that his presence was going to inhibit her.

'She won't talk to me if you're there,' she hissed, following him into the kitchen. 'Stay out here, please.'

'All right, but first I'm making coffee.'

Libby went back into the sitting room and resumed her place on the sofa. 'I won't apologise for my appearance, Sandra. I gather Hetty told you what happened.'

Sandra Farrow, a beautifully groomed, slim woman with silver hair pulled back into a pleat, nodded. 'I hope you didn't mind my calling her. But I felt I had to ask if you were really well enough to see me. She rather gave me the impression that you would leap at the chance.'

'I wonder why?' murmured Libby, as Ben came in with the coffee.

'Thank you.' Sandra smiled up at Ben. 'I remember you as a boy.'

Ben's eyebrows shot up. 'Do you?'

'Yes. I didn't know your mother then, but I used to see you around. And your older sister, too. She used to live at Steeple Farm, didn't she?'

'Oh, yes, of course, you would have been neighbours.' Libby hurried in to save Ben from having to answer questions about his sister, Peter's mother, who was passing her peaceful days in a very expensive home for the bewildered. 'Thank you for the coffee, darling. See you later.'

Ben took the hint with a smile, and disappeared back to the kitchen.

'What did you want to talk to me about?' Libby leaned back on her cushions and tried to give off waves of encouragement..

Sandra hesitated. 'It's rather … difficult. You know all about Vernon Bowling's murder, of course. Hetty said it was because of that you were attacked.'

'That's not proven,' said Libby.

179

'But you've been asking questions about it?'

'My cousin's been – um – seeing another member of your group,' said Libby elliptically.

'Oh, who's that? Sorry, none of my business.' Sandra coloured faintly.

'Go on. About Mr Bowling's murder.'

'Una said you were talking to her about it. Or about an aspect of it. And I know how successful you've been in the past –'

'Not really,' Libby interrupted. 'My friend and I just seem to get involved. The police do the real work.'

'But you do get involved, that's the point. And you obviously know quite a bit about this one.' Sandra shifted restlessly in the armchair. 'So did you know I was a member of the ukulele group?'

'Yes, so is your husband, you are a friend of Mrs Bowling's and a dab hand at darts.'

Sandra's eyes grew round. 'How ...?'

Libby smirked. 'As you said, we get involved. In fact, Una told me most of that, and Sid at The Poacher told me about the darts. And the Shott village church is in the pastoral care of my friend Patti Pearson.'

Sandra sighed. 'I knew it. As soon as Una said you'd been to see her. You've been looking into it, haven't you?'

'Not as such,' said Libby. 'One or two things came up, not to mention the fact that one local resident is blaming me for the ukulele group and the murder.'

'What?'

'She has her ears blasted with the ukulele group every Monday and says that I let the village in for it. I think she's even blaming me for the murder. But she's a batty old woman with bad eyesight, so I suppose I should feel sorry for her.'

'But it was the vicar who let us use the hall!'

'But the vicar's female. Female vicars are an abomination, apparently.' Libby grinned. 'It's all right. I know what this person's like, and so does everybody else. So, yes, I do know a bit about it. And my friends Lewis and Edie are part of the group, too.'

'And the concert is to be at your theatre.' Sandra shivered. 'If it ever goes ahead.'

'Now listen,' said Libby. 'You've come here to tell me something, or ask my advice, and all you're doing is offering cryptic remarks. Spill the beans.'

'There's something the police haven't released to the press.' Sandra took a sip of coffee. 'So you might not know about it. I only know because Denise told me.'

'The cannabis factory?'

Now the colour drained from Sandra's face. 'How …?'

'The man my cousin is seeing is Mike Farthing, who the police are convinced helped to set it up.'

Chapter Twenty-five

'Mike …' repeated Sandra. 'But he wouldn't …'

'No, that's what we think, but they were put on to him by someone, and now it appears they've found something. What my cousin and I are wondering is who made the suggestion about Mike being involved.'

Sandra looked down at her coffee. 'I was only going to tell you about the factory, but if you know …' She looked up. 'You see, Denise didn't really know anything about it.'

'But it was in her own attic!'

'Yes, but she just thought it was an ordinary laboratory. You know Vernon used to be a scientist?'

'I do. And where.'

'Yes, well.' Sandra looked uncomfortable. 'He always had his own personal laboratory. Apparently, at their last house it was a large shed at the bottom of the garden, but this time it was the attic.'

'And it's exactly the same design as Ron Stewart's house and attic. So who had the idea of the factory?'

'Ron's attic is a studio. As far as I can tell he already knew Vernon, and when his house was being built, introduced him to the architect. And Denise says it was Ron who suggested the laboratory.'

'Ah!' Libby's ears pricked up. 'So Denise thinks Ron was in on it?'

'I don't think so.'

'What I still can't understand is how she didn't know. What about the smell?'

'There's a very sophisticated heating and ventilation system up there.'

'And what about the floor? It must have been reinforced to

take the weight.'

'I suppose so. But that's not was worrying Denise. It was about someone else. She thought someone was after Vernon,'

Libby stared in silence.

Sandra put down her coffee mug. 'She thought he was worried about something and she heard the tail-end of a couple of telephone conversations.'

'I hope she's told the police,' said Libby.

'No, she hasn't. She told me because she began to get scared. She said she thought whoever it was might come after her as well.'

'Let's get this straight,' said Libby. 'She thought someone was – what? Threatening her husband? What was it she overheard?'

'She didn't tell me exactly, but it sounded as if it was threatening and he was on the defensive.'

'So she thinks whoever was on the phone is the murderer? Why would he come after her?'

'He might think she knows all about whatever it was.'

'And does she think that the "whatever" is the cannabis factory?'

'I don't know! I don't know that she does, either.'

'So what reason does she have to be scared? Has someone written to her? Called her?'

'I don't think so. But she's only just told me about this.'

'She really needs to tell the police.'

'She thinks it's too – too – too vague. She thinks they'd laugh at her. So,' Sandra slid a sideways glance at Libby, 'that's why I suggested you.'

'I see.' Libby gazed at the fire, thinking.

'But I didn't know you'd been, er –'

'Incapacitated,' said Libby. 'No.' She sat up straight, sending Sidney, who had just arrived on her lap, shooting off. 'Would she be willing to come and see me? I'd like to talk this over with my friend Fran and perhaps we could see Denise together. You could be there, too, obviously.'

'I'll ask her. She wasn't all that keen on asking you in the first place. I had to persuade her.'

'The woman sounds like an idiot, if you ask me,' said Libby. 'She should go straight to the police.'

Sandra sighed. 'I'll ask her. I'll tell her what you've said.'

'Good. And now tell me what you know about the members of the ukulele group and who you think might have bumped him off?'

Sandra looked aghast. 'Me? I don't know anything!'

'You know the members, don't you?'

'Not well. I haven't lived over there very long, so I only really met the people Alan knows. And the people on the darts team. That's how I met Denise.'

'Oh, not through the group?'

'No, she hates the ukulele. She said it drove her mad, him practising all over the house except when he went up to the ...' Sandra stopped.

'Laboratory, yes. So who does Alan know?'

'Only Vernon, really. And Eric Robinson, a bit. And Ron Stewart, although nobody sees much of him. He and Vernon were very close, I think.'

'We gathered that. And none of them would kill him.'

'Unless it was one of them he was scared of.' Sandra frowned.

'Do you know anything about them?'

'I don't *know* anything, but I've never been very sure about Eric. He treats his wife abominably. And I gather there's been some kind of estrangement with his children.'

'Sounds more like a victim than a murderer,' said Libby. 'And it doesn't give him a motive.'

'Unless Vernon was threatening to let out a secret?' Sandra looked hopeful.

'Then Vernon wouldn't be the threatened one, would he? He would be doing the threatening.'

'Unless, Eric knew something about Vernon – like the cannabis factory – and threatened to tell about that.'

Libby looked at her admiringly. 'You're getting good at this! Yes, that's a possible theory.' She sighed and rubbed her forehead.

Sandra jumped up, immediately contrite. 'Oh, I've tired you. No, don't try and get up. I'll be on my way, and I'll go straight to talk to Denise.' Impulsively, she bent to kiss Libby's cheek. 'You've made me think so much more clearly, thank you. I hope I can do the same for Denise.'

Ben came back into the room after seeing their guest to the door and found Libby still sitting up straight and busy making notes in the margin of a magazine.

'What's she persuaded you to do?

'Nothing. I had to persuade her.' Libby patted the sofa beside her and proceeded to tell him all that she and Sandra had talked about.

'The woman must be deranged! Of course she should go to the police.'

'I know, I know, but I can understand her reluctance. Some people never think that their evidence can be worth anything, and I expect she's still scared she's under suspicion about the factory.'

'So you've asked her here.'

'You and Ian have said I mustn't go a-scouting. I want to persuade her to go to the police. I'm going to ask Fran to be here, too.'

Ben sighed. 'All right, I suppose you'll be safe – unless the police suspect his wife killed Bowling.'

'Not as far as I know, but then, I don't know everything, do I? As Ian said.'

Fran enthusiastically agreed to be present for the proposed visit and reminded Libby that they were only just over two weeks away from Christmas.

'Oh, bloody hell. And I can't go shopping. What shall I do?'

'Internet. You did it last year. But you'll have to start now, or it won't all be delivered in time. And Ben can choose the Christmas tree for a change.'

Libby relayed this information to Ben and set about making a list of things needed for Christmas. She was halfway through this, with a bowl of soup to hand, when the phone rang.

'Libby, it's Sandra. Denise says yes, she'll come and see you. When would be convenient?'

'Well, I suppose the sooner the better. Is she free this afternoon? Are you?'

'I can be. I'll call you back.'

Fran agreed to come as soon as she could get away, and by the time Libby had ended her call, Sandra was calling back to say she and Denise would be there at three.

'It's the Monday ukulele meeting tonight, so I don't want to be too long.'

'Not at the hall?' said Libby.

'No, back at The Poacher. I don't think the vicar wants us back in the hall!'

'Oh, I'm sure that isn't true,' said Libby. 'Bethany's lovely. But I believe the police had it in quarantine, or whatever they call it, up until the weekend, so perhaps best you stay away. Anyway, I'll see you at three.'

Promptly at three, Sandra arrived with Denise Bowling. Fran had arrived at half past two, so Ben had taken the opportunity to go up to the Manor. Fran had set out the tea things, and the kettle was gently steaming on the Rayburn.

'This is Denise.' Sandra pushed a small, mousy-looking woman forward towards Libby. 'Denise, this is Libby Sarjeant.'

Denise held out a trembling hand and nodded nervously.

'And I'm Fran Wolfe.' Fran came forward smiling easily and ushered Denise into the armchair opposite Libby's sofa. 'I'm just making tea.'

Denise looked at Sandra, who took another chair and smiled encouragingly.

'So, Denise, did Sandra tell you I really think you should go to the police?' Libby leant forward.

Denise nodded, and swallowed visibly.

'Why don't you want to go?'

Denise opened and closed her mouth a couple of times, but no sound came out. Luckily, this fish-like scenario was stopped by Fran arriving with the tea. Denise shook her head at the offer of sugar and clasped her mug with both hands.

'Come on, Denise,' said Sandra suddenly. 'This is silly. You agreed to come and see Libby. You at least have to speak to her.'

'Yes.' The whisper could barely be heard.

'What are you scared of, Denise?' asked Fran gently. 'Not the police, surely?'

Denise first shook her head, then nodded. Libby and Fran exchanged exasperated glances.

'I think,' said Sandra, 'that although the inspector who came to see her at first was very nice, when the drugs people came, they scared her.'

'Ah.' Libby nodded. 'Yes, they were pretty horrible to Mike as well.'

'Mike Farthing?' Denise's voice finally came out as a squeak.

'I told you,' said Sandra. 'They think he had something to do with the – factory.'

'No.' Denise shook her head, more violently this time, and Libby raised her eyebrows at Fran.

'And you knew nothing about it?' said Fran. 'The factory?'

Denise drank some tea, sat up straighter in her chair, and nodded.

'You mean, you did?' gasped Sandra.

'No!' Denise shook her head impatiently. 'Yes, I didn't know anything about it. Not exactly.'

The other three waited.

'I knew there was something going on. I knew he'd got some very expensive equipment because I saw it delivered. I thought he was doing experiments with drugs – he never stopped doing experiments.' Denise continued to stare into the fire. 'After Dellington – well, it seemed he couldn't stop. Even though all those experiments were banned. He used to do things at home, in his shed at the bottom of the garden.'

'You don't know what those experiments were?' asked Libby.

'No. I didn't want to know.' Denise shuddered. 'We had so much trouble after Dellington. Those poor boys.'

'Did he tell you what he was doing there?' Libby was surprised.

'Oh, no, that wasn't allowed. It all came out afterwards. He used to get death threats, you know.'

'You have told the police all this, haven't you?' said Fran.

Denise looked surprised. 'No. He was killed because of the cannabis, wasn't he?'

'They don't know why he was killed,' said Libby, 'and it's highly likely that the murderer was a relative of one of the Dellington victims. They've uncovered one already.'

'Who?' Denise's face twisted. 'Tell me.'

'No, we can't,' said Fran.

'Why? How is it you know, then?'

Fran glanced at Libby. 'I'm afraid I can't tell you that. I'm sure Sandra told you we're involved in the investigation, so we're bound to preserve its integrity.'

The other three women stared at her.

'I say, Fran, that was brilliant,' said Libby. Fran blushed. 'Anyway, Denise, I'm sure Sandra said we'd help you if we could, but I really think you ought to tell the police yourself. We can pass on information, but they would have to talk to you themselves after that.'

Denise subsided. 'I know.'

'So, come on, then,' encouraged Fran. 'Tell us why you thought Vernon was being threatened and why you think whoever it is will turn to you next.'

Chapter Twenty-six

'Could I have some more tea?' Denise asked plaintively. It was obviously a delaying technique. Fran got up and collected the mug.

'Anybody else?'

Sandra and Libby shook their heads.

They sat in silence until Fran reappeared with a fresh mug of tea and handed it to Denise.

'Now,' she said. 'You were worried enough to tell Sandra and to let her bring you here. So tell us what the problem is.'

Denise sighed. 'I overheard some phone calls.'

'Do you know who they were from?' prompted Libby, when Denise seemed once more to have come to a stop.

'No. I only heard what Vernon said.'

'And what was that?' asked Fran, controlling her impatience better than Libby.

'It just sounded as if he was being threatened.'

'How?' Libby asked. 'For goodness' sake, Denise – I'm really sorry you've lost your husband, and I know you're upset, but you must try and help us out here. What were his actual words and how many times did you hear these calls?'

Denise did an impression of a rabbit in headlights.

'Would you rather tell the police?' asked Fran, still gently. 'We can call them now.'

'No!' It was almost a screech.

Startled, the other three women looked at each other.

'We'll have to tell them what you've said, though,' Fran pointed out.

Denise stood up, knocking her tea mug into the hearth. 'Then I shall deny everything. I thought you were going to help me.'

'We were.' Sandra also stood up. 'But I think we

misunderstood what you meant by help.'

'I agree.' Libby looked up at them both. 'I think you wanted help to cover something up, Denise, didn't you? So that someone couldn't come after you?'

'I'm going home.' Denise turned to the door.

'How are you going to get there?' asked Sandra.

'You're driving me.' Denise didn't turn round.

'Why should I? You've been rude to my friends – and to me. I feel no obligation to drive you anywhere.'

Libby could see Sandra was shaking and felt sorry for her. 'Give me the phone, Fran, I'll call a taxi for Mrs Bowling.'

When she ended the call she said, 'Ten minutes, Mrs Bowling. You can wait outside.'

'I'm waiting in here.' Denise still didn't turn round.

'I'd rather you didn't,' said Libby, and Fran moved to Denise and began propelling her towards the door, when she whipped round and lashed out at Fran's face. Fran ducked and Sandra leapt forward.

'Out,' she said, capturing both Denise's arms and shoving her to the door, which Fran managed to get open. Together, they pushed the furious woman outside and locked the door behind her. Fran moved to the window and Sandra collapsed in the armchair, her hands over her face. Libby got slowly to her feet and retrieved the mug from the hearth.

'Don't worry, Sandra. I'll make a fresh pot of tea.'

Fran turned a pale face towards her. 'I'll do it.'

'No, I'm perfectly capable as long as I don't move too fast,' said Libby. 'You ought to sit down too.'

By the time Libby had made fresh tea, the taxi had collected Denise Bowling.

'I'm so sorry,' said Sandra. She'd recovered her poise and tucked an errant strand of silver hair out of sight. 'I didn't realise …'

'You've only known her since you married Alan, haven't you?' said Fran.

Sandra coloured faintly. 'Yes. It's really quite odd, marrying when you get to our age, and there were several people in the

192

village – Alan's friends – who didn't take to it. Denise seemed different, but I realise I didn't know her very well at all.'

'I think Libby was right,' said Fran. 'She knows something and she wanted us to help cover it up.'

'But is she afraid of whoever it is or the police? Strikes me it's the police she's more afraid of.' Libby sat upright on the sofa and pushed her bandage back from her forehead.

'Or of the whoever it is finding out she's told the police,' said Fran.

'I wish I'd never got involved,' said Sandra, looking wretched. 'I just wanted to help.'

'I think,' said Libby, 'as long as she doesn't try and get back at you, you just stay away from her. We'll have to pass on what she's told us, and we'll have to give your name as corroboration, after that it's up to the police.'

Sandra nodded. 'I hope Alan won't be cross. He's never been fond of Denise.'

'Was he close to Vernon?' asked Fran.

'Not especially.' Sandra frowned. 'I mean, they knew one another, had a drink together, that sort of thing, but we never went to dinner with them or anything like that. I got friendly with Denise through darts. In fact, over the last few months it struck me that Alan rather disapproved of Vernon, and that was why he didn't really like me being friendly with Denise.'

'Has he ever said why?'

Sandra shrugged. 'I never asked him.'

'Well, I should,' said Libby. 'And if there's anything you think the police should know, get him to tell them. I don't suppose you were questioned because you weren't around the night he was killed.'

'And we will be now?' Sandra sighed. 'I suppose we must.'

'We'll tell our friendly policeman,' said Libby, 'and he'll decide what to do with it all.'

'Are you feeling better now?' asked Fran. 'Do you feel able to drive?'

'Oh, I'm fine,' said Sandra. 'I lived alone for years after all. I'm very independent. And at least I don't have to go near Shott or Bowling House on the way home.'

'Fancy naming your house after you,' said Libby. 'He wasn't self-effacing, then?'

'Actually, that's what's so odd. He was, rather. Quiet, you know. That's why everybody's so surprised about all this.'

'Well, I must be going,' said Fran. 'Can I do anything for you before I go, Lib?'

'Yes, so must I.' Sandra stood up. 'I don't know what to say. Thank you for trying to help, and I'm so sorry it turned out the way it has.'

Libby stood and gave her a hug. 'Not your fault. Keep in touch.'

'Are you really going?' Libby eyed her friend askance after their guest had left. 'Or was that just to get rid of her so we could talk it over?'

'Of course.' Fran resumed her seat. 'I thought we ought to discuss what we're going to tell Ian and who's going to call him.'

'You can do that. He'd probably come over and strap me into bed if I did it.' Fran raised an eyebrow. 'Oh, you know what I mean. So what do we tell him?'

'Everything. Perhaps a little truncated.'

'Omit Sandra's first visit and run the whole thing together?'

'Without the pauses,' said Fran. 'She really was a piece of work, wasn't she?'

'I can't believe Sandra was friends with her. I wonder what she'll do now.'

'Sandra or Denise?'

'Denise, of course. You don't think she'll disappear, do you?'

'Actually,' said Fran, reaching for her phone, 'I think she may do just that. I'll try Ian.'

She was able to reach him on his official police phone and after a brief conversation, she ended the call.

'He's sending someone to question her right now, so let's hope she hasn't already done a runner, and he's calling in here to get the lowdown.'

'Here? Where is he now?'

Fran grinned. 'In the churchyard!'

Ian arrived ten minutes later.

'It really is no use telling you to keep out of things, is it?' he said to Libby, as he sat down opposite her.

'Wasn't my fault,' she said indignantly. 'Sandra called me and brought Denise to see us.'

'It's true, Ian,' said Fran. 'It wasn't anything to do with Libby.'

Ian sighed. 'Well, whatever it was, it sounds as though you got hold of something.'

'Speaking of which,' said Libby, 'did you get hold of Denise?'

'I haven't heard anything to the contrary,' said Ian warily.

'Right. Well, what happened was …'

'And that's it,' she concluded five minutes later. 'Sounds very strange to us.'

'The strangest thing is the way she turned on you at the end,' said Ian. 'It definitely sounds as if she's hiding something.'

'What I don't understand is why she allowed Sandra to bring her to see us,' said Fran, 'unless it really was to see if we would help her cover something up.'

'I'm pretty sure of that,' said Libby. 'Look how hesitant she was at first, and she gradually realised we wouldn't do that, so she had to get out of the situation, somehow.'

'I'm wondering now if the taxi actually took her home or somewhere else,' said Ian. 'Do you happen to know the name of the taxi firm?'

'Of course,' said Libby. 'I called it.' She found the number in her phone and passed it over. Ian made the call.

'Odder and odder,' he said as he ended the call. 'She took the taxi to Derek Chandler's house.' He made another call, directing the officers who had gone to pick up Denise back to Itching.

'Oh, dear, Sandra lives in Itching,' said Libby.

'Does she now? And we haven't spoken to her or her husband. I think I'd better do just that. Meanwhile, you two, stay put.' He stood up.

'I've got to go home,' said Fran. 'I can't stay here.'

'And I'm going to the rehearsal tonight,' said Libby.

'Is that wise?' said Ian and Fran together.

'Of course. I'm being far too cosseted. I shall just sit and regard my poor cast with an evil eye and let Peter do the shouting. No music tonight, which is a relief.'

'Don't do too much,' said Ian as he went to the door. 'And thanks for letting me know.'

'Will you …?' began Libby, but Fran frowned at her.

'If I can.' Ian grinned. 'I may just see you on Wednesday evening.'

'Well, what about that?' said Libby, when he'd gone. 'He was actually grateful.'

'He often is,' said Fran. 'But I wonder why Denise has gone to Derek Chandler's? Sandra said she didn't have friends in the ukulele group.'

'For protection,' suggested Libby. 'He's a solicitor.'

'Oh, yes. But that's virtually admitting there's something to hide.'

'Why didn't she just go home and phone him, though?'

'Perhaps because she thought we'd send the police after her?'

'Which we did,' said Libby, with a smug smile. 'I do hope Ian tells us what happens.'

'Should we let Sandra know?'

'Good idea.' Libby found the number in her phone. 'I hope she's home. How long ago did she leave here?'

'She'll be home. It was well before we even called Ian.'

Sandra was home.

'I've just seen the police car outside Derek Chandler's house. He lives in our road. What's going on?'

'Denise went there instead of home,' explained Libby. 'The police want to talk to her.'

'Oh, lord.' Sandra sounded upset.

'It isn't your fault, Sandra. And by the way, Ian said he will be talking to you and your husband.'

'Ian?'

'Our DCI friend, Ian Connell.'

'Did he say when?'

'No, sorry. But if you see anything happening in your road, let us know.'

'Providence Row has never seen anything like it,' said Sandra with a wry laugh. 'I expect the whole village will know by tomorrow if anything happens.'

'Well, that's it,' said Libby, putting her phone on the table beside her. 'Now we just wait and see if anything happens.'

'Your cousin will tell you if anything else happens to Mike Farthing, won't she?'

'I expect so. But I don't think anyone else will be keeping us up to date, do you?'

'I suppose Dr Robinson might, because of the concert, but he'd tell Andrew, not us.'

'What?' said Fran. 'You mean if they have to back out?'

'Having the victim in the band is one thing, but if the murderer's in it, too, that might just be a tad too far, don't you think?'

Chapter Twenty-seven

Libby survived the rehearsal, but declined the offer to go to the pub afterwards and, to Ben's relief, obediently went to bed as soon as they got home.

On Tuesday, however, she was determined to resume normal service. She walked to the doctor's surgery on the corner of Maltby Close to have her bandages removed and the slight wound on the bump examined, bought a few things in the eight-til-late and went in to The Pink Geranium to see Harry.

'Coffee?' he offered doubtfully. 'Pete said you didn't go for a drink last night.'

'No, but I'm not having to stay off the alcohol for ever. I've been given the all clear on that, and I can even wash my hair, thank goodness.'

'I must say, it doesn't look its usual immaculately coiffed self.'

'You can't do much with a rusty Brillo pad,' said Libby, fondly patting her wiry mop.

'So, coffee or wine? Although it's a bit early for wine.'

'Coffee, please. I don't want to get blind drunk the first day I'm allowed to drink. What's been going on in the village?'

'Nothing much, or you'd have heard about it. Apparently our Beth, the goodly vicar, preached a very strong sermon against violence on Sunday and had a full house. She put that down to the fact that you'd just been to see her when you were clobbered. Fame by association.'

'I'd like to have heard that,' said Libby, accepting a mug. 'Pity Monica Turner didn't hear it. Although her violence isn't exactly physical, more vituperative. I'd love to know what she thinks about me being attacked. Probably stood on the sidelines cheering the bloke on. And I know Ian was in the churchyard

199

last night, so I bet that pleased her. He didn't tell me what he'd been doing, though Do you know?'

'How would I know? I'm closed Mondays, aren't I? And he hardly confides in me and Pete. So what was he doing with you?'

Libby related everything she and Fran had heard.

'So I'm waiting to find out what happened when the police caught up with Denise,' she finished. 'And who was threatening her husband.'

'She sounds certifiable,' said Harry.

'Mmm. And poor Sandra feels guilty.'

'Was she one of the knitting circle?'

'The knitting circle? What knitting circle?'

'You know, the old biddies who meet up every now and then. Hetty and Flo and the others.'

'Why did everyone seem to know about them except me?'

'I only know because they come in here sometimes. I do them a special lunch.'

'At a special price, I bet!'

'Of course! Your mate Edie comes over sometimes.'

'Yes, and Una from Steeple Lane and Dolly from the New Farm bungalows.' Libby shook her head and was delighted to find it didn't hurt. Well, not much. 'Anyway, what were you asking?'

'If she was one of their friends. There were two women who used to come together – one was Una, I think, and a very smart woman who was a bit younger than the others. Lovely silver hair.'

'That's Sandra. Doesn't she come with them any more?'

'Not when they come here, any road. She moved?'

'Yes, to Itching. Married again.'

'That reminds me – what's happened to the headmistress?'

'Cassandra? Oh, she's going back to London, but will be back for weekends to stay with Mike Farthing. Unless he's convicted of something.'

'I was thinking about that,' said Harry slowly. 'I can't believe the bloke's into anything dodgy. He stayed with us, after all.'

'Not a guarantee of innocence.'

'Snarky. No, listen. He's got people working for him, hasn't he?'

'Two lads in the office, I gather, who look after most of the mail-order business. I suppose there would be gardening type people, too. Why?'

'Well, why couldn't it be one of them who did whatever it was? I bet he's fairly computer clueless. They've taken the computer, haven't they?'

'I think so,' said Libby, frowning.

'And you said something about a heating and ventilating system.' Harry's bright eyes were watching her as it sunk in.

'Oh, of course! They would have the know-how to find and order the right kit, wouldn't they?' Libby pulled out her phone. 'I must tell Cass. And I wonder if Ian knows?'

'He might not, if the drugs boys are keeping things to themselves,' said Harry. 'But I wouldn't try calling him again. Didn't you say he said he might come in tomorrow?'

'Yes,' said Libby happily. 'Be nice to get back to normal.'

'If that's what you call normal,' said Harry with a snort.

Libby called Cassandra that afternoon, who confirmed that Mike had had to close the business – temporarily, he hoped – although his part-time glass-house staff were still coming in, as the plants didn't understand the concept of 'Closed'. Patrick and Gary, however, were not at work.

'Did Mike tell them not to come in?' asked Libby.

'I suppose so. Why?'

'Just wondered,' said Libby, not quite willing to share Harry's theory yet. 'Are you back in London?'

'Yes, just finishing wrapping Christmas presents. I'll be back at the weekend.'

'Right,' said Libby guiltily. 'I'd better buy some then.'

'Oh, Libby! You are *so* disorganised.'

On Wednesday, Ben drove them both to Joe and Nella's Cattlegreen Nursery to choose a Christmas Tree, and, leaving Ben to dig up the one they'd chosen, Libby wandered into the shop where Joe's son Owen had proudly made his famous hot chocolate for her.

'Lovely, Owen, thank you.' She wrapped her hands round the mug.

'So you gets bashed on the head, then? OK now?' Joe leant against the counter and peered at her.

'Yes, I'm fine, Joe. I don't really know what happened.'

'All that pokin' yer nose into murders,' said Joe, voicing the opinion of all Libby's well-wishers. 'Don't do yer no good.'

'No, I suppose not. Joe, do you know Mike Farthing?'

'Course I do. He does more plants, like, but sometimes someone might ask me for something, so I send 'em to him. Nice bloke. Why?'

'Oh, nothing, really. My cousin's really friendly with him,' said Libby. 'He certainly seems very nice.'

Joe narrowed his eyes at her. 'This something to do with that murder? The ukulele bloke?'

Libby felt her face growing hot. 'Um – sort of.'

Ben came in and smilingly accepted his hot chocolate from Owen.

'What's going on, Ben? Your lass getting into murder again?' Joe fixed Ben with a suspicious eye.

Ben sighed. 'Yes, Joe. Has she been asking questions?'

Libby opened her mouth, but Joe got in first.

'Yes – about Mike Farthing. Don't tell me he's mixed up in it?'

'We don't think so,' said Ben, glaring at Libby. 'He was just in the same ukulele group as the victim.'

'Ah. Surprised me, that did. Mike's a quiet sort. Don't get out much.'

'That's what he told us. That's why he joined, I think.' Ben took out his credit card. 'I've tagged the one for the Manor as well, Joe, so I'll come back in the van and collect them both.'

'Don't start spreading gossip about Mike,' he said, when they were back in the car. 'It's not like you to be so irresponsible.'

'I only asked if Joe knew him,' said Libby. 'I thought he might, being in the same sort of business. He just jumped to

202

conclusions.'

Ben sighed. 'Just don't say anything to anybody. Try and keep safe.'

'Well, Joe's hardly going to attack me, is he?'

'You never know,' said Ben darkly.

Libby spent the rest of the afternoon ordering Christmas presents online and revising her Christmas card list. After dinner, she and Ben walked to the theatre, where she was surprised to find Sir Andrew waiting for them.

'I came down to find out if there was any news about the murder,' he said, following them into the foyer. Ben switched on lights and went through to the auditorium.

'Not really,' said Libby, 'except that someone bashed me on the head. Mind you, we don't know if that was connected to the murder or not.'

Andrew paled a little and sat down abruptly on the edge of a table. 'My dear girl! Are you badly hurt? Should you be out?'

'I'm fine, Andrew. It was nearly a week ago now.'

'No idea who did it?'

Ben came back. 'Someone who doesn't like her poking about, we suspect,' said Ben.

'The murderer, then?' Andrew looked even paler.

'If it was he didn't hit me very hard,' said Libby. 'It seems odd, after he'd killed Vernon Bowling.'

'Perhaps,' said Andrew, showing signs of reviving, 'he didn't mean to kill Bowling, but lashed out in anger, and only meant to warn you?'

'Possible,' agreed Libby. 'Anyway, that's about all. The police have been making all sorts of enquiries, and questioning suspects, but nothing concrete so far.'

'Are you worried about the concert?' asked Ben.

'Well, I am, rather.' Andrew pulled out the chair beside him and sat on it. 'It seems to me, with a murder victim and a possible murderer in the band, it's not quite the right feel for a Christmas concert. I suppose there are no suspects who *aren't* in the band?'

'Not that we've heard,' said Libby, 'but the police wouldn't tell us that sort of thing.'

'You can't tell me that your lovely policeman – Ian, is it? – hasn't kept you up to date? Or isn't he in charge of the case?'

'Yes, he is, and yes, we've had conversations, more because of our personal connection to some of the suspects.'

'No!' Andrew looked horrified. 'I didn't know you knew any of them.'

'You knew we knew Lewis and his mother,' said Ben.

'Oh, yes, but they're not suspects.'

'And my cousin Cassandra – remember she came to the meeting? – she's – ah – in a relationship with Mike Farthing, another member.'

'Dear me.' Andrew frowned at his steepled fingers. 'So you're in the middle of it again?'

'Yes, she is, and she's been warned off again by me and the police.' Ben came up and draped an arm across Libby's shoulders. 'However, that's never stopped her before, and we think that our lovely policeman may be joining us at the pub tonight. So you'll be there, won't you?'

Andrew brightened up. 'Wouldn't miss it! I was going to see if I could call on Dr Robinson, but I'll stay here instead.'

'Are you going to watch?' asked Libby nervously.

'Of course!' Andrew twinkled at her. 'I love a good panto.'

'Then you might not love this one,' muttered Libby.

However, her cast behaved impeccably. Andrew sat next to Libby, and surprised her by whispering a couple of suggestions as they went along, which when implemented improved the scenes, especially, to Libby's astonishment, the slapstick scenes.

'I didn't know you did that sort of comedy,' she said, when they took a break.

'I've done everything,' said Andrew. 'I'd love to do a Dame again.'

'It's not unheard of for theatrical knights to play dames,' said Libby.

'True, but nobody's asked me,' said Andrew with a wink.

'Well, don't think I'm going to ask a theatrical knight to take part in an amateur pantomime!' Libby laughed.

'Oh, I don't know. There are lots of small independent theatres around the country that do. Pro-am, I suppose.'

'I think that's what we are, in a way. We have a pro MD and this year, a pro choreographer and dancers, and we have pro lighting designers. Even Ben's an ex-pro, so am I, and several others are, too.'

'And you do good shows.' Andrew patted her hand. 'I would like to see you do a straight play. I've only seen the summer show and this.'

'I'll let you know,' said Libby, 'if you're sure.'

'Of course, I am. Look, I'm going to pop down and see Harry now, and I'll join you in the pub at what – ten-ish?'

'Or a bit earlier if I can get away,' said Libby and stood up. 'Right back to work everyone. Go back to the beginning of scene three.'

In fact, it was just before ten o'clock when Peter, Ben and Libby walked into the pub and found Harry, Andrew, Patti, Anne, and Ian sitting round a table looking solemn.

'What's happened?' Libby came to a standstill.

Ian stood up. 'Denise Bowling tried to commit suicide.'

Chapter Twenty-eight

'What?'

'Sit down, Lib,' Harry pulled out a chair. 'I'll go and get drinks.'

'What happened?' Libby stared at Ian. 'Did the police drive her to it?'

'Libby, don't jump to conclusions,' said Ian gently. 'And it's thanks to your friend Sandra that she didn't succeed.'

'Oh.' Libby took a deep breath. 'OK, then, tell me what happened. From after you left us on Monday afternoon.'

'Should we go?' asked Patti. 'It's nothing to do with us.'

Ian shook his head. 'You've been in on our conversations for so long now I can trust you. But go if you want to, of course.'

Anne indicated her drink. 'We'll stay until we've finished these. All right, Libby?'

Libby nodded and looked back at Ian.

'Right,' he said. 'Well, as I told you we went to Derek Chandler's house in Itching, where the taxi had taken Mrs Bowling. The officers I'd sent to her house got there before me and were already talking to him.'

'Not to her?'

'No, she'd gone. He seemed very ill at ease, and apparently had denied he'd seen her at first. Then I arrived and he finally admitted she'd been there, but hadn't come in and had left immediately.'

'How?' said Libby. 'The taxi had dropped her off in Providence Row, you confirmed that.'

'We don't know. Apparently, your friend Sandra was watching and when she saw the police car go she went across to Chandler's house to ask after Mrs Bowling. He, of course, said she'd left. Sandra was worried about her and called her on her landline and mobile, neither of which were answered. By about ten o'clock she was driving her husband mad, he told us, so he drove her to Bowling House. There were lights on, but she couldn't make anyone hear, so she called the police.'

'But the woman wasn't even missing,' said Ben. 'How did she get them to take it seriously?'

'She was sensible enough to mention that the woman was the subject of a police investigation. Naturally, she didn't know my name – although she did say she thought it was "Ian" – but the despatcher knew enough to come through to us. I was off duty by then, of course, but they called me.' He paused to take a sip of coffee.

'And then what happened?' prompted Libby.

'They broke in and found her in her bedroom. She'd taken something with alcohol, but luckily was still alive, so an ambulance was called and the constables who found her did all the right things and kept her that way.'

'How dreadful.' Libby was pale. 'Was it our fault?'

'Nothing to do with you,' said Ian. 'I arrived just as they were taking her away and more officers had arrived, so they started another search and I sat down and talked to Mr and Mrs Farrow, who were both very shocked.'

'But why didn't Sandra call and tell me? This happened on Monday night, didn't it? You would have thought she would have called me yesterday.'

'Yes, I'm surprised she didn't, even though I asked her not to,' said Ian with a smile.

'Oh.' Libby looked affronted. 'Why?'

'I didn't want you to start poking about. Which you would, you know you would. You'd be looking for an excuse to go and see Derek Chandler, for a start.'

'Oh,' said Libby again, acknowledging to herself that he was probably right.

'Do you know why she did it? Was there a note?' asked Patti, who was looking distressed.

'No, but that's not as unusual as the general public think. It just appears as though she was in something of a panic.'

'Why? I mean how do you know that?' asked Libby.

Ian looked uncomfortable. 'I can't tell you that.'

'Derek Chandler must know. She came straight from seeing him.'

'And he's not talking,' said Ian.

'So is Mrs Bowling now a suspect?' asked Anne.

'For her husband's murder? It's a possibility,' said Ian.

'But that would mean she hit me on the head and she'd never even met me,' said Libby.

'Had any of the others?' said Ben.

'We haven't definitely linked your attack with the murder, Libby,' said Ian.

'But it's got to be almost a certainty, surely?' said Peter.

'That's speculation,' said Ian, with a smile. 'And we aren't allowed to speculate.' He turned to Libby. 'That's your job.'

Libby flushed. 'I know, I know. I can't help feeling rather guilty about Denise, though. If we hadn't upset her …'

'You wouldn't try and top yourself because someone upset you, you silly bat,' said Harry.

'Why would you do it, then?' asked Ben.

'Mostly because they've done something wrong and can't bear to live with it,' said Patti. 'And they can't see that people will forgive almost anything.'

'Not always,' said Anne. 'Sometimes it's depression. Real, clinical depression. No one knows how that feels unless they've been there themselves. It isn't just being miserable because of some awful life event, it's much worse. It's indescribable, actually, and those who take their lives in those circumstances should be treated with less blame.'

Everyone was quiet after that, until Ian said 'I doubt if depression was the cause in Mrs Bowling's case, however. I think it was fear.'

They all looked at him.

'You don't think it was a cry for help?' Peter suggested tentatively. 'I mean, I don't know, but …'

'I think it could very well be,' said Ian, 'but we haven't been able to speak to her yet. We would have insisted if there had been any doubt that it *was* a suicide attempt, serious or not.'

'It doesn't get you any nearer Bowling's murder, then, does it?' said Libby.

'Maybe.' Ian finished his coffee and stood up. 'Now I'll leave you to discuss it, and then let me who dunit by tomorrow morning.' He lifted a hand in farewell and left.

'Well!' said Libby, leaning back in her chair. 'That was a surprise.'

'It's horrible,' said Patti.

'I know, Patti. Are you regretting getting to know us?'

'To know you, you mean,' said Harry. 'The rest of us are blameless and incurious.'

'Yeah, sure.' Libby dug him in the ribs.

Patti laughed. 'No, of course not, but it does bring you up against the more unpleasant bits of life.'

'But you get that being a vicar, too,' said Libby. 'And speaking of which, I met Bethany Cole last week.'

'I heard,' said Patti. 'Just before you were attacked.'

'I don't think it had anything to do with her, though,' said Libby. 'She's nice, isn't she?'

'Do you actually know any male vicars?' asked Sir Andrew, who hadn't so far said a word.

Everyone looked at him in surprise.

'Yes,' said Patti, suddenly. 'You remember, Libby. I took you to meet him. Toby.'

'Oh, yes, when we were trying to find out about Wyghtham Hall. There you are, Andrew. We do know one.'

Andrew laughed. 'I'm glad us gents are keeping our end up. I wonder what the percentage is now?'

'I think in full-time posts about one in seven,' said Patti, 'and I think more in the south-east.'

'Is that because the south-east is more liberal?' asked Ben.

'I think you'd get an argument about that in a lot of parts of the country,' said Andrew. 'Manchester, for example.'

'Well, anyway, Bethany Cole had nothing to do with my being hit on the head,' said Libby, 'and I think we ought to change the subject.'

Everyone looked at her in surprise.

'What?' She lifted her chin defensively. 'I'm feeling guilty, all right?'

'You really have no reason to feel guilty,' said Ben later, as they walked home.

'She was more or less thrown out of my house, went straight to someone else for help, which she presumably didn't get, and then went home to kill herself. Why shouldn't I feel guilty?'

Ben sighed. 'Talk to Fran about it in the morning.'

Fran, of course, understood.

'What should we do?' she asked.

'Stay out of it, according to Ian, although he did say that he wanted us to tell him who the murderer is.'

'He knows we'll discuss it. All the others will, too. And we really *are* involved now.'

'I know. How do we do it?' Libby sighed. 'Shall we have a compare the suspects session?'

'If you like. I'm shop-sitting this morning while Guy stocks up on some more Christmas tat, but he'll be back this afternoon.'

'I'll come to you,' said Libby. 'I need to get back in the driving seat again.'

'It's only a week since your accident,' said Fran dubiously.

'I know, and I've been absolutely fine. I ran a rehearsal last night, I've been shopping and to the pub. I'm fine.'

'All right. But tell Ben, and leave before it gets dark.'

'It's dark by four, idiot! And I know the road between here and Nethergate like the back of my hand.'

'Just be careful.' Fran rang off.

'I'll come with you,' said Ben, when Libby phoned to tell him.

'Haven't you got anything else to do?'

'Not really, other than collect the trees from Joe. I can do that any time.'

'But we're having a – a –'

'Murder discussion. I know. So I'll go and keep Guy

211

company in the shop. I might have a bit of Christmas shopping to do, after all.'

The result of this was an invitation to dinner with Fran and Guy, which Libby immediately countermanded.

'No, my treat – dinner at either The Sloop or The Swan. You choose.'

By half past two Libby was ensconced in the window seat in the front room of Coastguard Cottage, Balzac the cat on her lap, her hands wrapped round a mug of tea.

'The view from here is lovely even in winter.'

'Except when it's so foggy you can't even see Dragon Island,' said Fran, who was ironing.

'It's a bit insubstantial today,' said Libby, peering.

'Come on, then, we didn't get together to talk about Dragon Island or fog. Review the situation.'

'Right,' said Libby, and dislodged Balzac. 'First of all, Mike Farthing.'

'He went early on that Monday night and other than a possible and improbable connection with the cannabis factory, has no motive.'

'He could have parked off the Canterbury road and come back through the woods behind Lendle Lane.'

'No,' said Fran, 'Ian has already told you, there were no cars parked along there.'

'And do we know definitely it was something to do with a heating and ventilating system?'

'No. We know there was one and we suspect it was ordered through Mike's computer.'

'By Patrick or Gary. '

' Carry on, then. Who next?'

'Derek Chandler. He was there that Monday night, but I don't know if he was in the pub when Lewis came in or not. He was an alleged scammer, although cleared of that and fairly close to Bowling.'

'Only motive counter accusations,' said Fran.

'OK Ron Stewart. Was he there?'

'If he was he was on his own. Didn't someone say he and

Bowling usually went together?'

'Even if he was there in the pub, he could have walloped Bowling earlier. But again, motive.'

Fran rested the iron and folded a shirt. 'Something to do with the factory. The house design … he had to know about the factory. His house came first, didn't it?'

'Do you think it was his idea?' said Libby. 'It could have been, couldn't it? You know – sex'n'drugs'n'rock'n'roll and all that.'

'I suppose so. I think Jonah Fludde were rather in the middle of the whole drugs scene of the early seventies. But how come he got Bowling interested?'

'Bowling was a user? I don't know. But cannabis isn't a hard drug.' Libby frowned. 'I suppose it couldn't be more than cannabis, could it? Ian would hardly have told us if they'd found – I don't know – evidence of manufacturing crystal meth or something, could he? It would make it all seem a bit more reasonable.' Libby shrugged, uncurled her legs and took her mug into the kitchen. 'And then there's dear old Bob Alton.' She went back into the sitting room. 'You know, I still think that's the most likely reason someone had it in for him. The needless deaths of those poor soldiers.'

'But not Bob!'

'We don't want to think so, but he said, didn't he, he wouldn't have carried on with the group if he'd known who Bowling was.'

'That's a far cry from killing him.' Fran shook out another shirt. 'And then there's Denise. Is the suicide attempt a confession?'

Chapter Twenty-nine

'I've interrupted, haven't I?' Jane Baker stood on the doorstep.

Fran smiled and held the door wider. 'No, come in. Libby and Ben are taking us to dinner at The Sloop, so we've got ages.'

Jane, now assistant editor of the *Nethergate Mercury* and its associated local papers, both print and online, edged into the room.

'Sorry,' she said to Libby. 'I wanted to show you the paper.'

'I saw it online,' said Libby, nevertheless taking the proffered paper.

'That was abbreviated,' said Jane.

Fran peered over Libby's shoulder. 'Nice picture.'

'Of Ben,' said Libby. 'What on earth do I look like?'

'Someone who's been attacked?' suggested Jane.

'Would you like tea, Jane?' asked Fran.

'If you're sure I'm not interrupting ...'

Libby grinned. 'Come on, you'd love to know what we've been talking about.'

'Well, I suppose I can guess.'

'I expect you can.' Libby looked at her speculatively. 'But how much do you know?'

'I know there's been a news blackout.'

'Ah. Since when?'

'Monday, as far as I can tell. The press office won't tell us a thing. All we're getting is the usual traffic stuff and drunks.'

Libby glanced at Fran who was coming in with fresh tea. 'In that case, I'm not sure ...'

'Has something else happened?' Jane leant forward.

'If it's under a blackout, we can't tell you,' said Fran. 'Sorry, Jane.'

'How do you know, then? Oh.' Jane nodded. 'Ian Connell.'

'And we – I – we're involved, of course,' said Libby.

Jane sighed. 'Of course. I'm well trained – I won't ask.'

Libby patted her hand. 'Anyway how did you know I was here?'

'I popped into the shop to show Fran the paper and Guy and Ben told me you were both here.' Jane sipped tea. 'I can't stay long in any case. Imogen's with Mum.'

'You haven't heard of anything more to do with Vernon Bowling's murder, then?' said Fran, going back to the ironing.

'Well, not as such … Do you know a Robert Alton?'

'Yes?' said Fran and Libby together.

'I thought you might know of him. He's a member of the ukulele group, isn't he? Or was.'

'Was?' said Libby.

'He told me he's left.' Jane looked from one to the other. 'Do you know anything about him?'

'A bit,' said Fran. 'What do you know?'

Jane coloured a little. 'I did a bit of research on the names of the people in the group – those that I had, anyway – and came up with the fact that his son was one of those killed at Dellington. You know about Dellington?'

'We do,' said Libby.

'So I asked him if I could talk to him. He was quite willing, although in the end I had to cut a lot of it as it could have been libellous. It's turned into rather a mild little comment on his previous life. Bowling's, I mean.'

'So Bob Alton's left? Did he say why?'

'He didn't want to be associated with the group any more.' Jane shook her head. 'It wouldn't surprise me if more people leave.'

'No.' Libby looked at Fran. 'It wouldn't surprise me, either.'

'The Concert' floated in the ether between them, unspoken.

'I must go.' Jane stood up. 'Thanks for the tea. You will let me know if there's anything I can publish, won't you?'

'Of course.' Fran went to the door with her. 'Love to Terry and Imogen.'

'Do you think I ought to talk to Andrew about this?' said Libby, as Fran went back to her ironing board.

'It might be an idea.' Fran looked up. 'It might also be a very good idea to talk to some of the people in the group to see how they feel.'

Libby gazed at her friend admiringly. 'What a brain!'

'Mind you – I suppose for decency's sake you ought to go to Eric Robinson first.'

'Well, of course. But suppose he says he's doing it anyway? You know, canvassing the members. He might say that he's already done it by holding that meeting in the theatre.'

'But things have changed since then.' Fran regarded the remaining ironing with distaste. 'I'm fed up with this.'

'So stop. I don't know how you manage to get so much ironing.'

'Guy wears shirts. And there's my linen tops, and tablecloths …'

'Tablecloths? Only at Christmas, tablecloths. Here, let me put the iron away.'

Ironing board, iron, and linen put away, they settled either side of the fire.

'So where do we go from here?' said Libby. 'Do we get in touch with Dr Robinson? We haven't checked him as a suspect yet, have we?'

'No, but unless he's got some sort of guilty secret, I don't know how he comes into it.'

'We ought to check them all,' said Libby. 'It could be any of them.'

'Let's stick with what we've got so far,' said Fran, 'and yes, call Andrew and tell him what's going on and suggest that you talk to Dr Robinson in your guise as member of the theatre board.'

'OK. Shall I do it now?'

'Have you got his number?'

'In my phone.' Libby dragged it out of the bag which had now replaced the ubiquitous basket.

'Hello?'

'Andrew, it's Libby. I'm sorry to bother you – have you gone home, by the way?'

'No, I'm still in the village. What's up?'

'Fran and I have heard that people are leaving the ukulele group. We were wondering –'

'If they should leave the concert. Yes, so was I. In fact, I was going to get in touch with Dr Robinson this evening. That's why I stayed down.'

'Oh. Are you going to ask them to leave?'

'I think I have to.' Andrew sighed. 'The initial murder was bad enough, but might have translated into a few extra sales from the ghoulish, but with others in the group under suspicion and now Mrs Bowling's suicide attempt, I feel it would be very bad taste to allow them to take part.'

'I agree,' said Libby, making a face at Fran. 'We'll leave it to you, then.'

'What do you mean, leave it to me?'

'We thought we might ask some of the members of the group what they thought about it.'

Andrew laughed. 'You mean you were going to use it as an excuse to go sleuthing!'

Libby couldn't think of anything to say.

'I think it will be better if I do it in an official way. It's a shame, and I shall have to pull in a favour from someone else to fill the gap, but I think it's for the best.'

'You're right. It's a shame, though.'

'You could come with me to see Robinson if you like.'

'Could I? As a representative of the theatre? Oh, but if you're going this evening I can't. Ben and I are in Nethergate. We're going out to dinner with Fran and Guy.'

'Perhaps I could make an appointment to go in the morning? Would that suit you?'

'Oh, you are lovely, Andrew! Yes, that would be wonderful.'

Libby ended the call and beamed at Fran. 'Did you get all that?'

'Andrew's going to see them himself?'

'Just Robinson to give him the sack. And he's going to try

and make an appointment for tomorrow so I can go with him.'

'Will that help?'

'I've no idea, but it can't hurt. I have a burning desire to find out who hit me.'

'I don't suppose it was Robinson.'

'No, but he knows me from the meeting in the theatre.'

'Yes,' said Fran. 'It has to be someone who knows you. But meeting Robinson won't help you talk to any of the others.'

'No, all right, it won't, but it's a start.'

'And what about Edie and Lewis? Should you talk to them? Edie might be disappointed.'

'I don't think she will be, somehow, but I'll give her a ring and forewarn her.'

'Do it now. I'm ready for more tea,' said Fran, getting up.

'Edie, it's me.' Libby spoke a little louder than she had to Andrew. 'I just want to tell you something. Andrew has decided that under the circumstances it would be better for the ukulele group not to perform in the concert.'

'Oh, that's a shame, dear. Although it wasn't the same last Monday. Lots of them weren't there. Not sure I shall carry on, as it happens.'

'That was one of the things that made Andrew decide. I told him people were already leaving.'

'Really? Who?'

'Bob Alton, for one.'

'Oh well, I will leave then. He was lovely, old Bob. The only one near my age.'

'Why don't you invite him over for a cup of tea? You said you would. Fran's seen him and says he's lonely.'

There was a pause, and Libby winked at Fran who was coming back in with fresh mugs.

'You got his number then?' Edie asked at last.

'Hang on, I'll ask. Fran did Bob Alton give you his number?'

'It's on the computer at the shop. He's ordered stuff from us in the past. I'll get it from Guy.' Fran took out her own phone.

'I'll let you have it when Fran's got it, Edie. So what do you think about the group being left out of the concert?'

'I think it's right, dear. I mean, if they're looking for a murderer in the group, well, it's not nice, is it?'

'Did you hear about my accident, Edie?'

'No!' Edie sounded horrified, and Libby explained.

'And they think it was to do with this murder? Well, I'm certainly not going back, then. And what about Mike? There's something going on there, too, isn't there?'

Libby sighed. 'Yes, but we're not sure what. I'll keep you posted. Oh, here we are, Fran's got Bob's number.' She read it out. 'So you have a chat with him. He might have thoughts about it all, too.'

She switched off the phone. 'I think Dr Robinson's going to find a lot of people agreeing with Edie and Bob.'

'I think so. And surely Ron Stewart would back out after this, anyway. He hardly needs the bad publicity.'

'Nor does Lewis, come to that,' said Libby. 'After he's a much more family-friendly personality than Screwball Stewart.'

Dinner overlooking the dark sea was an enjoyable experience, and Libby and Fran vetoed all talk of murder for the evening, to the relief of Ben and Guy. As they left, Libby said in an aside to Fran, 'I'll ring you as soon as I know about Robinson.'

'After you've seen him,' said Fran. 'If you do.'

When Libby checked her phone in the car on the way home, she found a text from Andrew, which simply read: 'Ten tomorrow. Pick you up at nine thirty.'

'I'm going out with Andrew in the morning,' she told Ben. 'We're telling the ukulele group they can't be in the concert.'

'Thank goodness for that,' said Ben. 'I was wondering when someone would realise that had to happen. Bad publicity for the theatre.'

'Why didn't you say anything, then?'

'I didn't want to upset Andrew, but I was beginning to think I'd have to, especially after this latest upset.'

'Denise's suicide attempt?'

'Yes. And how long Mike's involvement with the cannabis factory can be kept under wraps I don't know.'

'But he isn't!'

'Suspected connection, then. It's all very unsavoury. I should have insisted after the attack on you.'

'But we don't know that it was connected.'

Ben gave her a sideways look. 'Come on, Lib. We all know it was.'

'All right, it was. I still want to know who did it, though.'

'Ian's got his team on it, and they'll step it up after the suicide attempt. There'll be more to learn now. So go and give Dr Robinson the sack with Andrew and let it go. We can get on with Christmas and the panto and go back to normal.'

Libby made a face at him and turned to the window. 'We'll see about that,' she said under her breath.

Chapter Thirty

Libby walked down Allhallow's Lane to meet Andrew on the corner by the vicarage. The sky was a uniform grey and a sneaky little wind lifted tendrils of hair and blew up sleeves. A dark, sleek car purred to a halt beside her, and Andrew leant across to open the door.

'How did Dr Robinson sound when you asked for a meeting?' she asked as she fastened her seat belt.

'Resigned,' said Andrew. 'He didn't even ask me why.'

'So he knows what's coming. I wonder why he didn't talk to his members and suggest pulling out before this?'

'We don't know – he may have done.'

Libby shook her head. 'Not until yesterday afternoon he hadn't. I was speaking to Edie, Lewis's mum, telling her that Bob Alton, one of the older members, had pulled out, and she said she was going to do the same, but she didn't mention hearing anything from Robinson.'

'He probably called them all after he'd spoken to me. I suspect this meeting will be largely unnecessary.'

'But we might find out some more about the members,' said Libby.

'I can't see how. You can hardly ask the man if he thinks any of his members had a motive for murdering his friend.' Andrew indicated right towards Itching and Shott. 'Now, where's Hollow Lane?'

'Is it in Itching? Because it's a tiny village. I didn't realise Robinson lived here, too. Sandra and Alan Farrow do, and Derek Chandler. They live in Providence Row.'

'That doesn't help, Libby,' said Andrew as they emerged on to the main village street. 'Look, there's your Providence Row.'

'And there's Hollow Lane,' said Libby, pointing to a gap

between two stone-built cottages.

Andrew slowed the car. 'We can't drive down there. We'll have to park somewhere and walk.'

They found a space to park at the bottom end of the high street where there were no yellow lines and began to walk back.

'There must be another way in,' said Libby. 'Unless no one who lives there has a car.'

'Well, Robinson has one. I saw him get into his on the night of the meeting in the theatre, so you're right. There must be another way in.'

Hollow Lane was, unbelievably, cobbled. It led between the two side walls of the stone cottages, between two high garden walls, then widened a little and ran between terraces of cottages very like the ones in Rogues Lane in Shott. It struck Libby as dank and dismal as a Victorian etching.

Further along, the lane became steadily more rural, with occasional cottages and finally, one much larger house.

'This is it.' Andrew walked between two impressive iron gates up to a forecourt where three cars stood. 'Definitely another way in, then.' He went up to the front door and rung the bell.

Eric Robinson opened the door almost immediately, still aspiring to the image of a country gentleman circa 1950.

'I'm sorry we're late,' said Andrew, holding out his hand, 'but we came in from the Shott end of the lane. There must be another way in?'

Libby was sure she saw the suspicion of a satisfied smirk on Robinson's face as he shook Andrew's hand.

'Ah, yes, perhaps I should have told you. I'm afraid we always assume people know the way in. You go via Bishop's Bottom. Ah – Mrs Sarjeant.'

A woman rose to her feet as they were shown into an over-furnished sitting room.

'My wife, Veronica,' Robinson waved in her direction. 'Do you think we could have coffee, my dear?'

Veronica Robinson nodded, smiled tentatively at Libby and

left the room. Libby looked after her, slightly astonished. The woman looked as though she was dressed for a part in a period play, the perfect wife to play opposite the country gentleman.

'I expect you've guessed what this is about,' said Andrew, after they had taken their seats on squashy sofas.

'You want our group out of the concert.' Robinson nodded. 'I'm not surprised. At first we thought it would be fine, but as time has gone on ...' He stopped.

'Exactly. Various members of your group are under suspicion, Mrs Bowling has attempted suicide –' Libby watched for a reaction to this, but there was none, '– and Mrs Sarjeant here has been attacked.'

This time there was a reaction. Robinson turned to Libby, a horrified expression on his face.

'You – you were attacked?'

'Yes.'

Robinson looked as if he didn't know what to say, and was saved by the entry of his wife carrying a tray.

'Ah – yes, thank you, Veronica. Remiss of me – I didn't introduce you – this is Sir Andrew McColl and Mrs – er – Sarjeant.' A sheen of perspiration had appeared on his brow and Libby wondered why.

Veronica Robinson murmured something and sat down beside the table on which she set the tray.

'So,' Robinson turned back towards Libby. 'You were attacked? I do hope you weren't hurt?'

'She spent the night in hospital,' said Sir Andrew, in his best thespian manner. 'The doctors were quite worried.' Libby tried not to grin.

'I didn't know,' said Robinson. 'I'm so sorry. And this was – er – is connected to poor Vernon's murder?'

'Undoubtedly,' said Andrew. 'The police, obviously, are investigating. Ah, thank you, Mrs Robinson.' He took a cup from the woman, who, Libby now noticed, had unwashed hair and bitten nails.

'Well,' said Robinson, with a sigh, 'I can understand that the presence of the group might be an embarrassment in the concert.

I have actually warned several of our members that this was likely to happen.'

'And I believe some have already left,' said Libby, again watching carefully for a reaction.

'Indeed?' Robinson looked confused. 'I haven't heard …'

'Robert Alton, Lewis Osbourne-Walker and his mother and Mike Farthing.' Libby crossed her fingers, having no idea if Mike or Lewis wanted to leave, but assuming they would. 'Which robs the group of one of its celebrity members, of course. I suppose Ron Stewart will be staying with you, though.'

'Ah – yes. I have spoken to him, but none of the others you mentioned. Although I understand Mike himself is – er – under investigation?'

It was a question, not a statement. Andrew looked at Libby.

'Several people are,' said Libby non-committally. Robinson looked dissatisfied.

'The police seem to think it had to be a member of the group who killed him,' offered Andrew.

'I don't know why. Anyone could have got into that churchyard. I mean, why was he there anyway? It wasn't on the way to the car park.' Robinson looked at his wife. 'You don't think one of us killed him, do you, Veronica?'

Veronica looked plainly astonished.

'Well, do you?'

Veronica slowly shook her head. Libby caught a surreptitious glance at a photograph which stood on a small table beside the fireplace. It was angled away from her, but she determined to have a look at it before they left. There was definitely something going on here.

'I'm glad you've taken it so well.' Andrew stood up and Robinson looked confused. 'Leaving the concert, I mean.'

'Oh.' Robinson's shoulders slumped. 'I think I might break up this group. Concentrate on the Canterbury one.'

Libby also stood up. 'Those members of this group can always join that one, can't they?' She turned to Veronica. 'Thank you for the coffee, Mrs Robinson.' She went towards her, holding out her hand, which Veronica took warily. Libby glanced quickly at the photograph, then smiled at Veronica, detached her hand and went back to Andrew.

Robinson showed them out, looking depressed.

'What did you think of that,?' asked Libby as they walked back down Hollow Lane.

'He wasn't exactly the picture of calm, was he?' replied Andrew. 'And that poor woman!'

'I honestly didn't think there were any wives like that left,' said Libby. 'She's completely cowed, and doesn't even bother with her appearance. Do you think he beats her?'

'Libby!' Andrew was shocked.

'Lots of women are, and still stay with their husbands and partners,' said Libby reasonably.

Andrew shook his head.

'Well, what about his reaction to my attack?'

'Natural horror at a mugging?'

'More than that.' Libby gave a decisive nod. 'It looked as though he actually suspects someone in the group, and couldn't work out why they'd attacked me. Or else he knows who the murderer is, and knows that person couldn't have attacked me.'

'I think you're reading too much into it, Libby. The man's just had what would be a prestigious gig taken away from him, and now knows that the group's collapsing around him. He's just depressed about it.'

'Hmm,' said Libby.

The walk back down Hollow Lane seemed to take half as long as the walk up it. 'That's because we know where we're going,' said Libby.

'Should we go and see Derek Chandler while we're here?' she asked, as they came out on to the high street, with Providence Row almost opposite.

'What for?' Andrew stopped and turned to face her. 'Libby, this is not an investigation. Not for me, anyway. Now, I'm going to drive you back to Steeple Martin, then I shall say goodbye to Hal and go back to London.'

'Oh, all right.' Libby cast a disgruntled look over her shoulder at Providence Row and followed Andrew to his car.

Making an effort once they were on the way back to Steeple Martin, Libby asked who Andrew might get in to replace the ukulele group in the Christmas Concert.

'I'm going to have to pull in a few favours, as I said, but I don't want to use an unknown, tempting though it is to give someone a chance. After all, we've sold out, haven't we? Pity we couldn't do it for more than one night.' He looked sideways at his passenger.

'Even if you could,' said Libby, 'would your other guests be willing to give up more than one night?'

Andrew sighed. 'That's true. Well, I suppose I shall have to go through the address book when I get home. Or perhaps my agent's address book.'

'I wonder,' said Libby slowly, 'if perhaps Ron Stewart would do it?'

Andrew turned startled eyes towards her. 'What?'

'Well, he was prepared to do it as part of the group, and he was billed as such, same as Lewis. Couldn't we ask him?'

Andrew thought for a moment. 'I suppose we could. You've ruled him off your suspect list, have you?'

'No,' said Libby brightly. 'He's still right up there with Derek Chandler.'

'In which case, he might be hauled off in irons before the concert and we'd be worse off than before.'

'But we could ask him and see how he responded. Then we could find an excuse not to use him.'

'Libby!' Andrew banged an exasperated hand on the steering wheel. 'This isn't a game! I can understand how annoyed your Inspector Connell gets with you. Give it up and leave it to me.'

Libby subsided and gazed out of the side window as Andrew turned towards Steeple Martin.

'Drop me at the corner,' she told him as the car turned into the high street. 'Save you having to turn round.'

He stopped the car and leant over to give her a kiss on the cheek.

'Sorry I snapped. I'll let you know about the change of programme as soon as I can.'

Libby smiled, climbed out of the car and waved him off.

'And I'll go and ask Ron Stewart whether you like it or not.'

Chapter Thirty-one

'Libby, you can't!' Fran wailed down the phone line. 'That's ridiculous! What will you say to him?'

'I told you. As the ukulele group are now out of the concert, had he thought of doing a solo spot instead.'

'And – supposing he even sees you – what do you say if he says "yes"?'

'I shall tell him I'll put it before Sir Andrew and I'm just sounding him out.'

'He's Screwball Stewart for goodness' sake. It doesn't work like that.'

'Well, how does it work? You have to ask people to do things or they'd never get done,' said Libby reasonably.

'I'll tell you what would be better, if you must keep meddling,' said Fran. 'Why don't you ask Sandra when the group are having their next meeting. You could go along to that as the representative of the theatre – to apologise, perhaps.'

Libby considered. 'Not bad. Would you come with me?'

Fran sighed. 'I suppose so. Depending on when it is. And don't forget your rehearsal schedule.'

'I'm not likely to, am I? I'll call Sandra and let you know.'

To Libby's frustration, Sandra was not in.

'I'm sorry, but are you Alan?' Libby asked.

'Yes.' It was the voice of an old man, which somehow surprised Libby. 'And you must be the friend from Steeple Martin Sandra was telling me about?'

'Yes, Libby Sarjeant. I'm on the board of the theatre. I don't know if you've heard from Dr Robinson – um – recently?'

'He called just a while ago. We're not doing the concert, it seems.'

'Yes,' said Libby. 'I'm awfully sorry, but under the

circumstances ...'

'Bad taste, I know. Don't worry, my dear. We're having a bit of an emergency meeting this evening –'

'This evening? Oh, bother,' interrupted Libby.

'What?' Alan Farrow sounded put out.

'Oh, I'm sorry, Mr Farrow, but I was hoping I could come along and explain if you had a meeting. I feel bad about the concert.' Libby crossed her fingers.

'And you couldn't come this evening?'

'No, I'm sorry. Well, never mind, perhaps you'll convey my – er – sentiments to the group?'

'Of course.' Now Alan Farrow sounded bewildered.

'Thank you. And you'll tell Sandra I called?'

Alan Farrow assured her he would and rang off.

'So that's that idea scuppered,' Libby reported to Fran. 'It'll have to be the Ron Stewart angle after all.'

'No, Libby. That is quite ridiculous, and I doubt very much if he would see you anyway. He's probably surrounded by high-tech security and possibly guard dogs, too.'

Libby chewed her lip. 'How am I going to speak to him then? I must see if he's a viable suspect.'

'Libby – what's got into you? I know you always want to get to the bottom of things, but there's no way you're going to be able to get any further with this. Leave it to Ian and his minions.'

Libby sighed. 'All right. But I don't know how I'm going to live with that.'

But, as it happened, she didn't have to.

Just as she and Ben were leaving the house to go to the theatre that evening, the phone rang. Libby darted back indoors to answer it and tripped over the step.

'Yes?' she said breathlessly.

'Did I disturb you, Libby?'

'Oh, Sandra! No, not exactly. I was half out the front door on the way to rehearsal.'

'Oh, I see. Alan said you called. He told you about our meeting?'

'Yes.' Libby groaned inwardly. 'I was so sorry I couldn't be there.'

'Well, actually, that was what I was ringing about. Apparently The Poacher has an event on tonight, so we can't go there, and we're coming to Steeple Martin.'

'What? To the hall?'

'No – they've got something on, too. No, we're coming to the pub. Well, it used to be my local. Where I played darts. So, I thought, maybe …'

Libby thought furiously. 'What time are you meeting?'

'Not until nine. A lot of people had things to do.'

'I'll come as soon as I can after rehearsal,' said Libby. 'I might even let them off early!'

'And what,' said Ben, as she tucked her arm through his and set off down the lane, 'do you imagine you're going to find out?'

'I don't know. But at least I'll get a look at them. And maybe one of them will look guilty when he sees me.'

'And supposing not many of them attend?'

'I'll cross that bridge when I come to it,' said Libby. 'And I shall just send Fran a text.'

The pantomime cast were gratified but confused to be dismissed at half past nine and Libby left Ben and Peter to lock up the theatre on their own while she hurried down the drive towards the high street and the pub.

Sandra was in the snug, a room often appropriated by the theatre crowd, who were now milling disconsolately round the main bar. Libby went into the snug.

Eric Robinson looked up without enthusiasm, Mike Farthing with embarrassment, Sandra with a smile of welcome, and Lewis, to Libby's surprise, with a grin and a wink.

'What do you want to drink, petal?' He stood up and pulled out a chair for her, while the rest of the company looked on with sour expressions.

Libby put in her order and sat down.

'I've come to say how sorry I am about the change of plan.' She looked round the table. 'But under the circumstances, Sir Andrew felt he had no choice.'

The heads around the table nodded gloomy acquiescence.

Lewis came back with her drink.

'Do you know everybody, Lib?' he asked. 'I expect they all saw you at the other meeting, but you don't know people, do you?'

Libby could have hugged him.

Apart from the four Libby already knew, there were only four others. Alan Farrow, pleasant, balding, and moustachioed, Chester Lucas, a jovial black man with a huge smile, Derek Chandler, with a pinched face, rimless glasses, and a comb-over, and Ron 'Screwball' Stewart, tall, his legs stretched out in worn jeans, with the sort of face usually described as 'lived-in'. Libby eyed these last two with interest.

Chandler was almost too like the central casting version of a provincial solicitor, while Stewart was aiming for the same status as 'ageing rock-star'. They both seemed familiar, but Libby guessed that she would have seen pictures of Stewart over the years, and Chandler would probably have been at the previous meeting in the theatre.

'Er – I didn't tell you,' said Robinson, clearing his throat and looking shifty, 'Mrs Sarjeant was attacked last week.'

All eyes turned to Libby.

'It's all right,' she said hastily, 'I'm quite recovered, but I did have to spend the night in hospital.'

Chandler looked at Robinson. 'And is it connected …?'

'The police think so,' said Libby. 'They're assuming the same person who murdered Mr Bowling had a go at me.'

The members of the ukulele group exchanged furtive glances. There was definitely something going on here, thought Libby, although, to be fair, the Farrows and Chester Lucas just looked puzzled.

'You know,' said Sandra suddenly. 'I think it would be a good idea for Libby to look into this for us.'

The men all looked at her, astonished.

'Well, Libby's had a lot of experience investigating murders,' Sandra continued, 'as I'm sure some of you know. And it looks as if this whole situation is damaging us as a group, especially since … er … since –'

234

'Mrs Bowling's suicide attempt,' said Libby.

'And several people have already left,' said Robinson reluctantly.

Ron Stewart gave a grunt and sat up straight. 'What would you do?' he asked.

'How do you mean?'

'How would you investigate? The police are already asking questions.'

'Lib would be asking different questions,' said Lewis. They all looked at him. 'She's good, y'know. She helped me out of a bit of bother.'

Stewart shrugged and looked round at his fellow members. 'Can't hurt. Give it a go.'

Ron Stewart slipped to the bottom of Libby's suspect list.

'I'd be happy to ask some questions on your behalf,' she said, wishing Fran was there, 'but I'm not a professional. I'm just more likely to look at odd things than the police are.'

'I don't think it's a good idea,' said Derek Chandler in a thin voice. There was a sheen of perspiration on his upper lip. 'I think it could well work against the police investigation. We wouldn't want to impede that.'

'You've asked me questions, Libby,' said Mike. 'What did you find out?'

Libby recognised the challenge in Mike's normally peaceable face. 'Do you really want me to tell you in front of everyone?' she asked.

Surprised, Mike looked round the table. 'Well ...' he began.

'I would like to know,' said Libby, turning to Derek Chandler, 'why, after she left my house, Denise Bowling rushed round to see you before attempting suicide. Why would she do that?'

Chandler looked even more uncomfortable. 'It's none of your business.'

'Actually, it is. She had just been to see me to ask me to look into her husband's murder.' Libby crossed her fingers and didn't dare to look at Sandra. The rest of the table looked interested and slightly apprehensive. 'She became upset. So something said in my house prompted her to – to – to try and kill herself. I think that makes it my business.'

Chandler's eyes slid sideways to meet Robinson's, then across the table at Ron Stewart. 'She didn't tell me anything.'

'Did she ask you anything?' said Lewis. Chandler looked as though he'd been bitten by a butterfly.

'No.'

'Well, there,' said Libby. 'So asking me to look into your friend's death wouldn't work, would it? If no one would answer my questions. If everyone said it wasn't my business.' She stood up. 'Once again, I'm sorry about the concert. I'm even sorrier about Mr and Mrs Bowling and my own rather uncomfortable episode. I'd help if I could, but obviously it isn't a good idea.' She smiled round the table. 'I'll let you know who Sir Andrew is able to get to replace you in the programme.'

Back in the other bar, the usual suspects were gathered round their table by the fire.

'So?' asked Ben, as Libby sat down. 'Where did that get you?'

'Precisely nowhere,' said Libby, finishing the half pint of lager that Lewis had bought her and picking up the one waiting for her. 'I was surprised to see Lewis, but I think he came to support me – although how he knew I'd be there I don't know. And he's leaving the group anyway.'

'Well, you can ask him,' said Peter. 'Here he comes.'

'You stirred 'em up a bit, Lib.' Lewis sat down with a grin. 'They're arguing among themselves now. I told 'em I was leavin' and so was Edie. Very down in the dumps they are.'

'It strikes me that Derek Chandler and Dr Robinson don't really want anybody asking questions,' said Libby.

'Dead right, kid. Something funny goin' on, I reckon, although I don't think either of them would have killed Bowling, however much of a tonk he was.'

'Screwball Stewart surprised me, though. I wouldn't have thought he would welcome some member of the public asking questions. He normally keeps a really low profile, doesn't he?'

'What did he say?' asked Peter. Libby explained. 'Ah, well,

putting you off the scent I expect.'

'Well, I'd keep quiet,' said Ben. 'He's coming towards us.'

Ron Stewart stopped by the table, looming over Libby.

'If he hasn't found anybody for the concert,' he said, 'would you tell Sir Andrew I'll do a solo spot?'

Chapter Thirty-two

Everyone stared. Stewart kept his eyes on Libby's face.

'Well, I will, of course,' she said eventually. 'It's exceedingly generous of you. I – er – I don't really know what to say.'

He smiled briefly. 'Just say you'll tell him.'

Libby stood up. 'Tell you what – why don't I ring him now? It's not much after ten.'

Stewart raised an eyebrow. 'Fine.'

Libby moved away from the table and pressed buttons on her mobile. Andrew answered almost immediately.

'You're never going to believe this, Andrew, but Ron Stewart's just offered –'

'What did I tell you!' Andrew almost exploded in her ear.

'Andrew – no, listen. He offered. He's right here. Do you want to talk to him?'

There was a bubbling noise at the other end of the line, like a kettle coming to a boil.

'All right, put him on.'

'So gracious,' murmured Libby, and handed the phone to Stewart and tactfully went back to rejoin her friends.

'Did you suggest that?' she whispered to Lewis.

'No of course not. Wonder why he's done it?'

'Coming back,' muttered Ben.

Stewart handed the phone back to Libby. 'He wants to speak to you.'

'Andrew?'

'I'm sorry, Libby. I jumped to conclusions. He's offered to do an acoustic set with another member of – what's their name? His band.'

'Jonah Fludde. How very kind.'

'Yes, apparently,' Andrew coughed self-consciously, 'he's always been a fan of mine, and the charity is one he regularly contributes to, so he's prepared to do it.'

'How lovely.' Libby was aware of Stewart standing tall and silent, watching her. 'I'll talk to you about the programme and stuff in the morning, shall I?'

'Yes, and – thank you, Libby.'

'No problem.' Libby switched off her phone. 'Well, thank you, Mr Stewart. This is very generous of you. Will I be able to collect some publicity material from you at some point?'

He inclined his head. 'Tomorrow morning? Better not waste time. Come to the house. Do you know where it is?'

'Yes, thank you. I'll see you then.'

There was silence round the table as Ron Stewart walked back to the snug, said a few words, and then left the pub. Conversation broke out within both groups.

Libby told her table what Sir Andrew had told her.

'So Ron Stewart doesn't look like a suspect for Vernon Bowling's murder,' said Ben.

'Do you think he's got something to tell me, though?' asked Libby, frowning. 'After all, he suggested I should look in to the murder, and now he's invited me to his house. It's a bit odd.'

Lewis nodded. 'Certainly when you think how reclusive he is. It surprised me when he joined the group and was willing to do the concert. Even let Robinson use his name in publicity.'

'You let him use yours,' said Peter.

'Yeah, but I'm a media tart.' Lewis grinned across the table at him.

'Shall I go with you?' asked Ben.

'Do you think you should?' asked Peter. 'He's asked for Libby.'

'He could hardly object,' said Ben.

'He could,' said Lewis. 'He invited our Lib, and if he has got something to tell her, he probably won't if you – or anyone else – is there.'

'True,' said Ben, 'but I wish you weren't going on with this.'

'I know.' Libby squeezed his hand. 'But I'm very cross about having been bashed on the head, I feel guilty about Denise Bowling, and I need to find out about Mike Farthing on behalf of Cass. It's personal.'

'Will you ask Fran to go with you, then?'

'Same thing applies,' said Lewis. 'He's obviously got some – I dunno – thing about Libby. He asked her to investigate. Then when the group said no, he's found a way of getting her to see him privately. I don't think he wants anyone else around.'

'Why couldn't he just ask to see her then?' said Peter. 'Why go through all this rigmarole?'

'Because of who he is,' said Lewis. 'You ask to see someone private, like, and everyone's speculatin' like mad. This way, it's perfectly normal.'

'I suppose you're right,' said Ben. 'Still, at least we all know where you're going and when.'

'I don't think he means to attack or kidnap me,' said Libby, with a laugh. 'He wouldn't have made the arrangements in front of you all, otherwise.'

There were signs of the meeting in the snug breaking up. Mike Farthing came over to Libby's table.

'Er – I hope we weren't rude to you, Libby?'

'Not at all, Mike,' said Libby brightly. 'Actually, I might drop in on you tomorrow. I have to be out your way in the morning.'

'Really?' Mike looked nervous. 'Cass won't be there.'

'I know, but she'll be down later tomorrow, won't she?' Libby smiled, still brightly. 'See you tomorrow.'

'Now what are you playing at?' asked Ben when Mike had gone.

'Well, it makes sense, doesn't it? I shall be driving right past his nursery, so I'll pop in and see if I can't get something out of him without Cass being around.'

Lewis and Peter laughed. 'You won't stop her, you know you won't,' said Peter. 'It's a stubborn old trout.'

On Saturday morning Ben went off to fetch the Christmas trees from Cattlegreen Nursery and Libby phoned Fran to tell her what was happening.

'I can't come with you,' said Fran, 'I'm in the shop all day and it's already really busy.'

'No, that's all right,' said Libby, mightily relieved that she wasn't going to have to tell Fran she wasn't wanted. 'And I thought I'd drop in on Mike after I've seen Stewart.'

'Be careful, Libby,' warned Fran. 'Don't go doing anything stupid.'

'More stupid than getting bashed on the head? No, I won't, I promise. And everyone knows where I'm going, so if I need rescuing there'll be a posse all ready to gallop in.'

Libby took the more direct way into Bishop's Bottom, avoiding Itching and Shott. Ron Stewart's house looked more settled into its environment than Vernon Bowling's more recent structure, although it was obvious that both had been designed by the same architect, if not built by the same builders. As predicted, huge gates stood in a high brick wall halfway up a gravelled drive. Libby had to get out of the car to speak into a metal box, but before she'd said more than 'Hello', the gates began to open. She hurriedly scrambled back into the driver's seat and edged the car between them.

The drive widened out in front of the house, which was smaller than she'd thought at first. Built in the mock-Georgian style, Libby thought it would have looked more at home in an estate of upmarket executive homes, although the planting around it softened the edges. Ron Stewart stood at the top of a flight of shallow stone steps, hands behind his back.

'Hello,' said Libby breathlessly. 'Am I late?'

A sardonic eyebrow was raised. 'As we didn't specify a time, no. Come on.'

Libby followed him into a wide hall, from which a central staircase rose. Dark panelling aped an era different to the exterior of the house, and abstract art on the walls clashed with both.

'Thought you might want to see the studio,' Stewart threw over his shoulder. 'This way.'

He led the way to the back of the hall, where Libby was

surprised to find a modern lift. He grinned at her expression.

'Unexpected, isn't it? But people with a lot of gear come here. Don't want them lugging it all up those stairs.'

Libby got into the lift with him, and it rose smoothly, past an upstairs galleried landing and on to a much lighter corridor.

'Here we are. More me, if you know what I mean.' Stewart opened the door and they turned into the corridor, which led straight into a huge, light room filled with recording equipment, two vocal booths and vast mixing desks.

'Wow!' said Libby.

Stewart grinned and sat down behind one of the desks, waving to another chair. Libby sat.

'Now,' she said. 'What did you want to tell me?'

His eyebrows rose in surprise.

'I thought you wanted publicity material?'

'Of course I do,' said Libby. 'But you could have sent that over to the theatre.'

Stewart stretched his long legs out in front of him and contemplated the rips in the knees. 'Clever.'

Libby shook her head. 'Not very. You tried to get the ukulele club to ask me to look into Bowling's murder. There must be something you know that you don't want to tell the police, but you think I could help.'

He was silent for a long time, then looked up and waved a hand to indicate the studio. 'See this? He was very taken with this.'

'Yes?' prompted Libby, when he fell silent again.

'See,' he leant forward, his elbows on his knees, 'I've always smoked a bit.'

Libby, assuming he meant cannabis rather than tobacco, nodded. Went with the territory.

'So did Vern. Got into drugs when he was at that lab. We go – went – way back.'

'Did you know him at the time of the experiments?'

'Oh, yeah. They all blamed him, you know, although he was doing what the bloody government told him.'

Libby suddenly had a glimmer of sympathy for Vernon

Bowling. She hadn't thought of him as a victim, too.

'Anyway, when I had this place built he loved it, and started asking about strengthened floors and how it worked. I had no idea what he was on about, but I told him my architect designed it and knew what I wanted, so he got the name of the architect, and next thing I know is he's having a house built practically next door.' He shrugged. 'I didn't mind really, and I thought the missis might be able to be mates with Vern's wife. Course, we didn't really know her, then. We'd never, you know, gone out together. Different crowd. Vern and I used to get together, but that was about it.'

He leant back and stretched. 'I asked her to bring up some coffee, but I think she's forgotten. I'll give her a bell.' He picked up a mobile and pressed a key.

'Hello, sweets – you forgot that coffee? Oh, right.' He put the phone down. 'Coming right up.'

'So when Bowling built his house, did he tell you what he wanted to do with the converted attic?' asked Libby.

'Wasn't converted – purpose built, like this one. And no, not at first, but eventually he asked me about Mike Farthing.'

'Mike? Why?'

'Mike helped with a bit of the landscaping round here, so Vern wanted to ask him to help out at his place, too. And then he asked me if I thought Mike knew anything about plant ventilation systems. You know, for greenhouses.'

'I know.'

'So I asked him if he was setting up a nursery, or a conservatory or something. And that was when he took me up to the factory. Course, it didn't have plants in it then, but he explained it all.' Stewart shook his head. 'I told him he was mad.'

'So what happened when he asked Mike?'

'Mike must have refused to help. You know Mike, don't you? Can you see him doing anything like that? Course not.'

'He says he didn't know anything about it.'

'So he didn't even ask him. Not surprised.'

Libby thought for a moment. 'So he asked the boys in Mike's

shop instead, didn't he?'

Stewart looked surprised. 'I suppose so. How do you know?'

'The police took his computer away and shut the place down. There was something on that computer, and as Mike hardly ever uses it and all his mail order stuff is run by those two – Patrick and Gary, isn't it? – it wasn't hard to guess.'

Libby heard the lift door swish open and a woman appeared carrying a tray. Libby had expected Stewart's wife to be as much of a seventies throw-back as he was, but Maria Stewart looked like most of Libby's friends, middle-aged but not frumpy.

'Telling Libby here about Vern's house.' Stewart waved a hand in Libby's direction. Maria sat down and handed out mugs.

'Silly bugger,' she said. 'Needed his head examined. And all those others.'

'Others?' Libby looked from Maria to Stewart.

'Doctor, lawyer, merchant chief,' said Maria. 'He got them all hooked. But not on cannabis.'

Chapter Thirty-three

Libby gasped. 'Robinson? Chandler? They were users? Of what?'

Stewart shrugged his shoulders, watching her carefully. 'This and that. Course, so was I, but not on that scale. I introduced Vern to Chandler. He got me off a drugs charge a while ago, see. I didn't know what it would lead to.'

'What about the doctor?' Libby was frowning. 'And is he a doctor of medicine or what?'

'Psychology,' said Maria. 'Pity he doesn't psychoanalyse himself.' She brushed greying blonde hair out of her eyes.

'Now, sweets, we don't really know about that,' said Stewart.

'About what?' asked Libby, beginning to think she was floundering around in a completely different investigation.

'His mates all covered up for him,' said Maria, eying her husband defiantly. 'Abuse, it was.'

'Abuse?' gasped Libby.

'Now, now,' Stewart protested again. 'No one really knows.'

'All right – it was gossip. His wife –' Maria paused. 'Have you met her?'

Libby nodded.

'She goes to the same WI as I do.' She caught Libby's look of surprise and grinned. 'Didn't expect that, did you? Yeah, I belong. I know your friend Patti, too. We're ever so normal, really. Anyway, Veronica Robinson goes to the same WI as Sandra Farrow and I do. Or she did. She stopped coming because of the gossip – at least I guess that was why it was.'

'But gossip about what?'

Maria hesitated. 'Well, Ron's right, really. It is only gossip, but the word is that he used to beat Veronica up.'

'Oh, good heavens,' said Libby, her hand going to her mouth.

'But how do you know?'

'As we said, it was only gossip,' said Maria.

'It was hushed up,' said Stewart. 'The word is that he'd done it before, and his colleagues had rallied round.'

'I can't believe it! This is like a soap opera.' Libby shook her head. 'But they're still together?'

'Easy to cover things up when you can get someone to say your wife's loony tunes in his business.' Maria sat back triumphantly. 'I honestly don't know why Ron still knows them all.'

Stewart sighed. 'Performing, that's all.' He looked at Libby and grinned. 'That's why I'd like to do the concert.'

'Did Bowling know all this?'

'Yeah.' Stewart looked at his feet. 'He got to know everyone's secrets.'

Libby groaned.

'Makes it difficult, doesn't it?' said Maria. 'But we haven't told the police any of this.'

'They will already know about Robinson if his wife complained. It will be on record.'

'Not if Derek Chandler managed to get them to scrub it. And we don't know that the wife complained.' Stewart sighed and sat up. 'Now you know why I wanted you to have a look into it. One of those bastards is responsible, I'm sure, but no one will have told the police about any of this.'

'So.' Libby let out a breath. 'Are there any more skeletons in the cupboards? Any more suspects?'

'No.' Stewart shook his head slowly. 'Poor old Bob Alton, of course, but he wouldn't hurt a fly.'

'Because of his son? You know about that?'

'Oh, yes. He found out who Vern was when he saw our names on the list for the concert.' He shrugged. 'We weren't a formal group – when we met in The Poacher it was all first names.'

'What about Alan Farrow?'

'Alan?' Maria laughed. 'Driven snow! And now he's married to the lovely Sandra – he wouldn't jeopardise that.'

'So – just Robinson and Chandler?' said Libby.

'And me,' said Stewart with a grin. 'I knew about his factory and I've been done for drugs.'

'I can't see that you've got a motive, though.' Libby sighed. 'And Mike. I suppose he still has got a motive, if it was his computer used to research and buy the ventilation stuff.'

'Research, I think, not buy. So he'd kill Vern for that? Don't think so.'

'On the spur of the moment?' suggested Libby.

Maria and Stewart both shook their heads.

'Was he a ladies man? Could Denise ...?'

'No. And Denise wouldn't want to kill him. He was her source.'

'He – what? Denise, too?'

Maria nodded. 'Have you met her? All nervy, gets stressed-out, and starts yelling.'

'Oh – yes. I've seen her do that. I didn't realise.' Libby sighed again. 'So might he have found someone else – to get away from her, perhaps?'

'Did you ever see him?' asked Stewart.

'No, why?'

'Imagine Derek Chandler with ginger hair – what there was of it,' said Maria.

'Unprepossessing, then?'

'Off-putting to a degree.' Maria shuddered artistically. 'Creepy.'

'That's what I thought about Chandler,' agreed Libby. 'Well, thank you both for all this information, although I haven't got a clue what to do with it. And I can't see any reason at all for any of our suspects to have a go at me.'

'I knew about you and your investigations – so could any of the others. And you were involved with the concert,' said Stewart.

'It still doesn't makes sense,' said Libby, and stood up. 'I'll think about it. I shall have a word with Mike on my way home.'

They both took her down in the lift and saw her to the front door.

'Oh –' said Libby as she stood on the steps. 'Publicity material!'

'Oh, bugger!' said Stewart. 'Hang on.'

He disappeared in the direction of the lift and Maria laughed.

'He's getting more and more forgetful.' She moved nearer to Libby. 'And he's really nervous at the thought of performing – just so's you know. That's why he joined the uke band, to get him back into it.'

'Why – I thought Jonah Fludde still performed?'

'Occasionally at festivals, and he stays well in the background. He lost his nerve.'

'Was there a reason?'

Maria's eyes slid away from Libby's. 'Breakdown.'

'Ah.' Libby nodded and didn't know what else to say. Stewart appeared in the hall holding a brown envelope.

'I put all that together when I got in last night. Hope it helps.'

'It does, and we're all very grateful. If we hadn't already sold out this would have done it for us.'

They both waved Libby off as she drove back down the drive and through the gates.

'So that's what a superstar is like,' she said to herself.

As she drove towards Mike's nursery she found herself trying to remember something that had been said that felt important, but couldn't pin it down. But it niggled all the way towards Shott.

There were cars on the forecourt and the doors of the shop were wide open. To her surprise, Libby found Cassandra serving customers alongside a harassed-looking Mike. She stood aside and watched until they were both free and the shop was empty.

'I thought you said Cassandra wouldn't be here?' She went forward and spoke to Mike.

'I offered. Mike couldn't cope here in the shop on his own.' Cassandra was in full headmistress mode.

'Oh.' Libby looked at Mike. 'The boys. Have they been prosecuted?'

Mike looked nervously at Cassandra. 'I don't know how much you know …'

'I think I know that Vernon Bowling approached your boys, Gary and Patrick, who researched the heating and ventilating systems using your computer. That was why the police were so sure you had something to do with the factory. Is that it?'

'Yes. They took the computer.'

'I know. So how are you coping without it?'

'He's using mine.' Cassandra pointed to a laptop. 'I set him up with an email address, and he can access his old website via that. He'd written the login details down. Not really the right thing to do, but useful, in this case. We're coping.'

'Have they arrested Gary and Patrick?'

'I think so.'

Libby made an exasperated noise. 'Don't you know?'

'No.' Mike looked at Cassandra again. Libby could see that this was going to be the pattern of their relationship from now on.

'So that was it, was it?' said Libby. 'That was why they were turning you over? It wasn't drugs?'

'Of course it wasn't,' snapped Cassandra.

'But in a way it was, wasn't it?' said Mike, suddenly. 'They thought I'd been researching the systems for Vernon. They thought I was into drugs.'

'Well,' said Libby, narrowing her eyes at him, 'so many people are, aren't they?'

'I suppose they are,' said Mike gloomily. 'I'm sure there wasn't as much drug-taking when I was young.'

Cassandra was also watching him. 'I don't think she meant that, Mike.'

'Eh?' He looked startled.

'I think Libby meant so many of your friends.'

'My friends? Who do you mean?'

'Eric Robinson and Derek Chandler for two.'

Mike looked stunned. He really didn't know, thought Libby.

'Eric ... and Derek? Drugs?'

'Ron Stewart told me all about it. And Denise Bowling, of course.'

Mike looked as though he was going to faint.

'Do the police know this?' asked Cassandra.

'I've no idea. And if they do, they will be looking into it all very carefully.' Libby sat down on the only chair in the shop. 'And none of them could have a motive for attacking me.'

'There's an obvious reason for attacking you,' said Cassandra, looking down her aristocratic nose.

'Oh, yes?'

'You're nosy.'

'That's a bit harsh,' said Mike nervously. 'She's not nosy, exactly, she's – um –'

'Nosy,' Libby finished for him. 'I know I am, but I'm known for getting most things right. The only problem here is that nobody from the uke group knew me.'

'A lot of them saw you at that meeting in the theatre,' said Cassandra.

'But they didn't know I would be looking into the murder. And they didn't know where I lived, or that I would be out and about that afternoon.'

'Easy enough to find out where you lived,' said Cassandra. 'Somebody would only have to ask in the village shop. And a lot of people in the area would have seen you in the local newspaper – or even on the local TV news programme. You and a murder equals investigation.'

'So whoever did it jumped to conclusions?'

Cassandra shrugged. 'Looks like it.'

Libby scowled at her feet and decided not to mention the allegation of abuse against Dr Robinson, although she couldn't help asking, 'How well do you know Robinson?'

'I've told you before, not well at all. I didn't know any of them well. I joined because I didn't go out much and it was a way to meet people.' Mike smiled. 'And I found I enjoyed it.'

'You never met his wife?'

'Never. I didn't even know he had one.'

'Right.' Libby stood up. 'I'll get going then. I've got one more call to make before I go home.'

Cassandra looked a question, but didn't press it. Mike merely looked relieved.

The final visit, Libby had decided on the spur of the moment, was to Alan and Sandra Farrow. She pulled out her mobile before getting in to the car.

'Yes, we're in,' said Sandra, sounding surprised. 'I'll put the kettle on.'

Providence Row was another tiny cobbled lane leading off the main street in Itching. The Farrows' house was halfway up, a flint cottage under a slate roof. A smart red front door sported a holly and fir Christmas wreath.

'Come in.' Sandra led the way directly into a long room with gentleman's-club furniture. Out of French windows at the other end, Libby could see a frosty garden.

'Let's go into the kitchen. It's warmer there, we haven't lit the fire in the sitting room yet.'

The kitchen, very new and glossy, also looked out on the garden, where Libby could see Alan Farrow pottering in the doorway of a small shed. Sandra knocked on the window, he turned and waved.

'So was there something you wanted to ask me?' said Sandra, pouring tea from a knitted-cosied teapot very much at odds with the new kitchen.

'Well, sort of,' said Libby, accepting a cup. 'You know you said you were friends with Denise through darts and – didn't you say she was lonely?'

'I thought she was, yes.'

'You never suspected she might be on drugs, then?'

Sandra almost dropped her cup. '*Drugs*?'

'Apparently.' Libby was watching closely. 'No indications?'

Sandra sat back in her chair shaking her head. 'None. Mind you, I wouldn't know what I was looking for. What was it? The cannabis?'

'And worse, I gather,' said Libby. 'I'm afraid she *did* know about the factory after all. But she never let on to you?'

'Never. I can't believe it. Yes, she was a bit – well – nervy. Highly strung. But I suppose that was the drugs.'

'Mmm.' Libby was silent for a moment. 'Do you happen to know how she is? Is she home?'

'No, she's been – ah – detained. Psychiatric ward. So sad.' Sandra indeed looked on the point of bursting into tears. Luckily, Alan emerged through the back door rubbing his hands.

'Tea?' he said, beaming at the two women. 'Capital.' He shrugged off an old tweed coat and sat down next to his wife.

'Alan,' she said, turning to him. 'Denise was on drugs.'

Alan Farrow looked at her for a long minute. 'I know.'

'You knew?' gasped Sandra.

Alan turned to Libby. 'When they first moved here I met Vernon in The Poacher and we got chatting. We met a few times, and one evening Denise came in. She was in such a state.' He shook his head. 'Vernon hustled her out. Eric Robinson was there, too. He said "Drugs, poor woman". I supposed he knew. Being a doctor.'

'But he's a psychologist' said Libby. 'Not an ordinary doctor.'

'All the more reason for him to know, surely?' said Alan.

'I suppose so.' Libby pinched her lip. 'Well, I'm no nearer knowing who hit me over the head or murdered Vernon Bowling, assuming it was the same person.'

'Are you sure it is the same person?' asked Sandra. 'And one of the ukulele group?'

'That seems to be the way the police investigation is going,' said Libby. She swallowed the rest of her tea. 'I'd better get going. I've been out all morning and I've got to get this publicity stuff off to Sir Andrew.'

'So Ron Stewart's really going to do a spot at the concert?' said Alan.

'Yes, he really is.' Libby smiled. 'As long as he doesn't get arrested before then.'

'Arrested?' Sandra looked horrified. 'Oh, no! You don't mean ...?'

'I was making a joke, albeit in rather bad taste,' Libby explained. 'Sorry, Sandra.'

Libby drove back home to Steeple Martin thinking over her three visits. She'd got rather more information than she'd bargained for, but none of it seemed to give anyone a motive for the murder of Vernon Bowling. All the secrets that he might have known about were also known by other people, so there was no reason to try and silence him. So why him? There must be another reason buried somewhere in his life. And if there was, surely the police would find it. They would be going through every aspect of that life, financial, personal, public and private.

She thought about his connection to Dellington. At first, that had seemed to be the obvious motive, as a reprisal for the death of a relation or loved one, and that could mean anyone, anywhere. She supposed the police would have traced descendants or relatives of all the victims of the experiments, and for all she knew they already had someone they were keeping an eye on – had even perhaps arrested. Detective Chief Inspector Connell sadly didn't tell her everything.

She reached the crossroads at Steeple Martin and drove across and into Allhallow's Lane. Before she could continue to number seventeen, a familiar figure in a red coat riding a mobility scooter screeched to a halt in front of her. Libby stood on the brakes.

Chapter Thirty-four

'The police are still hanging around my house.' Monica Turner thrust her face up to Libby's window. 'Why?'

'It's not your house,' said Libby wearily. 'They're still looking at the churchyard.'

'Why are they in the Close, then?'

'Because that's the way in, of course.' Libby glared back and Monica Turner waved her umbrella.

'Don't you take that tone with me!' she yelled, spittle forming at the corners of her badly lipsticked mouth.

'And *you* don't take that tone with me,' countered Libby. 'Who do you think you are?'

'Your better and elder, that's who!' The other woman was panting now, and Libby was getting worried about her.

'Look,' she said more consolingly, 'they'll be making an arrest soon, then they'll be gone. I dare say it's annoying, but you want them to catch the murderer, don't you?'

Monica Turner just stared at her, and Libby began to get worried. To her relief, Bethany Cole suddenly appeared from her blue gate.

'Mrs Turner,' she said approaching the red-coated fury. 'I think you're blocking Mrs Sarjeant's way. Can I help at all?'

'No.' Monica Turner swung her scooter sideways, banging Libby's bumper and nearly running Bethany over. 'Mind your own business.'

Libby got out of the car and watched the scooter bumping along the high street towards Maltby Close.

'Thanks, Bethany. I didn't know quite what to do. Glad she didn't run you over. Her eyesight's so bad.'

Bethany shook her head sadly. 'I know. I can't help being quite glad that she doesn't come to my church.'

'She's what used to be a typical female churchgoer years ago, isn't she?'

Bethany nodded. 'The sort who would be in love with the vicar.' She giggled. 'I was always sorry for those vicars. Well, if you're sure you're all right, I'll go pottering on my vicarly way.'

'Yes, I'm fine, Bethany. Thanks for coming to my rescue.'

Ben had lit the fire and was sitting on the sofa reading, Sidney curled up on his lap.

'You were a long time,' he said. 'Do you want tea?'

'Don't get up,' said Libby taking off her latest cape. 'No, I've just had one with Sandra Farrow. And coffee with the Stewarts. Is it past lunchtime?'

'There's some soup on the Rayburn. I've had mine.'

Libby fetched herself a bowl of soup on a tray, then regaled Ben with the results of her morning's interviews.

'So there are lot more unsavoury characters than just Vernon Bowling and Derek Chandler,' said Libby, and stopped, her spoon halfway to her mouth.

'What?' said Ben. 'What have you thought of?'

'Something the Stewarts said. They said Bowling was like Chandler only with red hair. What he had of it, they said. So – what if it was the wrong victim? Like in Othello, you know. "Murder's out of tune", when Cassio isn't killed.'

'That's a bit far-fetched, isn't it? The whole group had been together. Nobody would have mistaken one for the other.'

'But what if it wasn't a member of the group? I was thinking that on the way home. Perhaps the police have found something we don't know about? And Chandler had more reasons for people to murder him, didn't he? Trying to diddle people out of money?'

'But I thought after Flo blew the whistle they got their money back?'

'That's true.' Libby put down her spoon. 'Bother. But has it occurred to you to wonder why he's still practising?'

'I thought someone said he was actually cleared?'

'Oh, so they did. Bother again.' She finished her soup. 'The thing I was actually thinking about on the way home was that

258

the police have probably found other leads in Bowling's life, not just the cannabis factory and the ukulele group.'

'I should imagine the uke group was a very small part of his operation,' said Ben.

'Yes,' agreed Libby gloomily. 'He probably had contacts all over the place. It started at Dellington, I suppose. Experimenting with all those drugs. Oh, and it wasn't just cannabis.'

'And he was probably part of a much wider organisation.' Ben stood up. 'Time to give it up, I think, don't you?'

'If I could forget that a member of this bloody drugs cartel bashed me over the head, yes.'

'Which does seem a bit amateurish,' said Ben. 'You'd expect professional drugs barons to be a bit more sophisticated.'

'Yes, but it could be someone much lower down. Ron Stewart said if he'd heard of me, so could anyone who lives in the area – someone whom Bowling supplied. Yes – that's it!' said Libby excitedly, spilling some soup. 'One of his customers got into an argument with him – perhaps couldn't pay him – killed him and then thought I'd find out.'

'It works,' said Ben. 'It works better than anything else.'

'In which case, I expect Ian or someone has thought of it and they're chasing down any customers they can find.'

'I don't suppose he actually left customer records,' said Ben, amused.

'No,' sighed Libby. 'Oh, well, perhaps Ian will let us know at some point.'

'I doubt it, unless they can prove someone hit you on the head,' said Ben. 'Now. Would you like to go to Hal's tonight? He called and said he'd had a cancellation.'

'Oh, yes, please. Although that's not really fair, is it? I bet he had a waiting list.'

'Don't look a gift horse in the mouth,' said Ben. 'Now you'd better ring your mate and tell her about your morning.'

Fran was interested but distracted.

'I'm sorry, Lib, it's frantic in here. Give me a ring tomorrow.'

'Never mind,' said Ben. 'Look, how about doing the tree?

And we can do Mum's tomorrow when we go up for lunch.'

As usual, Sidney was keen to help decorate the tree, which stood on the table in the sitting-room window. Outside, ice began to form in the ruts of the lane and darkness crept in. Behind them, the fire burned and there was the occasional comforting sound of settling ash.

'Nice,' said Libby eventually, standing back. 'Very traditional.'

Ben put his arm round her. 'And normal. Now let's have a cup of tea and put our feet up.'

Harry's table was free at nine o'clock. When Libby and Ben arrived, Peter was already seated at the big table in the window with a bottle of wine. He beamed and gestured to the other chairs.

'I didn't expect the best table,' said Libby, taking off her cape.

'I expect he moved someone,' said Ben, as Adam came up to take coats. 'Hi, Ad.'

Adam gave his mother a kiss. 'He's even done you your Pollo Verde. He cooked in the kitchen of the flat.'

The Pink Geranium was a vegetarian restaurant, so Harry had to keep separate cooking utensils if he was cooking Libby her favourite dish.

'Serve him right if I hadn't wanted it,' she said with a grin. 'Anyone want nachos first?'

They were well into the first bottle of red wine when Libby's phone began to ring.

'I'll switch it off,' she said, fishing it out of her bag. 'Oh, no, I must take it. It's Ian.'

'Where are you,' he asked, 'and what have you been doing to poor pensioners?'

'Eh? Pensioners? What are you talking about?'

'A Mrs Monica Turner. She called the station and insisted on speaking to me – making a complaint about you. That's why she was actually put through to me.'

'A complaint? About me?' Libby's voice rose and Peter and Ben flapped hands at her. She stood up and went out of the door.

'Honestly, Ian, that's rich. You ask Bethany Cole. Monica Turner is lethal on that mobility scooter – she practically caused a crash today.' She told him what had happened. 'So why was she complaining about me?'

Ian sounded amused. 'Apparently you're to blame for all the disturbance in the village, including the murder.'

'I know – she told me that, too. Honestly, Ian, the woman's batty. Oh – and we're in the caff. Harry had a cancellation.'

'Oh,' said Ian, now sounding wistful.

'Have you finished at work? Why don't you come and join us? It is on the way home, isn't it? We'll wait for our main courses until you get here.'

'I don't think I should be eating with such rogues and vagabonds,' said Ian, 'but it sounds too good to miss. See you in twenty minutes.'

Libby returned to the table looking smug. 'He's joining us,' she said.

'Don't pump him,' said Ben.

'Poor bloke,' said Peter.

Another bottle of wine had already made its way on to the table by the time Ian arrived.

'Do you realise we only ever see you in a suit?' said Libby as he sat down. 'Do you ever wear anything else?'

'When I'm off duty.' Ian cocked an eye at her. 'And I'm never off duty when I'm with you.'

Libby pulled down the corners of her mouth. 'That makes me sound like a suspect.'

'What you get up to is often suspect,' countered Ian.

'Stop bickering, you two,' said Peter. 'Will you have just one glass of wine, Ian?'

Ian laughed. 'Yes, please. Then I'll stick to water. Are you waiting for me?'

'Yes!' said Harry appearing at the table. 'So get on with it.'

'Charm itself,' said Ian, grinning up at him. 'Quesadillas de hongo, please.'

'So is there anything you can tell us?' asked Libby when Harry had gone and Ian's glass was filled.

'Not much. Have you got anything to tell me?'

Libby looked at Ben and Peter. 'Might have. But I expect you know it all anyway.'

Ian sighed. 'What have you been doing?'

'Andrew took me with him to see Dr Robinson yesterday – as a sort of apology. then they met in the pub last night to discuss it – the uke group, I mean – and I met them there. And Ron Stewart asked me to look into the murder.'

'He what?'

Libby nodded. 'And then the others said they thought not. So Stewart offered to do a solo spot in the concert –'

'Whoa, steady. I'm not following this. Apology for what?'

'Andrew's dropped them from the concert. Under the circumstances.'

'Very sensible,' said Ian. 'And you say Stewart's offered to go on instead?'

'More or less. But really he wanted to talk to me. So I went to see him this morning.'

'Really.' Ian looked sceptical. 'More than he did with me.'

'Well, yes. That's why he wanted … well, he told me quite a lot of things. But I expect you know all about them.'

'Try me.'

'Denise,' said Libby. 'You know about her?'

'Ye-es,' said Ian cautiously. 'What do you know about her?'

'She knew about the factory and is a drug user.'

'Yes, we knew that. Even if we hadn't already suspected it, the minute she was taken to hospital it was confirmed.

'Oh.' Libby looked at the table, unsure whether she should go on.

'Did Stewart talk about any of his fellow members of the group?' Ian prompted gently.

'Yes.'

'Well, I expect we *do* know, but tell me anyway.'

'Derek Chandler and Eric Robinson.'

'Robinson?' Ian's eyebrows rose. 'Now, we hadn't heard that.'

'There was something else, too.' Libby had grown pink. She

wasn't actually enjoying this.

'Go on.'

'Libby,' Ben broke in, 'I don't think this is quite the right time and place for this. Can't it wait until after we've eaten?'

Ian smiled apologetically. 'My fault, sorry, Ben. No more – er – shop.'

Libby was unnaturally quiet throughout the meal, until her three friends took pity on her. The restaurant was emptying now, and Ben suggested they move to the sofa and chairs in the other window. Adam brought coffee and went off to commune with the PhD student, and Harry joined them, still in his checkered chef's trousers.

'This is to go no further,' said Ian, 'whatever it is Libby's heard. So what was it, Libby?'

'Gossip. The Stewarts heard that Robinson had been accused of – um – abuse. By his wife. They heard that his colleagues had covered up for him in a previous incident, and that Chandler got the new accusation hushed up.'

'Domestic abuse? The police don't always get involved,' said Ian.

'They did say it was only gossip,' said Libby, 'but Maria Stewart and Sandra Farrow went to the same WI as Veronica Robinson, and then Veronica stopped going.'

'But we interviewed Robinson and his wife together,' said Ian, frowning. 'Why is she still there if this is true?'

Libby shrugged. 'In the same way that all beaten wives stay with their husbands?'

'Possibly.' Ian picked up his coffee cup. 'Any other bombshells to drop?'

'Chandler and Robinson were users,' said Libby, eyeing him warily. 'And it was more than cannabis.'

'Robinson, too?' Ian sighed. 'Stewart told you all this?'

'Yes, because he was one too, and he said Vernon knew all the secrets.'

'They all had a hold over each other. No wonder one of them killed him.'

'Do you think that's it, then?' said Ben.

'Looks like it,' said Ian. 'But there are other avenues of inquiry.'

'People not in the ukulele group?' said Libby. 'Relatives of the Dellington victims?'

Ian smiled. 'You know I can't tell you anything, Libby.'

'Could you tell us about the murder weapon? Seeing that it might be the same thing that hit me?'

Ian shrugged. 'I would if I could, but we can only guess. There was a piece of decorative stone obviously missing from one of the graves, and traces were – er found.'

'In the wound?' said Libby. 'So it was opportunistic, then.'

'That's complete speculation, Libby.'

'But quite valid,' said Libby. 'Nothing else you can tell us?'

'You know I can't. I only let you in on what you already know about.'

'And get help from me!' said Libby huffily.

They all laughed.

'Poor old trout,' said Harry. 'Have a brandy.'

Chapter Thirty-five

'All the same,' said Libby, as she and Ben walked home, 'I was surprised that Ian didn't seem to know about Robinson.'

'He knew about Chandler being a user, though,' said Ben. 'When you told him, he said "Robinson, too," so he must have known about Chandler.'

'They'll find evidence, won't they? DNA or something. I expect they weren't looking before. And bother! I forgot to ask about Gary and Patrick.'

'Who?'

'The boys who worked for Mike and got Vernon Bowling's heating and ventilation system for him. At least, I think they got it. They researched it, anyway.'

'Ah. And as for DNA, I expect they're still waiting for results. It takes a long time, doesn't it?'

'But it's three weeks since the murder! That's ages. And the other thing I wanted to ask was did Bowling and Chandler look alike.'

Ben looked amused. 'You know, I don't think Cassio and Roderigo looked alike in Othello.'

'Oh, you know what I meant – the wrong man was murdered.'

'In Othello's eyes, yes.'

'I wonder if there's anything in that?' mused Libby. 'If someone was paid to kill Chandler and got Bowling by mistake?'

'I know it's possible, but it's rather far fetched, isn't it?'

'You don't know it wasn't like that!' Libby was indignant. 'He was mixed up in drugs. It could have been someone from that world. Easily.'

'All right, of course it could.' Ben hugged her. 'Now let's get

265

home and have a nice cup of cocoa.'

Libby dug him in the ribs.

On Sunday morning Libby rang Fran and filled her in on everything that had happened the previous day.

'There's something very wrong about all this,' said Fran when she'd finished.

'What do you mean, wrong? Of course it's wrong! It's murder.'

'No. It just feels wrong.'

'Are you having a moment?' asked Libby after a pause.

'I think I might be,' said Fran, 'which is good in a way, because I'm out of practice.'

'So what can you see?'

'Nothing. It's just a knowing. I've told you before, I seem to know things as fact without any basis for them. And this feels wrong.'

'But wrong in what way?' asked Libby, exasperated. 'The wrong man? The wrong murder? What?'

'All of that. Almost as though we – or the police – should be investigating something entirely different.'

'Well, that will please Ian,' said Libby. 'He was going off to look into the Robinson case today, although I still think it was odd that he didn't know about it before.'

'If there was no formal complaint it wouldn't appear in the files,' said Fran, 'and Chandler could easily have had someone in his pocket in the force, couldn't he?'

'Another user, perhaps? Oh, dear, now we're building fantasy clouds again, as Ben would say.'

'Speaking of Ben, are you off to Hetty's for lunch?'

'Of course. She'd be devastated if we didn't go. Why?'

'I wondered if Flo and Lenny were going?'

'No idea. They do sometimes, but again – why?'

'I –' Fran stopped. 'Do you know, I've no idea either.'

'You *are* having a moment. Or several.' Libby did a bounce of excitement. 'This hasn't happened for ages. What do you think it means?'

'I don't know.' Libby could almost see Fran shaking her head in confusion. 'It might not mean anything.'

'How about Maltby Close? That leads up to the church, the hall and the churchyard and the police concentrated on the residents when they first discovered the murder. Could that be it?'

'It could, I suppose.' Fran paused. 'No, nothing. Look, I've got to go. We're busy in the shop again.'

'OK. Let me know if you think of anything else.' Libby switched off her phone and moved restlessly to the window. Outside, the sky was an unremitting grey, but the ice in the ruts had melted. She switched on the tree lights and sighed deeply.

'What's the matter?' asked Ben, appearing from the kitchen.

'I don't really know. Fran has just been having a moment and I can't think what it means.' She recapped the conversation for Ben and looked at him hopefully.

'Don't ask me,' he said, sitting down in front of the fireplace and rustling the Sunday newspaper. 'I don't understand Fran's moments at the best of times.'

'Oh, come on,' said Libby, 'you were the one who introduced us. When she was working for Goodall and Smythe – not to mention you.'

'I know, but it doesn't mean to say I understand them. You're better at interpreting than I am.'

'I think that's simply wish fulfilment or something,' said Libby with a sigh. 'Occasionally they provide a hint, and my imagination does the rest.'

'Except for the occasions where she has actually saved someone's life,' said Ben. 'Go on, go away and fidget at it, but don't be late for lunch.'

Libby stood still in the middle of the sitting room. 'Indecision,' she said. 'I don't know what to do.'

'You could, of course, leave it alone. Ian's looking into whatever leads you gave him yesterday, so he's bound to turn something up soon.'

'But Fran says he's looking in the wrong direction.'

'Fran's not infallible.'

'No.' Libby made up her mind. 'I'm going to see Flo. Maybe she can help.'

'They're coming to Hetty's for lunch.'

'Why didn't you tell me earlier?'

'Why? What does it matter?'

'Oh, nothing.' Libby made for the door, picking up her cape on the way. 'I'll be back to wash and brush up before lunch.'

From the frostiness of yesterday, the day was now unseasonably warm. The high street was quiet, the only shop with lights on the eight-til-late, with the large, colourful pantomime poster prominently displayed in the window. Libby paused to smile at it before crossing the road to Maltby Close.

The sound of singing floated towards her, and she realised Matins was about halfway through. That meant, thankfully, that Monica Turner would be somewhere in Canterbury attending her church.

'Hello, gal.' Flo looked surprised to see her visitor. 'We're seein' you later, aren't we?'

'Yes, I know, Flo, but you see ...' Libby trailed off. 'Oh, hello, Lenny.'

Lenny twinkled at her. 'Come in, love. You're lookin' a bit put about.'

'I am,' said Libby. The room, as usual, was over-warm, so she shed her cape and took the chair offered by Flo. 'I mean ... you know Fran has her – um – moments?'

Flo looked at her shrewdly. 'Yes. Never been sure if I believe in 'em, but there've been times, haven't there?'

'Oh, yes,' said Libby, 'there've been times. Well she's had one about this murder. At least, we think it's about the murder.'

'And where do we come into it?' asked Flo.

'That's exactly it, Flo. I've no idea. She started off by telling me it was all wrong. That Ian was more-or-less looking in the wrong direction. And you came into her head.'

Lenny looked shocked. 'Well, we didn't do 'im in, gal!'

'No, of course you didn't, but why did you come into her head? You hadn't got anything to do with it.'

'Course we do,' said Flo, lighting a cigarette and squinting against the smoke.

'Eh?' said Libby and Lenny together.

'That Chandler. Him who tried to diddle me. And says 'e didn't.'

'Oh.' Enlightened, Libby heaved a sigh of relief. 'Of course. So do you think it means Chandler killed Bowling?'

'Don't ask me, gal. But it do provide a link, don't it?'

'It certainly does. I just wish Fran's moments were a bit clearer.'

'I 'spect she gets pictures and they remind her of things – you know, without her realisin'.'

'Sub-consciously.' Libby nodded. 'Yes, you're probably right. Well, now we've solved that, I'll go back to Ben. He's fussing.'

'What about – you? Gettin' involved. Well, 'e won't stop you now, will he? Go on, then, see you later.'

Libby retrieved her cape and set off back down Maltby Close. Some of the windows displayed fairy lights, some miniature Christmas trees, others the ubiquitous spray-on snow. She was obscurely comforted by this, the evidence that those who could be said to be in their declining years (although there was nothing declining about Flo and Lenny) were still decorating their homes for, and enjoying, Christmas.

A car swept round the corner and had to brake sharply. Without looking, Libby knew this was Monica Turner, back from church in Canterbury. Sure enough the lady, still in her red coat, glared at her through the windscreen. Beside her sat mousy Vi Little, hanging on to the door handle for dear life.

Libby smiled sweetly and looked over her shoulder as she heard the heavy church doors opening.

'This should be interesting,' she said out loud, as Monica Turner turned her attention to driving her car straight at the congregation emerging from the church. They all stood still, mouths agape, until at the last moment she wrenched the wheel round and drove round to the back of the Close and the residents' car park.

Bethany saw Libby watching and waved. Libby wandered

over, exchanging greetings with a few of the members of the congregation.

'She often does that,' said Bethany, still in her cassock and purple stole of Advent. 'One day she'll lose control and mow us all down.' She looked Libby up and down. 'How are you now?'

'I'm fine. I'd just like to know who did it.'

'The murder and you, I suppose.'

'I think so. The police think it's the same person, but I don't see why.'

'I'm sure they have their reasons. And what about your psychic friend? Hasn't she any ideas?'

A tall dark man with a goatee came up behind Bethany and tweaked her thick blonde plait. She turned and smiled at him.

'This is my husband John, Libby. John, this is Libby Sarjeant.'

'Oh, the lady who got knocked on the head. How are you now?' He shook Libby's hand.

'Very well, thank you. I must go. It's Sunday, and that means lunch at the Manor.' She smiled at them both and turned to go.

'I hope you find some answers,' said Bethany quietly. 'I'm sure you don't believe in it, but I'll pray for you.'

Libby reflected on this as she once again made her way down Maltby Close. Were Fran's psychic moments and Bethany's prayers going to help her find answers? And would it matter if she didn't? The police would, eventually, and meanwhile there was real life to be getting on with, a pantomime to produce and Christmas to be got through.

Her thoughts turned to Denise Bowling. This was one Christmas she wouldn't forget, poor thing. Cooped up in hospital, refused help by her husband's friends – she stopped short. That was it. Denise had gone to Derek Chandler for help that evening and he had refused. And why had Denise gone to him in the first place? Protection? Which he wouldn't provide? So she'd gone home, and … She started walking again. Why had Derek Chandler refused to help?

'Obvious,' she said out loud. 'He didn't want to get involved with the police. Because he was a drug user.'

But that wasn't enough. He'd been a drug user long before this and, as a solicitor, he must have been involved with the police regularly, not to mention when the accusations were made against him by Flo, so it must be something else. Which was, of course – murder!

She hurried back down the high street and up Allhallow's Lane.

'I've got it!' She burst through the door; Sidney leapt off Ben's lap and hid under the table.

'Got what?' Ben put down the paper and Libby explained.

'It's possible,' he said, 'but why?'

'Bowling threatened him? About the old lady scam. Remember, Denise heard her husband being threatened over the phone.'

'Did you tell me that bit?'

'Oh, it doesn't matter – she did. And that must have been him.'

'Tenuous.'

'All right,' said Libby exasperated, and plonked herself down on the pouffe.

'Also, Chandler would be cutting off his source of supply, if Bowling *was* the source.'

'It would make more sense if Chandler had been murdered,' said Ben, returning to the paper. 'Are you going to go upstairs before we go to Hetty's?'

Libby trailed thoughtfully up the stairs contemplating this notion. Yes, it would make more sense, but there were still problems. And the same problems applied whoever was the victim. Unless the murderer was a member of the ukulele group, how would they know that Bowling or Chandler were going to be in Steeple Martin that night?

Of course, thought Libby, as she changed into suitable clothes for lunching at the Manor, there had been a good deal of local publicity about the Christmas concert and the fact that the group were taking part, including, if she remembered rightly, many of their names. So people could have known. But no one but a member of the group would have seen Bowling go into the churchyard – or, indeed – persuaded him to go.

She made an exasperated sound and struggled to get a brush through her hair. It really was time she let this go.

Libby and Ben walked back along the high street towards the Manor drive. Suddenly, Libby was aware of a familiar sound behind her – part hiss, part hum. She turned round and confronted Monica Turner in her mobility scooter.

'Hello again, Monica,' she said pleasantly. 'Tell me, just why did you hit me over the head?'

Chapter Thirty-six

Libby was aware of Ben cautiously moving round behind Monica, who continued to stare at Libby without saying a word. Libby noticed, however, that she was shaking.

'You see,' she continued, 'when I heard your scooter behind me, I suddenly remembered hearing it that night, just before I blacked out. So I knew it was you. Why?'

Monica shivered. 'Your fault,' she muttered, her hands closing on the controls of the scooter. Ben sneaked an arm in and switched it off, miming a phone call as he did so.

'What was my fault? The ukulele group?'

'Those people. The noise. The disruption.'

'There was hardly any noise, I heard them. And they never went on after nine thirty – ten at the latest. So you were angry because they were there? And so why,' said Libby, taking a deep breath and crossing her fingers, while watching Ben make a thumbs-up sign, 'did you kill Vernon Bowling?'

This time, Monica jerked into life. 'I didn't!' she howled. With lightning speed, she switched on the scooter and swung it violently to the left, where it careered into the middle of the high street – and Flo and Lenny.

Surprisingly, Flo managed to leap aside, while Lenny got caught on the hip and went sprawling on the ground. Ben leapt for the scooter, which was now coming back towards him, and grabbed the controls, while Libby, Ali, and Ahmed from the eight-til-late and their customers all hurried to the aide of Flo and Lenny. Flo was swearing.

'You go to Ben, gal,' she said, when she caught her breath. 'I always knew the old girl was barmy, but … go on. I'll get someone to take us to Hetty's. Police'll be on their way, won't they?' she looked quizzically at Libby's white face. 'Yes. Off you go.'

Libby arrived to where Ben was holding the controls of the scooter, while Monica Turner sat slumped inside.

'She hasn't said a word.' Ben shook his head. 'Ian's sending a car.'

Almost as he spoke, a sleek black car drew up alongside them. To Libby's surprise and relief Sergeant Maiden – or was it Inspector Maiden now? – got out and smiled.

'We'll take over, Mrs Sarjeant,' he said. 'Good afternoon, sir.'

'Do you know ...?' asked Libby.

'Mr Wilde explained, ma'am. I believe DCI Connell will be in touch very shortly.'

Libby and Ben stepped back as Maiden and a plain-clothes female police officer gently manhandled Monica Turner into the back of the unmarked police car.

'What happened?' A breathless Bethany Cole appeared at her side.

'I'm not sure,' said Libby, feeling weak and a little inclined to cry. Ben put his arm round her.

'I really think we'd be better going up to my mother's now,' he said smiling at Bethany. 'I just need to see how the other walking wounded are.'

But Flo and Lenny had been loaded into the doctor's car, they discovered; the doctor having seen the whole thing from the front window and were being driven to Accident and Emergency in Canterbury.

'Best thing, I suppose,' said Libby, after they thanked the assembled Steeple Martin residents. 'Hips are no joke at Lenny's age.'

Hetty took her reduced lunch party philosophically. 'They can have it cold termorrer, unless they get back here this afternoon,' she said. 'But they'll want to keep 'im in at 'is age, the old fool.'

'It wasn't Lenny's fault,' said Libby. 'If anything it was mine.' And she burst into tears.

Hetty and Ben were still mopping her up when Ian walked

into the kitchen and surveyed the scene with surprise.

'I know,' said Libby with a sniff. 'Not like me.'

Hetty supplied large glasses of Mouton Cadet, plus a small one for Ian, and put the meat and vegetables back into the warming oven.

'Tell me what happened,' Ian asked, so Libby did.

'And she said she didn't kill Bowling. As if she really meant it. But why did she hit me, then? She said it was my fault.'

'In her head, it is,' said Ian. 'Apparently, once she'd got over the shock in the police car, she began talking. That nice DC Spinner had the nous to put her on speakerphone and get through to me. The whole office heard it and it's been recorded. So I came straight here.'

'So what was it all about?' asked Ben. 'Why did she attack Lib? And why did she kill Bowling?'

'She didn't. In her head she was killing Derek Chandler.'

Libby let out a deep sigh. 'See? Othello after all.'

'What?' Ian looked confused.

'Wrong man,' said Hetty surprisingly. 'Roderigo instead of Cassio.'

Libby and Ben smiled.

'So what does she say happened?' asked Libby. 'I suppose she knew Chandler was a member of the uke group?'

'Yes. And she *had* been swindled out of her savings by him, although she wouldn't admit it.'

'Why didn't she get them back? Flo and Vi got theirs,' said Libby.

'Because she was too proud to admit she'd been taken in. And when she saw Bowling go round to the back of the churchyard she thought it was Chandler, whom she'd only ever seen briefly. She used to watch them every week.'

'Behind the net curtains,' said Ben.

'Exactly. Anyway, according to her, she followed Bowling – or Chandler – to the churchyard and began berating him about her money. And probably demanding it back. From what we could gather, of course, Bowling was saying he didn't know what she was talking about and she lost it. Much as she lost it today. Then she found out it wasn't Chandler after all, and for some reason blamed you for it. You were the reason the group had come to the village, therefore it was all your fault. She rather degenerated into a lot of biblical ramblings at that point.'

'Oh, dear,' said Libby. 'She won't – um – she won't –'

'Go to trial? I shouldn't think so. I expect the doctors will find her unfit to plead, especially at her age.'

'What I still don't understand,' said Ben, 'is why Bowling went into the churchyard in the first place.'

'This is the biggest irony of all,' said Ian with a sigh. 'Bob Alton's son is buried there, and Bowling used to go and pay his respects. Robinson told us that when we asked if any of them knew why he would be in the churchyard. I don't suppose he ever got over those deaths at Dellington.'

''I remember now – Fran said he came from Steeple Martin. Did Bob Alton know Bowling used to visit the grave?' asked Libby.

'I don't think so.'

'No.' Hetty shook her head. 'He would've been angry about that. He hated Bowling.'

Libby, Ben and Ian looked at her in surprise.

'Edie's had 'im over fer tea. I met 'im there. Nice bloke.'

Ian left shortly afterwards, Ben, Hetty and Libby ate their delayed lunch, although Libby for once didn't have much of an appetite, then Libby called Fran.

'Hey listen. The murder. It was "Murder's Out Of Tune" after all.'

It was Monday evening before Ian was free to give his now familiar round-up and explain some of the things that still puzzled Libby. Hetty magnanimously allowed the gathering to take place at the Manor, and Ben wheeled Lenny in his borrowed wheelchair up the Manor drive. His injury hadn't been as bad as at first feared, and he was rather enjoying his new invalid status. Fran and Guy drove over from Nethergate and Edie and Lewis from Creekmarsh. Ian arrived as Ben and Libby were dispensing drinks.

'You know this is very irregular,' he said accepting a mug of coffee from Hetty.

'Oh, come on,' said Harry, lounging with his feet almost in the fireplace. 'You know you do it every time.'

'First of all,' said Libby, 'I want to know what it was Denise Bowling wanted from me, and who it was she heard threatening her husband.'

'I thought you wanted to know about the murder?' said Ian slyly, and laughed when she looked indignant. 'All right, all right, although it isn't remotely connected to the murder or the attack on you. As you all know by now,' he looked round the group, 'Bowling wasn't only growing cannabis. He apparently got into drugs in a big way while he was at Dellington, and as a scientist he was very good at the manufacture of various illegal substances. He also had contacts in the wider drugs market. Denise, we discovered, had been a cocaine user for a long time, and the telephone call she heard, as far as we can make out, was from someone threatening exposure or demanding payment.'

'Why did she think whoever it was would come after her?' asked Harry.

'For the money, and possibly revenge.' Ian shook his head. 'She's a little more lucid, now, and she seems genuinely frightened. And then of course, there's the blackmail.'

'Blackmail?' came the chorus.

Ian smiled. 'Yes. I'm sorry we didn't tell you before, but we can't tell you everything.'

'We know,' said Ben. 'Carry on.'

'He'd kept several of the demands – goodness only knows why – in his factory. We've traced them to Chandler.'

'Chandler?' said the Greek chorus.

'We began to look more carefully into the accusations made against him by you, Flo. There was a very sophisticated, almost untraceable paper trail to the account attributed to the mysterious swindler, who in the end turned out to be Chandler after all. The mistake he made was to use his own name and company as a sort of double bluff. He knew this sort of scam well, and thought it would remain hidden.'

277

'So why was *he* blackmailing *Bowling*? Wouldn't it be the other way round?' asked Peter.

'He lost money and his habit was costing more and more. He isn't saying much, but we gather it was counter-accusation. Bowling threatened to blow the scam apart, Chandler threatened Bowling with revealing the truth about the drugs manufacture and supply.'

'So I suppose Bowling continued to supply Chandler in return for his silence?' said Ben.

'Is that why Denise went to Chandler when she left us?' asked Libby.

'She was scared he would keep asking for money and she hadn't got any. And she needed a new supplier. She thought Chandler would be able to help. And all he wanted to do was keep out of it.'

'There's still one thing we don't know. Who tipped off the police about Mike Farthing?' said Libby.

'We still don't know,' said Ian. 'It was an anonymous phone call. At a guess, Ron Stewart. Or his wife.'

'But Ron said he didn't think Mike had anything to do with it.'

'His wife?' said Ian. 'As I said, we can't know. I doubt if it was the two boys who worked for him, they'd know it could be traced to them.'

'No, they might have been covering their tracks,' said Peter. 'A double bluff.'

'Could be,' said Ian. 'Whoever it was, it was a malicious thing to do.'

'What about that Turner cow, then?' asked Flo. 'Libby said she thought she got the wrong bloke?'

'She did. Chandler had visited one of the residents of Maltby Close on a legitimate matter some time ago, so she'd seen him. That, incidentally, was what gave Chandler the idea of milking the elderly residents. Monica Turner was, in fact, one of the first to fall for it, then Vi Little and some of the others. Flo didn't.' He grinned at her. 'So when it all came out, Monica was furious. Especially when she saw him, as she thought going into the church hall for rehearsals. She did, of course, but her eyesight's bad and she confused him and Bowling.'

'We all knew her eyesight was bad,' said Libby. 'So what finally made her confront him?'

'When she saw him go into the churchyard that night. She didn't know why, of course, but in her confused mind, he was – what was it, Harry? – an abomination. He was desecrating the place.'

'That's what she said to me,' said Libby.

'She demanded her money back, Bowling said he didn't know what she was talking about it – and that was that. We found the weapon quite openly sitting in her fireplace. She was still talking about you being –'

'Another abomination?' suggested Libby, and everyone laughed.

'I still don't know why I thought about Flo and Lenny yesterday morning,' said Fran later.

'Perhaps it was a warning? That they were going to be mown down? You've had those before,' said Libby.

'Perhaps,' said Fran with a sigh. 'Would have helped if I'd been able to interpret it, though, wouldn't it?'

'Never mind,' said Libby, 'Lenny's enjoying the attention.' She looked round the little party in Hetty's drawing room. 'Do you think we'll ever get through a year without a murder?'

'Now that's tempting fate,' said Fran.

The Christmas concert went very well, the high spot, despite appearances by some prestigious theatrical names, being Ron "Screwball" Stewart's spot with his fellow Jonah Fludde band member.

Theatrical and political luminaries floated round the bar afterwards drinking Sir Andrew's excellent champagne and complimenting Libby, Ben and Peter on their theatre. 'A little gem' was frequently repeated.

Harry arrived in time for Sir Andrew's speech and was rewarded by a warm smile. Fran and Guy, over for the evening and staying with Hetty (her spare rooms were bigger than

Libby's) people watched with amusement, and Lenny sat in state with his leg on a footstool, while Flo fended off solicitous strangers.

Libby looked round with satisfaction at the tastefully decorated foyer and smiled. And nobody mentioned murder.

END

Chapter One of

Murder in the Blood

Lesley Cookman

The sea lapped gently into the granite cave, dark as ink. The moon, orange as a dying sun, touched wavelets and turned them into dull fire. Caught on an unseen finger of rock, the body bobbed gently to the surface.

There are secret places in the Mediterranean. Along the coast of Turkey, in the foothills of the Taurus mountains, lie villages the tourists do not see. Ramshackle hovels of brick, breezeblock, and corrugated iron line the unmade roads, the odd discouraged goat tethered in a patch of dirt droops its head. Everywhere, acres of white-roofed glass houses. Further inland, the pine-covered slopes rear up above the rusted metal hoops of abandoned polytunnels and half-built concrete houses left to the elements. Along the better-surfaced roads, small groves of pomegranate and olive trees proclaim the more affluent villages, with their newly built villas proclaiming themselves to be 'Satilik' – For Sale, and a sudden clutch of billboards advertising hotels. There are still hovels, but the goats look more cheerful, and chickens cluck drowsily in the sun.

It was to one of these villages that Guy Wolfe had brought his wife and friends. Women in headscarves and baggy trousers carried baskets and bundles through the tiny centre with its statue, pharmacy, and market; a road led winding to the beach. There were small family-run bars and hotels, a few sunbeds on the beach, and a few boats tied up to a leaning wooden jetty.

Libby Sarjeant stretched her arms above her head and sighed. 'This beats the Isle of Wight.'

Ben Wilde, her significant other, smiled. 'At least we're not investigating murders and family feuds.'

From another sunbed, Fran Wolfe sat up suddenly and stared at the sea.

Peter Parker lifted his sunhat from his face and gave his partner Harry Price a dig in the ribs. Five people watched Fran apprehensively.

Eventually, Libby could bear it no longer. 'What is it, Fran?'

Fran gave the appearance of someone jolted to reality. 'Eh?'

'What happened?' asked Guy.

Fran looked confused and shook her head. 'I don't know.'

Libby sighed. 'It was a moment, wasn't it?'

Fran's unwanted psychic gift often resulted in what her family and friends called her 'moments'. These ranged from seeing a picture of a plant to a vision of murder, sometimes with attendant feelings of suffocation.

'Yes,' said Fran slowly. 'Someone was drowning.'

The other five groaned.

'No, my lovely, please,' said Harry, sitting up and glaring at her. 'We're on bloody holiday.'

'I can't help it.'

'Don't worry about it,' said Libby crossing her fingers. 'There must have been lots of drownings around here in the past. I expect that's what you saw.'

Fran smiled at her gratefully. 'That'll be it. Thanks, Libby.'

Guy stood up. 'I think we now deserve a drink. It must be nearly lunchtime.'

The little party stood up and gathered various belongings.

'Are we coming back to the beach after lunch?' asked Harry. 'Do we leave the towels here?'

'I thought Captain Joe said he'd take us out on the boat this afternoon?' said Peter, perching his hat on the back of his head.

'So he did.' Harry slung his towel over his shoulder. 'Come on, then, last one to the bar's a sissy.'

The tiny hotel sat right on the beach, its bar at the front. The six friends perched on bar stools and ordered the local beer. The owner, known to all British guests as Jimmy, due to his unpronounceable Turkish name, handed them glasses frosted from the fridge.

'You enjoying your holiday?' he asked them, as he had asked every day since their arrival. 'You glad Guy bring you?'

'Yes,' they all assured him. 'Very glad.' Guy had mentioned the previous summer, when they were visiting the Isle of Wight, that he knew of a small bay in Turkey little known by the general run of tourists. After the events of the past year, they had decided to award themselves a holiday, and even Harry had closed his beloved restaurant, The Pink Geranium. And Guy had been right.

The sweep of the bay, backed by the foothills of the Taurus mountains, was dotted with twenty or so 'paynsions', hotels, and bars, and one supermarket. At least, that's what it called itself. Guy had seemed to know at least half the proprietors, and they had all greeted him with fond cries of recognition, even though his last trip there had been years ago, before he had met Fran. The other guests were mostly regulars, who guarded their little treasure jealously and were quite happy with the two-hour journey through the mountains from the airport, which put off the tour operators and all but the most intrepid holidaymakers.

Now they ordered soup and *borek*, the Turkish version of cheese straws – only more substantial – and salad, to see them through the afternoon boat trip. A couple of the other British guests joined them, and one, a solitary Englishman wearing a panama hat who rarely spoke, sat at the farthest table from the bar.

'Who is he, Jimmy?' asked Libby. 'Has he been coming here for years like the others?'

Jimmy shrugged. 'No. I do not know how he came here. He book over the phone. He know people in the village, I think.' He shrugged. 'Very quiet.'

One of the other guests leant forward. 'We gave him a lift into the village the other evening when we went to The Roma.' The Roma was a Turkish/Italian restaurant that provided a change from those in the bay. 'He barely said a word, but he seemed to know where he was going.'

'Oh, well,' said Harry, 'nothing to do with us.'

'No ...' said Libby thoughtfully, and was drowned out with protests from her friends. Libby's nosiness was legendary.

An hour later, and they were gathered on the wooden jetty while Captain Joe, bearer of another unpronounceable name, let down his little gangplank for them to board his boat, the *Paradise*. There were several small boats competing for trade from the tourists, all taking trips round the coast to visit bays only accessible from the sea, where one could swim, eat freshly caught fish, and drink beer or raki, according to taste. This afternoon Joe was taking them to a small bay rarely visited, where there had been recent sightings of turtles.

The boat chugged off towards the headland, where a rocky island guarded the entrance to the bay.

'Reminds me of our Dragon Island in Nethergate,' said Libby to Fran, as they approached it.

'Same sort of shape,' agreed Fran. 'I love that someone's planted a Turkish flag on top.'

'They do that everywhere, don't they?' said Libby. 'I must say, I'm glad Guy brought us here. I want to come back, don't you?'

But Fran wasn't listening. Her back was rigid and she was staring at the sheer rock face rising from the sea. Turning her back on the island, Libby tried to see what she was looking at. And realised that Captain Joe was turning the boat slowly inshore.

The six friends stood together peering into the darkness of the cleft in the rock and saw what Fran had seen. Bobbing face down on the surface of the water – a body.

Libby Sarjeant Series

A Libby Sarjeant Murder Mystery
LESLEY COOKMAN
Murder in
Steeple Martin

A Libby Sarjeant Murder Mystery
LESLEY COOKMAN
Murder in
Midwinter

A Libby Sarjeant Murder Mystery
LESLEY COOKMAN
Murder by
the Sea

A Libby Sarjeant Murder Mystery
LESLEY COOKMAN
Murder in
Bloom

A Libby Sarjeant Murder Mystery
LESLEY COOKMAN
Murder in
the Green

A Libby Sarjeant Murder Mystery
LESLEY COOKMAN
Murder
Imperfect

A Libby Sarjeant Murder Mystery
LESLEY COOKMAN
Murder to
Music

A Libby Sarjeant Murder Mystery
LESLEY COOKMAN
Murder at
the Manor

A Libby Sarjeant Murder Mystery
LESLEY COOKMAN
Murder in
the Monastery

A Libby Sarjeant Murder Mystery
LESLEY COOKMAN
Murder at the Laurels

A Libby Sarjeant Murder Mystery
LESLEY COOKMAN
Murder by Magic

A Libby Sarjeant Murder Mystery
LESLEY COOKMAN
Murder in the Dark

A Libby Sarjeant Murder Mystery
LESLEY COOKMAN
Murder in a Different Place

A Libby Sarjeant Murder Mystery
LESLEY COOKMAN
Murder Out of Tune